Flora's
Money

For Jimmy!

Ray Pavely '11

Flora's Money

A Novel ~
Illustrated
by the author

Ray Rueby

Flora's Money

All Rights Reserved © 2007 by Ray Rueby.
No part of this book may be reproduced or transmitted in any form
or by any means, without permission in writing from the author.
All characters and events in this book, with the exception of established
historical facts, are fictitious and any resemblance to
actual persons, living or dead is purely coincidental.

Tobey Arts
32 Tobey Court
Pittsford, New York 14534
tobeyarts@hotmail.com

ISBN 978-0-9740428-1-7

First Edition

Also by Ray Rueby
THE MAGIC of YOUR NAME
Business – Nonfiction

Printed in the United States of America

For Nancy, editor,
kind critic &
congenial curator

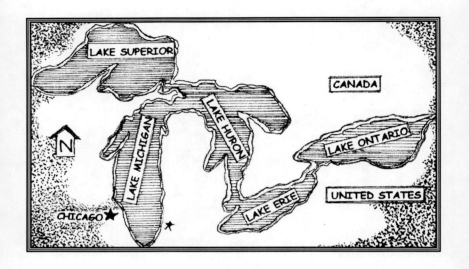

Contents

Part One ~ Hamelet   Page 1

Part Two ~ Chicago   Page 56

Part Three ~ The Raid   Page 113

Part Four ~ Repeal   Page 225

Part One ~ Hamelet
1921 -1932

FLORA'S MONEY, the main characters ~

ARIE - Grover's sweetheart
CARLOS - Arie's brother
FLORA - beautiful dreamer
FRANK - federal agent
GORKI - gypsy trucker
GROVER - Flora's pal
GUS - crime boss
HECTOR - Flora's lover
JED - Tri-Motor pilot
JERRY - town cop
JIGGS - mobster
JUDGE - counselor
MADDIE - Jerry's wife
MANNY - Golden's manager
MILLIE - hapless waitress
OREN - Flora's guardian
QUENT - front-man for Gus
RAMSAY - Grover's brother
RHONDA - Flora's maven
THEO - Academy Professor

CHAPTER 1

1921, southeast Lake Michigan, first light. Professor Theo climbed down the swaying rope ladder, amidships on the side of the rusty freighter, its engines at dead slow so a crew member could row him in to the nearby beach. Partway down the ladder, Theo's ankle-high shoes slipped off the rope rungs and his short legs thrashed the air. For a moment he hung by his hands, struggling, until he got his feet back in place and was able to continue. Determined, he kept going down to the waiting skiff twenty feet below, in spite of his dangling valise and satchel, hastily tied on his back by a deckhand, bumping him from neck to rump.

"Easy—got ya!" the sailor in the little boat grunted as he slipped his muscular arms around Theo's waist, in behind the bags, and gently pulled him backwards from off the

FLORA'S MONEY

ladder, then turned and eased him down on the unsteady floorboards. "Sit—hold on," the sailor said. "I'll get you to the beach. You can walk into town from there. Not far."

Twenty minutes later, Theo stepped from the boat into the shallow waves rippling the shore and began slogging across the sand, carrying one of his bags in each hand. His shoes, and trousers up to the knees, were soaked but he accepted the nuisance as all part of his adventure of disembarking in a remote place without a dock. Near the first of the cottages and village buildings, set back a quarter mile from the water's edge by the wide beach, he put his bags down to take a short rest and look around. There were no people about. He saw three gulls careening and swooping low around a lighthouse tower so far down the shore he could barely hear their cawing. The fishy smell of the wet sands was an acrid reminder of other shores, far away. Out on the calm lake he could see the skiff being hoisted aboard and the ship slowly steaming in the morning mists, its trail of black smoke fading as the vessel continued its voyage to the south.

Perspiring from exertion, Theo took off the blue beret pulled low over his right ear and uncovered his thick black hair. He tucked the cap into a pocket. His wrinkled brown suit and white shirt, minus the detachable collar he saved in his valise, hung loosely on his slender body. Thirty-five years old, his attentive eyes and mature face featured a ruddy complexion, a proud high-bridged nose, and a moustache with a short, neatly-trimmed beard.

On May 2, 1921, seven weeks earlier, Theo had gone on leave from teaching language and the arts at the Faculte des lettres, University of Paris, and departed from his bachelor rooms nearby to begin his first trip to America. Well-funded

FLORA'S MONEY

with family money, he planned to tour the Great Lakes area for several weeks and then end his journey at this rural place where he could experience a different culture and expand his outlook as a teacher. Arrangements were already in place for him to spend at least two years here as a schoolmaster in this village called Hamelet. He had traveled first class by steamship from Le Havre to Boston, then headed west, with side trips on local trains before reaching a port city on the shores of Lake Huron, north of Detroit. From there he booked a simple cabin on an ore-carrying freighter set to depart for a routine trip up through Lake Huron and the Mackinac Straits, then south on Lake Michigan as it headed for the steel mills, a route that would take the ship right by Theo's destination at this village. For ten dollars extra, the captain had agreed to drop Theo off there by small boat.

Theo picked up his bags and started to walk again. *So!* Here I am, he thought, approaching a bucolic place very unlike Paris, and in a foreign, but friendly land. Already my journal has many notes and tales about Americans I've met, especially the crewmen on that freighter. And now I am here, far from the boulevards along the Seine.

So, indeed. Has this been a journey of folly? But no! Students of Hamelet, be advised! Your new Schoolmaster has arrived! Ah, such pomposity, he told himself, chuckling—my secret will be that I am the learner and they the Faculte!

Minutes later, Theo noticed a man, about his own age, coming from the village and striding directly toward him. He wore a work shirt and slacks and no tie; as he got closer he flipped a quick wave and said to Theo, "Hi, friend. You just got off that ship? Right?" Surprised, Theo nodded as they both stopped and faced each other, a few feet apart. "Where

FLORA'S MONEY

you from," the man continued, "or maybe I shouldn't ask? Never mind. Got any thirst fixers you want to sell?" He looked down at Theo's bags as he spoke.

"Why no, not really."

"Okay. Well, are you maybe a drummer—pushin' dresses, maybe, or hardware?"

"This is my first visit to America, I'm a teacher, not a musician," Theo offered, perplexed, then added, "I've just come from France, to be the new schoolmaster here."

"Oh, really? I heard about that. Well, most gents comin' in here so early, or very late, for that matter, are in the booze business, and since we started Prohibition a year ago in this country it's my job to keep an eye out and—well never mind."

Theo laughed and said, "You thought I was a bootlegger? Are you in that business?"

"Not on the business side. I'm the town cop, name's Jerry. Welcome to Hamelet." He reached out and shook hands with Theo. They both smiled.

1925, four years later, Hameletbeach, 2 a.m. "Hey, you awake—are those gun shots?" Grover asked in a whisper. He sat up in his cot, listening, in the darkened bedroom he shared with his brother Ramsay in the unpainted little cottage.

FLORA'S MONEY

"Huh, yeah—somebody's shootin' out there," Ramsay replied. He rose up on his elbows, yawned and said, "wonder what they're up to, this time."

"Dunno—another bootlegger argument, prob'ly," Grover said. The boys had been awakened minutes before by the noise of two cars, one chasing the other and speeding along the shore down at the water's edge. They could hear the engines revving unevenly as the drivers skidded and swerved their vehicles through the sand. Then they heard the two shots, close together, as the cars turned, passed close by the cottage and moved on towards the dirt roads through town.

"Maybe the cops and feds are after 'em," Ramsay said. He reached up to the small shelf mounted on the wall over his head, found a match, scratched it on a stone lying next to a candle stub jutting up from a saucer, and touched the flame to the wick. A flickering glow began sparring with the black shadows in the cold room.

"Can't be. Uncle Jerry's the only cop here in Hamelet—you know that," Grover replied, keeping his voice low, "and it sounds like him comin down the hall—if the feds were out there he'd be with 'em." The door to their room opened and their uncle came in, a blanket wrapped around his shoulders over his nightshirt.

Startled by the light, he growled, "Hey boys! Blow out that damn candle—you know better than that. I think they've gone on, but if they come back they won't bother us—long as they think we're all asleep and keeping out of their business."

Ramsay snuffed out the light, and said, "Sorry, Jere. You goin' out there?"

"Naw, too late now. Go back to sleep. Remember, no

FLORA'S MONEY

lights." He left the room and shut the door.

"Well, a booze-runner sneaking in a load from a boat down on the beach in the middle of the night is one thing, but bullets, jeepers," Ramsay said softly, and then added, "Hey—what are you doing?" He could just see Grover reaching over in the dark and lifting up the bottom of the window shade.

"Just lookin' that's all."

"Stay low. Keep your head down. See anything?"

"Nope, nothin' out there, just dark—and it's snowin' some, too," Grover said. He slipped back under his puffy quilt, topped with his spread-out mackinaw.

Ramsay muttered, just loud enough for his brother to hear, "Maybe tomorrow, after Jere goes to work, we could look around out there for tracks and see if they left any booze bottles behind."

"Why would they do that?" Grover asked, his voice muffled by the covers.

"I heard that sometimes, if the cops or some other gang's after them, they drop the booze and run for it. Maybe, if we find some, we could try a little."

"Nuts. We ain't old enough to drink. You're only fourteen, and I'm twelve."

"So what? I'd like to try it," Ramsay said. "Professor Theo said that when he grew up in France, everyone in his family, even the kids, drank wine every day for dinner—and some days even for lunch. And everybody knows he makes his own wine in the shed out behind our school. He may even sip a little gin, too, for all we know."

"But whisky can make us sick, you know. That's what Aunt Maddie says."

"Well, we might find a few bottles that we could sell,"

6

FLORA'S MONEY

Ramsay said quietly. "I don't believe that sick talk. I know whisky is a lot stronger than wine, but I heard it can make you feel happy, and tingly—maybe I could just try a gulp or two, see what it's like."

The same night, in her room in town, Arie, ten years old and one of Grover's classmates at the Academy, also woke up when she heard the shots. She guessed what was happening and knew what to do. When scary sounds from the bootlegger people erupted late at night around sleepy Hamelet, screeching tires, loud engines and gun noises, she did as her big brother Carlos had taught her when she was younger: hug her rag doll, pull the bed quilts close around her ears to reduce the noises, and hum Dolly to sleep. She thought about Carlos away for the week, night-flying the mail somewhere, and not in his bedroom down the hall, and about Bertha, her minder and their landlady, downstairs in her bedroom, hard of hearing, sleeping through it all. Arie cuddled her doll, restless.

1931, Hamelet, another winter morning, six years later. Flora, nineteen, attractive, and notably tall, dressed like a man for safer bumming-it to Chicago, quietly left her uncle's place before daylight. Upstairs over his general store, the flat had been her home since she was six. She wore an extra-long army overcoat, once used by a gangling doughboy in the Great War, and clunky rubber-boots. A stocking cap hid her flaxen curls.

With one of her mittened hands she carried a burlap bag holding her regular clothes, personal things and three jelly sandwiches, two apples and some homemade cookies. No one but her uncle knew she was leaving except Grover, a life-long pal, young enough to be a kid brother. He heard her plan, encouraged her to go, and insisted she take nine dimes, all the cash he had.

In the bag, Flora also carried a cocoa can with a pry-out lid. Empty of any chocolate powder, the can had served her as a penny-and-nickel bank for years. Now it was put to use as a disguised purse, holding eleven dollars and ninety cents, including a five dollar bill from Uncle Oren and the dimes from Grover. It also held a locket containing a tiny photo of her deceased parents. She walked a block to the main road and stood on the curb in the snow until the Sinclair tanker truck she expected came splashing through the slush. Flora waved. It stopped in front of her, motor continuing to chug. She opened the door, easily stepped up on the high running board, and got in.

Flora was born in 1912. Her mother, a tall brunette from Quebec, worked as a clerk in the Emporium, the first and only general store in Hamelet. It was opened in 1895 and given its grand name by Oren, a young merchant from Milwaukee, unmarried, who had arrived a year earlier. Flora's father also worked for Oren in the stable behind the store as a blacksmith for farm horses and selling fuel to motorists from the single gas pump out front. Oren became a close friend of Flora and her parents. As a toddler, Flora made him an honorary uncle and began calling him Uncle Orangie. In 1918, when she was only six, both of her parents died in the flu pandemic that also orphaned Ramsay and Grover and killed thousands of others throughout the world. A grief-stricken Oren brought

FLORA'S MONEY

his widowed sister in from her run-down farm, outside town, to live in his apartment over the store and take care of the youngster.

When Flora was nine she began to spend a lot of her free time from school helping out in the Emporium, doing boring jobs she grew to dislike. She swept the floor in the store, unpacked all kinds of merchandise, including dry goods, liniment, overalls, stove parts and crates of soft drinks. As she grew taller, she sometimes toted customer purchases out to their parked farm trucks or horse-drawn wagons—or helped carry items to wherever people lived in town or nearby, striding along, easily toting sacks of flour or pecks of potatoes, a bundle of garden tools or other hefty items.

One thing she did enjoy, even as young as eleven, was getting to drive Oren's Chevy pick-up truck. With him riding as passenger and teacher they would jounce around the sandy roads for hours, winding through the dunes on a Sunday afternoon.

Ramsay, Grover and Arie played with Flora when they all were kids, and later, in their teens, included her on class outings to the beach in summer, and dune sledding in winter, year after year. When she was fourteen years old, she was the tallest of the thirty students in Hamelet Academy and her healthy body was well on its way to maturity. By the time she was sixteen she topped six feet, had attractive features in place, with light golden hair and a graceful body. Strangers who saw her walking around town often mistakenly assumed she was as old as she looked. Flora's humor helped her through those awkward years, and compassion for her peers, all smaller than she, came to her easily and encouraged her to be more protective than competitive, in school and out.

Romantic girl-boy contacts in Hamelet were constrained

FLORA'S MONEY

and usually limited to innocent innings of touch and go. Flora, not shy, was certainly attractive to males, but never connected with any young man she could consider a steady boyfriend. Growing up she did feel the human urges involved, but because of the small number of youths in the area, and the dearth of intimate social opportunities, she only sampled the teasing and the talk parts of the human ripening processes.

Flora's world as a teen female in a rustic American village, in the nineteen twenties and early thirties, was unvaried: in winter, along the deserted beaches, and clogging the dirt streets throughout the town, there were silent and freezing weeks of wind carved snowdrifts. Spring brought gusty showers and sun-teasing days clawing between dark clouds, followed by summer afternoons with toe-scorching sands baking in the sun until, finally, the warm season faded into fall with chilly portents of another dreary winter to come.

Girls her age, vacationing in summer with their parents and boyfriends from Chicago on daytrips to Hamelet's beach, often told her about the exciting wonders of illegal speakeasys and the numerous restaurants, museums, theaters and other entertainments to be enjoyed in the big city. She wondered what it would be like to learn how to drink and go dancing with the handsome men she saw in the fan magazine photos from the rack in Oren's store. She had never seen a movie, since there were no nickelodeons or movie houses in her town, but the stories about the glamorous stars and the wondrous moving pictures gave her curious tingles. Dance music and romanticized dramas beamed from Chicago stations, that she heard everyday on the sample radios on sale in the Emporium, and the records of crooner's love songs she played on wind-up Victrolas on display, all worked their magic, elating and stimulating her imagination.

One morning, a few months after her graduation from the twelfth grade at the Academy, Flora walked past the hand-cranked cash register in the Emporium, before unlocking the front door. It was then she saw that, perhaps the night before, Oren had framed and hung her diploma for all to see, on the wall behind the counter. Touched, she stood there staring at the certificate, unsure what she was feeling. Moments later, she took a deep breath and decided, finally, after weeks of uncertainty, that she wanted more; working full time at the Emporium, and living in such a small and somber town, was not for her. That was the day she began to actually plan and save for the journey that would take her to a new life in Chicago.

RHONDA

CHAPTER 2

Flora hitchhiked, and did a lot of walking to make her way into a bleak and frigid Chicago the day she left home. As a first-time visitor to a major city, she was awed by the hordes of people scurrying about on endless sidewalks, the scary heights of buildings glaring down at her, and the clouds of exhaust billowing from under the vehicles and carried by the cold winds. Late that evening, after being dropped off well into the city by the last of several trucks and flivvers to give her a lift from Hamelet, she stopped at a diner and decided to spend a nickel to warm up with a cup of coffee and eat her last sandwich. Flora asked the waitress how to get to the ladies-only residence hotel she had heard about, where she could share a room at a low rate. It was many blocks distant, but Flora left the diner and eagerly continued hiking and

FLORA'S MONEY

gawking. About fifteen hours after leaving home, she found her way to the hotel and rented a shared-room, with two beds, for two dollars a week, in advance. Three days later she landed a job in a beanery for twenty cents an hour, plus meager tips and a limited breakfast.

Her mate in the drab room was a congenial red-haired divorcee named Rhonda. She was a clerk in a ladies' hat shop by day who knew how to enjoy the neighborhood speaks after dark, work the guys for drinks, then pay them off with conversation. Glad for such an attractive companion as Flora, Rhonda became her nightlife maven. Right away she began teaching her how and what to drink, which joints to avoid, and many other big-city smarts. As the weeks went by, she also gave Flora tips on dressing better on a very low budget, and took her to secondhand shops where bargains on once-classy clothing were on sale—including items large enough for Flora's dazzling figure.

After Flora had been in the city a few months, Rhonda heard about an opening for a lady bartender in an already thriving speakeasy on Rush Street and urged Flora to go over and apply. She knew that Flora's quick wit, face of a merry goddess, fair hair and her tall shapely figure would be good for any classy saloon.

She got the job. The bar was located one flight up, on the top floor of a former factory building, once the home of a small business called Golden's Coffee Distributors. Twenty years earlier, the owner of the venerable coffee roasting and wholesaling firm, a Mr. Golden, who also owned the building, took a flier on the burgeoning movie craze and decided to put some of his life savings into opening a nickelodeon as a sideline. He did so well he closed the coffee operation within a year and moved to a small town west of Chicago

13

FLORA'S MONEY

to build and operate an elegant movie house. The improved films coming from Hollywood in those days soon started him on his way to becoming quite wealthy.

Golden didn't try very hard to find a buyer for his old building. When he first left the place he had movers haul out his favorite swivel chair, selected files and a framed photo of Woodrow Wilson. The out-dated roasting equipment was left behind. He also told them not to bother moving the hundreds of empty coffee cans, one-pound size, already labeled, and barrels of snap-in lids made so that one could be pressed into place in the recessed opening in the top of each can.

In the late 1920s, a successful bootlegger king named Gus began opening up illegal saloons of his own around Chicago to make more money. On his orders, one of his men was out looking for new locations and found the old coffee company; he called his boss and said, "Gus, I think this is perfect. A busy spot, lots of action around there. It has two floors, both empty. The stairway starts in the front entry and takes you right up to a big room, and a few smaller offices, on the second floor. We repaint the place inside, put the bar and tables in, take down the old sign over the door, and we're ready to go."

"Good. Is there anything left in the first floor?"

"Some old machinery, junk and piles of empty coffee cans—lots of cans. And like we discussed, the first floor could be left just like it is—customers feel less obvious when they go in and out. And you can buy this real cheap as an abandoned building."

"Did you say there was an old sign hanging on the front? What's it say?"

"GOLDEN'S—in faded white letters about a foot high."

FLORA'S MONEY

"Hmm, not bad. Leave it there. Let's call the place that. Catchy, easy to remember."

Flora did well at Golden's. Her friendly manner with the mostly-male customers, and her quick wit and splendid appearance helped cover her lack of experience in tending bar. The afternoon she applied, an incident with a customer standing at the bar helped: an awed gent about five-foot-three, seeing her for the first time as she talked to Manny, the manager, gazed up at Flora and asked, "How-the-hell-tall are you, anyhow?"

She responded with such a pleaser among the regular bunch of elbow-benders, up and down the bar, that her remark was joked about for days. First, she looked down at him with an indulgent smile then cooed in a very nonchalant manner: "I'm seventy-five and three-quarter inches high, in sandals. That works out to almost six-foot-four. And how long are you, little man?"

"It is impossible to tell whether Prohibition, now in its seventh year, is a good thing or a bad thing. It has never been fully enforced in this land—and the percentage of whiskey drinkers in the United States now is greater than in any other country."

Fiorello La Guardia, 1926

CHAPTER 3

In her first week at Golden's, Flora met Jiggs. He was an overweight and balding man, in his forties, who liked to brag about being one of the key men for the bootlegger-owner of the place. Manny, the manager and Flora's boss, reported to Jiggs. Right from the start, and during the many months she spent behind the mahogany strip, Flora acquired fans among the regular customers. The news spread quickly around the joints in the area that here was a jovial barmaid of spectacular components.

Jiggs also became one of her boosters and began spending more and more time sitting on a bar stool there, drinking alone, and watching her work. She always managed at least a tiny smile at his raunchy wisecracks, because he was a boss, but it was an effort to be nice to

FLORA'S MONEY

him — until the night he came up with an amazing offer.

It was very late and, as usual, Jiggs sat by himself at one end of the bar. Two couples, the only other people in the place, sat at the other end drinking and chatting softly among themselves. Flora had slowed down, too. Two yards from Jiggs, she stopped, leaned against the back bar shelving, easily placed one foot up on the edge of the glass-rinsing sink under the bar, took a deep breath and yawned. She looked away from Jiggs, absorbed in her own thoughts and idly plinked the upside-down lip of a stemware glass with a finger as it dangled just over her head, with dozens of other glasses, from a suspended wooden rack—up at arm's length for most bartenders, not so for Flora.

Jiggs nursed the most recent of the many tumblers of bourbon he had drained that night and stared at her backside; due to her one-legged stance it was displayed in a tightened silky skirt at a pleasantly rounded angle. He raised his eyes, took a gulp of his drink, grinned and said brightly, "Hey—Flora!"

She turned her head, looked back, gave him a weak smile, and said "Hey, Jiggs," in a meaningless way, like two people do to just exchange sounds, periodically, for the umpteenth time after sharing rather limited space for far too long.

"Busy night?"

"Uh-huh. Earlier it was. Remember?" He nodded, and took a sip.

"So, girl, how do you like it here?"

"Great," Flora answered flatly. She sighed, took her foot off the sink, leaned forward a little and placed her palms on the bar. He watched her for a moment, letting his eyes wander over the jutting effect made by her change of position.

FLORA'S MONEY

Flora considered going down the bar and pretending to be busy polishing something, but he spoke before she started to move, "Uh, girl, you got a good place to stay?"

Unconcerned by such a personal question, she shrugged and said, "Not bad. Nothin' fancy." Always a nuisance subject for her—part of the of moon-howling by a lonely drinker—but she knew it was best to give a friendly, but devious, response to intimate questions in the-where-do-you-live category.

Jiggs persisted, "Just a room? Or is it more like an apartment—don't get me wrong, I mean, are you happy there? I'm not askin' where. Don't get me wrong."

"Sure, Jiggs. It's okay. A basic room; the sink is in the corner. The john and tub are in a closet. Great view of an alley." She smirked.

He repeated himself, "Don't get me wrong," then added, "Can you keep a secret?"

Flora yawned and said, "Hell, yes."

She stretched her arms over her head, yanked them down and looked at him, waiting and thinking about moving down the bar and ending the chat. Jiggs sipped again, twice, finished the drink and reached out, offering her the empty glass for a refill. Trapped, she took it, did the needful and placed the new drink in front of him. While she had been making it, he sat quietly, gazing up and around her aura, like a kid admiring an over-decorated Christmas tree. Then he continued: "Well, it is a secret, but today I closed a deal and bought an apartment building. Little way from here, in a nice area." The remark about buying an apartment building was what got her attention.

"You did? My, how nice for you. Do you live there?" she asked.

18

FLORA'S MONEY

"Naw. It has eight apartments. I'm just going to rent 'em all."

Flora put on a furtive look, as if sharing a state secret, stepped closer, leaned toward Jiggs and whispered, "What's the matter? Can't you afford to live there?"

For a moment, he frowned, confused, then he shouted "OH! HEY, that's a good one! I get it!" Delighted, he grinned, laughed, winked and took a big swallow.

"So what are the apartments like, Jiggs?" she asked in a quiet voice.

"Classy—all furnished, ready to move in—bedroom, kitchenette, sittin' room, private bath, and all that. I may move in later on, but not now. Some of the apartments are empty. If you want it, I'll give you a good deal. No strings, just a business thing, you know?"

She quickly refilled his glass, thinking about the so-so cubby she had, handed his drink to him and said, "Deal? Like what?"

"For you, there's a front apartment, second floor. How about free?"

Flora stared. "No strings, you said. My body's not part of any deal, you know!"

"Abso—" Jiggs said, inserting a hiccup, "—lutely, Flora. Move in. Free. No cleanin' or collecting rent. Nothin like that. And there's even a lot to park your car in, right next door. Free!"

Flora laughed. "Car? I don't have one and I've only driven a farm truck, out in the sticks, never in traffic like here."

"Ah, we'll fix that. You should have a car, Flora." Offering a car, to sweeten his offer, was no problem for Jiggs. He just happened to have an extra one. The summer before, a runner from the Southside was way behind in some payments for booze—and then got in deeper after several rigged hands of poker with Jiggs and his cronies. Word on the street, later, was that the guy had abruptly disappeared as did his 1928 Packard Runabout roadster. Six months later, Jiggs drove the car in from a warehouse he owned in nearby Cicero and parked it in a commercial garage in Chicago. By then the car had been repainted an elegant forest-green, been fitted with different license plates, and was ready for him to sell or use on occasional ego trips—like enticing Flora into his web.

"You're a good kid—just a kid compared to me, Flora, I mean, well—" he muttered after a swallow of bourbon, "and I know a guy that can drive you around and give you whatever practice you need. He's a regular chauffeur. But as for me, no strings on the apartment, Flora. Sure, maybe later you get to know me better. Maybe invite me over for a drink sometime." He shrugged and added, quietly, almost to himself, "Hey, I'm harmless." Then he took a big breath, exhaled and asked, "So, what d'you say?"

Flora squinted, just a little, and said thoughtfully, "Sounds great, Jiggs, but maybe we better think about this for a bit. Okay?"

The next night, Rhonda came in and sat at the bar. Flora came over, bent down to put her head closer, and heard Rhonda say quietly, "That deal you asked me about on the phone this afternoon—Jiggs and his extra apartment: go easy with him, babe. He can be mean. But since he's a boss, maybe he'll get sore if you say no. I'd say, what the hell, take the place, enjoy it—but don't let him in the joint or anywhere near your bed."

Flora made a big frown and said, "That'll never happen."

Bathtub Gin was often mixed in the family tub. Popular recipe: ample neutral spirits (from a drug store), distilled sugar, touch of juniper berry juice, top off with water. Noted for producing hangovers; use at own risk.

CHAPTER 4

With his mother attended by the town midwife, Grover was born in 1913 on the kitchen table in his family's four-room cottage on the beach just outside Hamelet—the same as his older brother, Ramsay, when he arrived two years earlier. After turning the care of the mother, Hilda, and the boys, over to a neighbor lady, the midwife made out the birth certificate, gave it to Grover's father, Ansel, and walked back to her vegetable farm north of town in time to milk her cow before the sun set.

Ansel and Hilda had run a little bakery in Hamelet, year after year, making plain breads and a limited variety of cookies. When the Great War came along, Ansel was not drafted, due to poor eyesight, yet he died in late 1918, as Hilda did two weeks later, both victims of the lethal flu pandemic that

FLORA'S MONEY

swept throughout America and abroad, during the war and into 1919. Their bakeshop was closed during their months of illness, and never reopened. The boys escaped the flu and were looked after, at first, by Ansel's brother, Jerry, the only living relative they had, and sympathetic neighbors.

Uncle Jerry was unmarried, had been drafted into the army during the war, and served in the infantry in France. When he came back in July, 1918, he was hired as Hamelet's only policeman.

After Hilda's funeral, Jerry made arrangements for Madge, a young war widow he knew in Hamelet, to move into Ansel and Hilda's cottage to look after Grover and Ramsay. Her pay started as a place to live and a few dollars a week from Jerry for expenses. Within a year, the two were married and Jerry moved from his bachelor room in town to begin a new life with Madge and the boys. Jerry and his wife never bothered to apply for legal adoption papers for them. Since they already had the same last name, folks came to think of them all as the cop's family and Ramsay and Grover grew up calling their folks Jere and Maddie.

Hamelet was a quiet place, most of the time. There was seldom much contact with outsiders, other than a few summer visitors who came on one-day visits to enjoy the beach or to rent one of the outlying beach cottages for a week or two. It was never crowded anywhere in the area. Some people in town took in roomers all year around, but there were no hotels, resorts or specified campsites for visitors to use; and, of course, there were no saloons there during Prohibition.

Two dollars a day for unskilled labor was not unusual and money was scarce even before the Depression years began. People considered strolling around town on a Sunday afternoon as a diversion; a typical night out was walking to each other's houses, playing cards, having coffee or a few home brews, then going home well before midnight.

When Grover was thirteen, it was his folks' turn to have friends over for a Saturday night penny-ante poker game, and they came in spite of the high winds and heavy rains that had stalled over much of the area since the previous Thursday. Folks in Hamelet were seldom dominated by bad weather. They were used to it, but the prolonged days of thunder and lightning of that storm were beginning to make the grown-ups edgy.

Oscar, the town pharmacist and his wife, Leona, came over that night to play cards. She worked with him in the only drugstore in town. Leaning into the wind, they had made their way from their flat in town, on foot and wrapped in rubber raincoats.

Fergie, a widowed friend employed at the state prison, located about ten miles away, was also there. He had driven out in his Ford, parked it in the lane out back and dashed through the rain and into the kitchen.

Ramsay and Grover had spent some time before anyone arrived, out on the porch in a dry spot back by the wall, watching the cascading waves roll in, and screeching as the scary lightning out over the horizon streaked across the black sky. When the adults started playing cards the boys went inside and stayed there to watch the game.

After many hands of poker, and much friendly banter in loud voices to be heard above the storm, Oscar finished a new round of dealing, laying five cards in front of everyone seated around the kitchen table, and announced, "Everybody in, I see." He looked at Jerry, on his right. "Draw?"

"No. I'm set. But I'll sweeten the pot with two more," Jerry replied, dropping two pennies on the little pile. Then,

FLORA'S MONEY

for a laugh, and to draw attention to what he was trying to sell as a pat hand, he spread his cards into a tight fan and held them privately, just off the end of his nose, and winked at his wife seated next to him.

"You in, Madge?" Oscar asked.

"Yup. And I raise it four more! Tra la! And no draw either, thank you. My, listen to the wind blow out there!"

"What's she got, Osky, five aces?" Leona kidded, popping a Lucky Strike between her lips and flicking up a flame on a wooden match with her thumbnail.

"Naw, Lee, she's bluffin," Jerry said. "Course, only she could get five aces when there's no wild cards allowed in this hand."

"Hah! Never mind. I know what I'm doing, dearie—I think. It's wild enough outside," she added, grinning at her pun.

Oscar looked at the next player, his wife Leona, and said, "Okay, Lee, it'll only cost six little ones, unless you want to raise, too. What's your pleasure?"

"Well, I was going to ask for three, maybe four cards, but I guess I won't. Not if it'll cost me six cents up front. I'll fold."

A sudden roll of booming thunder made the house vibrate; deep thuds and rumbles continued on down the beach. Everyone winced and rolled their eyes at the others.

"Okey-dokey. Cost you six, Fergie. You in?" Oscar asked.

"No, guess not. I pass. Almost eight o'clock, time for me to drive over to work for a while, anyway—extra duty tonight. Hold my stack, Oscar. When I return I'll give you guys a chance to win some of it back, if it isn't too late."

"Sure you will, Ferguson, ol' bean," Jerry tossed out.

FLORA'S MONEY

"Look at Oscar, he's already frothing at the mouth to get back what he lost last week."

"Aw Jerry, that's just your home brew droolin' down his chin!" Madge giggled.

Fergie got up, took his uniform coat from the back of his chair and slipped it on as he walked toward the back door where he picked up his poncho and slipped it on over everything. "See you in a couple hours, folks," he said quietly, going out. They all nodded, with polite smiles but their faces became even more somber after he went out.

Madge got up and stood by her chair. No one spoke. From outside they could hear Fergie start his Ford in the lane behind the cottage. They all watched as his headlights flashed into the room and reflected off the rain-spattered windows when he turned and drove away. Oscar shook his head and said quietly, "Damn. How does he stand it? I'll take running my store, any day. So, now what everybody? Maybe we should have a break. And hey, you notice? The wind seems to be easing up."

"Hope so—but golly. Us sittin' here having a good time, while over at the prison Fergie is—you know—don't seem right," Madge said softly.

"Now, Madge," Jerry said, "he's doing his job—he's a regular guard and doesn't pull the switch, you know. And this time, the prisoner is one of those gang-guys who shot a cop just doing his job, trying to stop a bootlegger's truck downstate—hell, could've been me. But okay, let's finish this hand and maybe go sit outside for a spell, if it isn't too wet out there."

Over an hour later, Oscar and Leona sat on collapsible beach chairs out on the porch, their empty beer glasses on the floor nearby. Jerry perched on the top step, sipping the

FLORA'S MONEY

last of his third glass of beer, the empty pitcher beside him. The rain had stopped and the wind had gone down, but there was still a nervous rumble, now and then, off in the distance. Ramsay and Grover sat on the bottom step, pushing idly at the wet sand with their bare feet.

A small lamp in the front room cast a narrow aisle of light through the open door and across the floor toward the steps, leaving the rest of the porch in shadows. With little desire to talk, everyone just sat and gazed across the beach at the lights that showed from a few house-windows in town, and the sign reading DINER that was lit up by two bulbs mounted on the top edge of the panel. After a while, Madge called Grover to come back into the kitchen with her, as the others remained out on the porch. Standing there she switched off the kitchen light and said, "Let's just sit in here for a while, Grove, and enjoy the dark. Kind of cozy, don't you think?" He shrugged and remained silent. She hoped the brief dim-out wouldn't be as upsetting for the boy, if there wasn't much light in the room. They had been through nights like this in the past, but not very often in Grover's memory. She gently led him over to sit down at the table. "Don't mix up the pennies," she said softly, and reached over to pat his hands lying loosely, one atop the other on the tabletop.

"Maddie, what's it like?"

She sighed, and said, "You mean—"

"Over at the prison place. Do they really murder the prisoner with electric wires?"

"Well, it's not murder, exactly. The bad man, the prisoner, is the one that broke the law and did the murder. He shot a policeman and the poor man died. Like Jerry said, the cop was just doing his job and well, the bad guy has to be punished. I know it seems hard, but he was tried by a judge,

26

FLORA'S MONEY

with a jury and all—and they do it that way to—well, if they didn't have laws, you know, there'd be a lot more innocent people robbed, or killed and all that. Understand?"

"I guess so." They sat in silence, waiting.

Maddie and Grover hadn't been paying any attention to what they were saying outside, at least not at first. But since they were so quiet they couldn't help but hear Oscar ask, "Do you ever have to go over there on these nights, since you're the Hamelet policeman?"

"No, that's state business. And the prison is not in our town area, as you know. They handle it all, at least so far—uh, there he goes."

The dim beam of light angling across the floor from the living room blinked off, and the town lights were also snuffed out for several palpable seconds.

About ten-thirty, Fergie drove back into the lane behind the cottage, parked, walked between the puddles and came in the kitchen door, sleeves rolled up, uniform coat and tie apparently left in the Ford. The bright light in the kitchen ceiling was on and dance-band music from WGN was coming in from the Philco radio in the front room. The other four adults were all sitting around the table, behind little piles of pennies, holding cards and turning to smile at him as he walked in. His empty chair was waiting for him.

Since it was not a school night, Ramsay and Grover were still up. Ramsay sat on a stool, waiting to watch more of the card game. Grover was making loud scraping noises, sliding a covered stewpot full of popcorn seeds, back and forth over one of the burners on the kitchen stove, busy listening for the first popping noises to start.

FLORA'S MONEY

Grover glanced over at Fergie for just a second, not sure what he was expecting, but feeling relieved that he looked just the same. Fergie nodded at him, with a little smile, then he sat down and announced, "Well, storm's over, finally."

A half-full pitcher of homemade beer sat on the edge of the player's table, next to the waiting popcorn bowl.

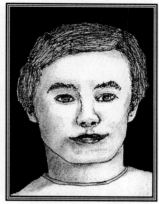
GROVER

CHAPTER 5

By the end of the third grade at the small Hamelet Academy, Grover was advanced to grade five by Professor Theophile. Theo, as he preferred to be called, his only teacher from grade one through twelve, also gave Grover a new tablet to take home, saying: "Use this for writing, drawing, and private notes. You don't need to show them to anyone, not even me, unless you want to." Later, he suggested to the bright youngster that he might want to call his work *Grover's Omnium-Gatherum*.

Grover liked the title and decided to use it, even though he had to ask what the last two words meant. Theo told him to look it up. He did and found this: omnium is Latin for *all* and gatherum is a mock-Latinate alteration of *gather*. Keen, Grover thought. He began filling a tablet right away.

FLORA'S MONEY

After that, all through school, Theo supplied Grover with another tablet whenever he needed one, each time saying things like, "You tell me you enjoy writing and art. Fine. Keep at it. Write down your thoughts. Save your drawings. And carefully choose each word for your stories, like you would select fieldstones to build a wall—be positive that each word fits, and continues to raise the wall higher. Save the pages. When you're older you'll be glad you started the habit."

Years later, whenever Grover opened his tablet file drawer and was reminded of his old friend and mentor, he realized how right Theo had been. As his collection kept growing, Grover learned that to put thoughts on paper, privately, in story-form or pictures, stimulated his thinking and opened doors to imaginative ideas. In time, he willingly shared the tablets with Theo. Grover's first entry starts here, followed by one four years later:

FLORA'S MONEY

Grover's Private Omnium-Gatherum, 1924 ~ Age 10-1/2

I go to Hamelet School, in grade 5. The teacher is Professor Theo. He lets us call him Theo as long as we say yes sir or no sir in class. He gave me this whole tablet to write stories or draw in, at home or anywhere. I can do stuff just for me or let him see it if I want to.

I hate penmanship class. All you do is write dumb things over and over. The ink drips a lot after you dip the pen and my wiper rag gets my fingers black. I like to use pencil. Arithmetic is OK. I do problems easy and get answers faster than other kids. I like science class, but my favorites are reading and art. Theo draws real good.

Last week we had Armistice Day to memorize the soldiers that died. The veteran band played tunes on the beach near our house. They had chairs for the band and let people sit around on the sand. The leader stood on a box. I sat on the end of the same box and heard everything loud. Ramsay climbed on the cannon by the flagpole to watch and Uncle Jerry made him get down. My friend Arie is calling me. I guess I'll go out and play with her until Maddie gets supper.

Ramsay, this is my Private Tablet. Do Not Read This!!

FLORA'S MONEY

Grover's Private Omnium-Gatherum, 1928 ~ Age 14

This town isn't named after Shakespeare's prince, as far as I could ever find out. There's nothing tragic about our Hamelet. Besides, we spell it different, with a middle E. The exact year the village was started has always been uncertain, but everybody says the place does have a long history. Trouble is, hardly any of the data was ever recorded in special books like they have in Elkhart, or maybe Kalamazoo, big places like that.

Hamelet has about ten blocks of old houses, with some vacant lots, and about a dozen shops, including a drugstore, a diner with a counter and stools and a sign in the window that says: Famous For Hamelet Omelets. All these houses and buildings extend out on three sides of a block long park in the center of Hamelet. The fourth side is open to the town beach, with a wide view of sand, sky and water.

We have a grocery store, and the Emporium that sells almost everything folks around here need, and a Sinclair gas station with a shed where everybody gets their cars and trucks fixed. There used to be a bank, but it shut down years ago after some guys drove through town, robbed it, and only left enough money to return savings to the few customers that it had. It never reopened. We also have two churches and a graveyard.

FLORA'S MONEY

Our firehouse is manned by some of our neighbor guys. The town hall, post office and Uncle Jerry's police station are all located in the same building with the fire truck. There's only one schoolhouse for all the grades, one through twelve. It was originally a mansion built in 1870, with the carriage house later fixed up to be the town library. I spend a lot of time there, reading. They say the mansion was left to Hamelet by a rich man who made lots of money selling sand and gravel that he didn't own, to county road builders, about 1910. He just sent his men out to the dunes not far from town and had them shovel the loads onto wagons pulled by his teams of oxen. Then the men walked behind the wagons to wherever the roads were being built and shoveled it off.

Professor Theo told us about a tall tale he heard that he says might have been passed down by elder storytellers of the Indians who roamed the forests around here, long before Hamelet was started. The yarn claims that the first people to ever live in this part of the wilderness were a young man, and his wife, who got mad at the people in their tribe up north and decided to come looking around this area for a new place to live. So, he had his wife pile up their pots and blankets and most everything else they owned, and tie the heap on a frame thing, laid over some trailing poles, called a travois. The usual way then was

FLORA'S MONEY

to hang one end of each pole on either side of a horse and drag the other ends on the ground, with the load on top, and with only one person riding the horse. As the man of the family he rode the only horse they had. She walked behind and carried all the things that wouldn't fit on the travois—her husband's weapons, his shell collection and their pet cat if they had one.

So, off they went, looking for teepee spots with a nice view. This lasted until about the third day when the lady abruptly became ill—that is, according to Theo, she got sick of watching her man loll and loaf while she toted and trudged. So she dropped the load of future artifacts on the ground and maybe said, "This is it, chief, I quit."

Now, centuries later, when someone asks how Hamelet happened to be where it is, some grown-ups claim the spot she picked in those woods, to pile her goods, later became the site of an early office of something called the Women's Anti-Saloon League, and our town kind of grew from there. I guess that's supposed to be a joke.

Oh, and how did our Hamelet get its name? I don't know, and I haven't found anyone who is really sure. Theo and I found it listed in the big dictionary he has, but all it said was it meant village. We already knew that, and it said it had Germanic origins, but that didn't help either.

34

FLORA'S MONEY

One oldtimer told us that many years ago, maybe eight or nine years back, some locals started what they called the Greater Hamelet Historical Committee. He said they even started collecting donations to open a little museum in some old barn where local antiques could be displayed, and the committee could have meetings, and maybe a clambake once in a while. But since then most of the members have died off or moved away, and now there's no one left here who knows where the money went, or if there ever was any donated.

So, how did the name Hamelet get picked? I still don't know.

CHAPTER 6

In 1929, when Grover had just turned fifteen, and Ramsay was seventeen, their uncle Jerry was in the Hamelet post office one sultry afternoon, looking over the wanted photos of Chicago-area gangsters. Seeing nothing new, he glanced again at the other notices and, mostly out of boredom, he flipped through all the sheets that were tacked to the bulletin board in front of the counter.

It was then that he saw a federal notice of property disposal underneath several other papers. He saw that the bid request had come from Washington and concerned fifty acres described as 'wilderness land.' The exact boundaries of the property were stated in a confused manner, apparently using longitude and latitude numbers taken from a very old nautical chart. But, to Jerry's surprise, there was a small map that placed the land out on the shore only a mile from town, and that helped him figure out exactly where the land was located. Intrigued, he wondered if anyone else in town had bothered to read the bid.

Jerry stared at the paper and thought that the land had to be out by the point, but there was no mention of the old shut-down lighthouse or the other abandoned shacks and outbuildings still out there. He removed the tack and took the bid document back to his office in the police rooms down the street. As he re-read the bid, he began thinking about the fifty dollars in small bills his late brother Ansel had left in his care for Ramsay and Grover, just before dying in 1918. Jerry still had the cash, hidden in their cottage; he had kept it safe for eleven years, determined to use it on the boys in the best way he could.

Unsure what to do, Jerry talked it over with Maddie; then he visited the only lawyer in Hamelet, the town Judge and an old friend, and asked him about the possibility of using the meager legacy to try getting the property for the boys. Intrigued, the Judge made some notes and told Jerry he would do some discreet digging and get back to him.

Ten days later, the Judge walked over to Jerry's office and told him he had found out that the high bidder could retain the property forever, as long as he or a member of his family lived on the site—and, of special interest, the whole place would enjoy special exemptions from most real estate taxes. Then, leaning across the table where they sat alone in Jerry's office, the Judge lowered his voice and whispered, "The lighthouse and anything else still out there was all written off, apparently, back in 1904 when the operation was deactivated by the government! As far as the government is

FLORA'S MONEY

concerned, the property is just a bunch of woods and sand, a wilderness—nothing on it. Hell, my advice is to give it a shot. Think about it. Talk to Maddie. If you say go, I'll write up the bid no charge, for Ansel's sake. I remember he helped save lives more than once—as a volunteer on the lifeboat-rescue crew we used to have on the beach back before most of the guys went off to the war."

"I think we've already decided, Judge. Let's try it. We'll probably never get it," Jerry said, "but maybe, who knows? It could be great for the boys."

Nine weeks after sending in the government bid, Maddie and Jerry were stunned when he received a letter direct from a federal agency in Washington. It advised him that his bid of fifty dollars, as high bidder and a U.S. Army veteran, had been accepted, making him the owner of the entire fifty acres—and apparently the unmentioned lighthouse and structures still on it. With Maddie's agreement, Jerry then had the Judge draw up the papers making them legal guardians of the boys so Ramsay and Grover could become co-owners of the bid property as soon as they were old enough to legally take over.

When everything was worked out, the Judge said to Jerry, "Keep a low profile on this deal. Never contact Washington about it. Everything is legal and proper, in my judgment, but you never know when some politicians down there might want to get their hooks into something like this, and maybe change the rules, or whatever. Someday that shore area might be worth a lot of money. Best you don't try to sell it until the boys grow up—or maybe never. Just take possession now and hang on. Fix up the place and let them live there, at least in the summer; the sooner the better. Tell the boys, if anyone asks, that they inherited the place. Then stop there. Warn

FLORA'S MONEY

them to never reveal how much the bid was, or any of the details. I'll chat with them about it, too. So congratulations, and regards to Maddie."

Jerry told Grover and Ramsay the news about the winning bid the same afternoon he received the government letter containing the official results, and the brothers were elated about being allowed to move into such an enchanting place and be on their own. It was less than a mile down the beach from Jerry's cottage, and they both had grown up with the deserted tower as their particular playground. It was their place to wade, fish, launch homemade toy boats—and play at ruling a mighty kingdom from the rocky ledges comprising the base of their special castle.

As young boys, Ramsay and Grover had managed to find ways to wiggle between the planks nailed over the one small window by the door at the base of the lighthouse tower—and run up and down the circular stone steps inside, shouting to make lonely echoes in the dank, shadow-filled stairwell. Sometimes, other boys from town would join them to play at battles in and around their pretend castle, with blunt wooden swords all the boys made themselves. As gallant knights, some of the boys would often tie two corners of an old towel around the neck to make grand capes.

Young girls came to play, too, but only on sunny days for their outings with their own family members. Some of the girls made miniature sand castles, squealing and splashing in the puddles of tepid lake water along the layers of rock at the tower base.

Yet, in spite of the family outings now and then, a lot of the time the lighthouse had few visitors and sat silent and alone, year after year, lifeless and of little interest to the other locals. Ramsay and Grover were the exceptions. By

39

FLORA'S MONEY

the time they reached their early teens the unique ledges at the base of the tower had become their favorite hangout, and the surrounding sands, the majestic lake and the rocky shores their kingdom.

On the wonderful day when Jerry and Maddie broke the exciting news about winning the government bid for the lighthouse, astonishment and big smiles by the boys, along with their excited questions, took over, especially when he told them that they could begin to clean up the tower and move in right away. After a few minutes Maddie said, "Okay, settle down. We want to talk to you about this before you start hauling your things out there. Jerry?"

"We'll be watching you," he warned them, "no hell-raising, no visitors, especially girls, inside, or anywhere, without one of their adults, or one of us around. Right, Maddie?" She nodded and made eye contact with each boy.

"And remember," Jerry continued, "you have to behave just like you would here in the cottage with me and Maddie. I'll help you out at first with a few bucks' worth of groceries, about the same as I've been spending to feed you now. But you'll have to earn what you can to help pay for things out there. I'll help you do any fixing up, if you need me—but it'll take time. Bringing electricity out there, or much in the way of heat, or even getting a water pump rigged up are out of the question for now.

"When it gets too cold," he added, "and the snows start, you should come back here till spring, at least till we can get better heat in the shack. For the warmer months I know where I can get a wood stove you can cook basic stuff on, and maybe warm up part of the shack a little. The top room in the tower can be used for sleeping, and a fantastic everyday room. And I'll help you fix up the old outhouse in the woods.

40

FLORA'S MONEY

In the meantime, you'll have to make use of the bushes back in the trees, like beach users always do. And don't forget to take your baths or Maddie will get mad. Come back here or use the lake!"

"And Jere," Ramsay said eagerly, "once we get the place cleaned up some, what if we put up a sign for people who want to climb the tower steps and enjoy the view? Maybe charge a nickel a person. And maybe sell some lemonade."

"Golly, Rams," Grover said, "we want to get it fixed up first, don't we? We don't want a lot of strangers sneaking around when we're tryin' to get settled and all, do we?"

"Maybe we could earn enough to buy some souvenir stuff to sell," Ramsay replied.

"You can always limit visiting hours on the sign, if it gets too busy," Jerry said with a smile, "crowds normally aren't a problem around here."

Then Grover asked, "Do we know how much of the land goes with the lighthouse? You've always had keep-out signs and lots of barbed wire strung around out there. And you always made it clear that we shouldn't fool around in those woody areas, because maybe there was poison ivy around and some old wells we might fall into. I remember, you took us in there once. Yuck."

"We don't know yet," Jerry replied, "the Judge said he'll stop by soon with some of that detail. He's trying to track down some old survey records that may help. In the meantime, he said, don't tell folks about the amount of the bid. Understand? There are going to be enough envious people around town, even though few of them ever went near the tower very much. But as the news spreads that you've moved in, some folks might get jealous. We don't want to stir up a fuss." Both of the boys nodded, then stood up.

FLORA'S MONEY

"Gosh, Jere, this is fantastic," Grover said, "The lighthouse has always been my best place—read, draw, watch the birds—can we all go over, right now?"

Jere and Maddie stood up too, and she said, "I'll come over later."

"Okay," Jerry replied, "and let's take the hammer and the crowbar to get those planks off so we can open up the place and air it out. And we have to be careful up top when we take off the boards covering the windows—and no telling what shape the stairs are in."

Ramsay grinned and bragged: "Don't worry, Jere, we already know our way around in there." Maddie made a mock-frown.

"Oh, indeed," Jerry remarked, patting each of them on the shoulder. Then he turned away, gave his wife a quick kiss, nodded quickly at the boys and went outside, blowing his nose as he went. Maddie gave the boys each a hug and said, "I'll see you over there."

When the boys came out with the tools, the three of them walked over to the tower. The young lords, with the king's help, freed the besieged castle by removing the boards nailed over the front door. The boys ran up all the steps and helped Jerry open some of the windows up top—as soon as he made it up there, too. After that his majesty left and went back down, saying it was time for him to go back to work in town.

That day and the next, the pair of royal heirs carried on the attack, trotting back and forth across the sands, again and again, carrying supplies up the numerous steps many times—and sleeping on the floor up-top that night.

FLORA'S MONEY

Late the next afternoon, neither of the conquerors was about and sunlight streamed through the first four of the windows to have the boards pried off. Boy treasures now occupied the knights' quarters and this was the scene in the castle's round room: two wooden orange-crates, standing on end with the board-separator in the middle of each box acting as a shelf, held well-worn books, including *Gulliver's Travels, The Time Machine* and one tattered *Encyclopedia Britannica* volume (D through E), a Sears Roebuck catalog and a half-roll of toilet paper. Stacked next to the crates was a pile of articles saved from the Chicago *Sunday Tribune,* including several sepia rotogravures of paintings by American artists. Next to the pile, a Mickey Mouse big-little book (four inches square and two inches thick) sat on several copies of old *Popular Mechanics* magazines. A flat wooden box, over a foot square, with a hinged cover, held several of Grover's tablets of writings and drawings. The box, once used to display packets of flower seeds in the Emporium, had the Mandeville & King logo printed on a label across the front. It also held some hand-sharpened pencils and blunt crayons, a tin box of watercolor squares and two frowsy brushes, an Indian-head penny and a grubby slide rule. Sitting loose on the floor were six candle stubs, a nickel box of matches, and two former cigar-boxes holding tiny parts for Grover's construction-in-progress of a crystal-set radio.

A bushel basket held two plates, one fork, two spoons, three bottles of NeHi orange drink (one empty), a half-full Crackerjack box, a torn and scuffed baseball, a jumble of BVD underwear and an empty goldfish bowl. Heaped by the wall were two one-piece bathing suits for boys and a handknit sweater (all made of wool, with a few moth holes in each) and two olive-

FLORA'S MONEY

drab army blankets, a frayed patchwork-quilt and two lumpy pillows without cases. A squashed derby hat sat atop the pile.

Earlier that afternoon, Maddie was there, helping them clean up. Insisting she come along, they hurried her into town and hustled Jerry from his office to the marble-topped soda fountain in the drugstore, saying they wanted to toast the two of them, their treat, (after taking a quarter, dime and nickel from their official treasury: a total of ninety-three cents kept in an old sock).

Then Ramsay ordered four flagons of mead from their family friend, Oscar the druggist. He laughed and served each of them a Coke, flavored with chocolate syrup, in the traditional glass. With a flourish, he put two straws in each one.

Later, the boys came back to the tower by themselves and climbed up to the round room. Grover sat down on the floor and began sorting though their gear and wondering what to do next. Ramsay went over to the other side of the room and reached into the pocket of an old jacket. It was on the floor, where he had put it that morning, hidden behind some of the removed boards from the windows. He took out a corked pop-bottle, holding about two inches of a brown liquid, and said with a grin, "Hey, now we can have a real toast!"

Grover looked around, stared, and said, "Where did you get that?"

"Never mind. I kind of borrowed it from a jug Uncle Jerry had in the closet over at the house. It's whisky, want some?" Ramsay replied. Then he pulled out the cork he had used as a makeshift stopper, sniffed the

FLORA'S MONEY

contents and offered the bottle to Grover.

"Uh, you first," Grover said. "Jeepers, you shouldn't have swiped it."

Ramsay shrugged, took a sip and smacked his lips thoughtfully for a moment. Then he tipped the bottle up and swallowed a mouthful—gagged, made ahem-noises, twice, looked wide-eyed at his brother, gulped and managed to say, "That's smooth!"

Grover said, "Smooth? Hey—know what, you forgot to make a toast."

THEO

CHAPTER 7

At 8:15 on a fall morning in 1929, Professor Theophile stood in front of all thirty of the boys and girls enrolled in Hamelet School. As usual for one of his group assemblies, he had the older pupils, like Grover and Ramsay, sit in chairs at three long tables lined up parallel to the four windows, and the kids in the lower grades perch on stools, here and there, brought over from their low tables in the corners of the room.

Theo looked around, smiling, and announced: "As you've all heard, Grover and Ramsay now live in the old lighthouse. We know it so well from the outside and soon we'll have a tour inside, once the boys have it ready for visitors. Now then, a quick background. The first lighthouse in America was put to work in 1716 on Brewster Island in Boston Harbor, and our tower was built in 1868. Since then, hundreds of U.S.

FLORA'S MONEY

light stations were built and staffed by local and federal governments, all around our seacoasts and on inland waterways. In fact, active and inactive light stations are still scattered all around this lake.

"Lighthouses have always led a precarious existence, constantly exposed to harsh weather with eroding waves, or torn down because they have been outmoded by more modern navigational aids on ships as well as shore beacons. Many towers like ours that have been turned off are being preserved as museums, inns or private homes. In daylight, the lighthouses left standing, whether active or not, are often used by both on-shore travelers and sailors as daymarks to help them find their way. In 1904, our light was shut down by the government, the keeper retired from service, the Fresnel lens and lighting equipment removed and the windows boarded up.

"It is about sixty-five feet to the top of our tower. It was originally planned to be over eighty-feet high, but after construction was about halfway up a change was made, perhaps due to budget reductions by the government. Anyhow, the main room up top was built at a lower level than first intended. It was a good change for the boys because with the round walls tapering in toward the top, their living room space up there is over fourteen feet in diameter. If they had built the tower higher, the lightroom up top would have been smaller. If anyone doesn't follow that I'll make a diagram later.

"The boys have a wonderful front porch for sightseeing on the observation gallery. It has a railing that encircles the tower just below the windows and is accessible through a low door off the top room. The tall windows, all around that room, are set right in the stone, to make them strong enough to resist storms and often very strong winds.

FLORA'S MONEY

"Once lit, every night at dusk when it was an active lighthouse, our light began a sky sweep that lasted till dawn—and class, we'll discuss lighthouses again after the boys have let us tour theirs. Now, before we go on to other things, are there any questions?"

Buster, a fifth grader, raised his hand. He peered through his thick glasses, looking concerned, and asked, "Professor, I've heard that some ghosts of drowned sailors live in the top room of the lighthouse and after midnight they say you can hear echoes of them screaming for help down the stairway—is that true?"

Everyone laughed. "Would one of you care to answer that question?" Theo asked, looking over at Ramsay and Grover.

Grover nodded and said, trying to sound serious, "Well, Buster, actually I haven't heard them call out the word HELP, though they do moan a lot. But it doesn't bother us much anymore, does it Ramsay?"

His brother hesitated for a moment, to heighten the suspense, then making his voice shrill he said, "Naw. It doesn't scare us. They only do it during thunderstorms when there's a lot of noise, anyhow—and if we do hear them moaning, and screaming sometimes, we just pretend it's the wind from the storm!"

Buster joined Grover outside, after school that day, as he often did. At first, they walked along the dirt street in silence until Grover began to whistle soft little trills and swirled sounds, easy, relaxed and informal. Right off, Buster asked, "How did you learn to whistle like that—can you do birdtalk—can you teach me?"

FLORA'S MONEY

Grover looked at Buster and said, "I don't remember ever learning to whistle. For me, it's been like breathing. I don't think about it; I just pucker up and blow easy—like humming." Taller than his young friend, Grover looked down at him and said, "Sometimes, I whistle tunes I've heard on the radio or the Victrola—or just make something up as I go along. You've done it with a kazoo haven't you?

"And if I hear birds when I'm alone, in the woods or on the beach at dawn or dusk, I listen and try to copy their language rather than whistle songs that they probably don't know. Birds do most of their gabbing early in the morning, or just before they hit the hay in their nests, and of course they don't whistle our tunes."

"I can do a duck," Buster said.

"Anybody can quack. Whistling takes more practice."

"I know. How do I practice?"

"First, just listen to the birds sing as they sit up in the trees, or maybe on a roof. You have to believe that they're whistle-talking to each other. I can see them look down when they hear me butt-in and chirp something. They even cock their heads a lot as though they're listening to me. Then we have a friendly chat. I listen to them and then imitate what I hear, as best I can. We repeat the tweeting back and forth, until one of us gets bored and takes off; they flutter and fly, I walk."

"Golly, Grover. Really? They must like you, huh? "

"Well, sometimes they do misunderstand something I whistle when we're having a chirpy chat, and for some reason it makes them mad. Then they might get snappish, suddenly sound shriller and quickly leave the scene—just like people having an argument sometimes do. Right?"

FLORA'S MONEY

Buster stared for a moment and asked, "Do birds really say words?"

"Probably," Grover said, "I can't prove it. And there's no bird dictionary that I know of, but I don't think they worry about grammar and stuff like that. But when they talk at you, listen carefully. Experiment with puckering as you blow. Try to make whistle-sounds that have the rhythm, speed and up and down that resemble what you hear. Before you know it, you'll start to hear them pause after they tweet at you, as though they're waiting for your reply. When you hear that, you know that at least you've got their attention. Honest. Now, if this happens, you may wonder how it can be a conversation between you and the birds if all you're doing is repeating what they're saying. I haven't figured out an answer to that, yet. Maybe, like people they don't really listen very closely to what others say.

"But, anyhow, you should try different ways to blow and expand your chirps. Squeeze spit close to inside your lips, keep it there and blow. This adds bird trills, swirls and warbles to your message. But watch out you don't spit on anyone walking by.

"Chat with birds whenever you can, for practice. You'll find some birds talk better than others, and like to repeat things a lot, just like us. And if you converse with birds just arrived from a foreign country, don't worry; I think bird talk is the same all over."

By then, they had walked to Buster's corner where he had to turn to go to his house. He stopped, gazed thoughtfully at Grover for a moment and said with a frown, "I hate crows. They're mean, so I just ignore them when they do all that scratchy hollerin'. Crows just aren't nice to anybody, seems like."

Grover nodded and said, "I know. Not even to each

FLORA'S MONEY

other. They're scary."

Then Buster, suddenly distracted by something, looked almost straight up and said, "Is that a hawk up there? Can you talk to him?"

"No, I've never been near enough to a hawk to know what they sound like. They always just circle around so high up, looking to swoop down, grab a little creature for food and zoom off again."

"Gee," Buster blurted with a grin, "maybe they can't say much because being so high and going around in circles so much makes them dizzy!"

"Hey, you may be right," Grover replied, grinning along with him.

Buster puckered up and blew soundless puffs for a few moments—until a shrill and spit splattering teapot-twerp slipped out. He looked at Grover, astonished.

"Hey, keep it up. See how easy it is!" Grover shouted.

Waving his arms, hands outspread, Buster turned and bellowed, "Thanks, Grover, lookit me, I'm a bird!" Still flapping his arms, puffing and spluttering, he began to skip and run toward home.

Grover walked on, smiling. After a bit he began whistling a melody from a Gershwin tune he had heard on the radio.

One April day in 1930, Ramsay decided to explore the dark woods behind their lighthouse and see what he could find. Jerry had always forbidden them to go there for fear they might get lost, fall into sinkholes or be caught by shifting sands from the dunes. But now that they owned much of the area he felt challenged to sneak in and take a look.

After prowling through the brush, dunes and dense

FLORA'S MONEY

pines, he did find a tumbledown shed, the size of a large barn, that shifting sand had nearly buried on two sides. The whole structure leaned out of square and the roof sagged low in the middle. He picked up a hefty stick, pried three planks off an opening that once might have held a framed window, climbed inside and peered around in the gloom. He was astounded to see the bulging hull of a long wooden boat propped up on three logs in the middle of the single, large room. A smaller boat sat next to it, upside down. A heap of oars and assorted spars lay nearby on the stone-paved, sandy floor. Thick dust and lacy spider webs were everywhere. Waving aside some of the clingy strands, he stared over the gunwale of the long boat and counted eight rows of wide plank seats where oarsmen and passengers would sit. The faded lettering on the stern panel spelled out HAMELET RESCUE.

"Damn, a lifeboat! From the old squad," he whispered, then said out loud, "wow!"

Enchanted, Ramsay began poking around in more of the shadowy room. Heaped next to one wall he found a shoulder-high pile of old, rotting straw. He paused, curious, when he saw the corner of a wooden crate protruding from the pile.

Kicking aside the smelly stuff he uncovered three wooden boxes he thought might be old whiskey cases, each one completely nailed shut. He used his pocket knife to pry open a slat on one box and, holding his breath in disbelief, lifted out a fancy bottle, cork sealed, full and, he guessed, about a quart size. He counted eleven more bottles inside, each one packed between separating slats. The language on the bottle label mystified him until he saw the words *French Champagne Cognac*. Cripes, he thought—thirty-six of them,

52

FLORA'S MONEY

must be worth tons of money! Wide eyed, he gasped and squealed out loud, "CRIME-A-NETLY!"

Ramsay hastily lugged the cases outside, one at a time, and buried them deep in loose sand next to rocky outcroppings behind the big shed, a spot he made sure he could find again. Then he went home without telling Grover or anyone about the three boxes.

The next day Ramsay brought his uncle and brother to see the two boats he had found. Jerry said the place looked like it was once a summer storehouse for blocks of lake ice that used to be harvested by crews every winter and packed in straw in the shed. But he had never looked in the old ruin before, and didn't know the boats existed.

Later, along with three men from town, they opened a wide sliding door in the old building, leveraged the lifeboat onto rollers and dragged it down next to the lighthouse. There they propped it up again, safely back from the water's edge. The group easily picked up the skiff, carried it down to the shore, and placed it next to the lifeboat. When they turned the little skiff over they saw it had oarlocks, a slot for a small keel and blocks mounted forward, inside the hull, to hold a short mast.

News of finding the rescue boat spread quickly. The Judge walked down to take a look and confirmed that town volunteers, including the boys' late father, Ansel, had used the boat before the war to save sailors in trouble. Others came to see the relic and several men offered to help fix it up, once plans for its future were worked out. That was okay by Ramsay. But he claimed the skiff for himself, and no one objected.

Within a week he had it rigged with a short mast, a homemade sail, oars and a keel board. The skiff soon became Ramsay's passion and something to do after the boring year

FLORA'S MONEY

he had gone through since graduation. On sunny afternoons he tried cruising off shore, sometimes with various friends, male or female. Grover went along a few times in the early morning, to spend a few hours fishing with his brother. But that amusement didn't last.

With no jobs in the area, most of Ramsay's friends had drifted away seeking work. He had often heard rumors that there was a lot more to life nearer the big cities, exciting places he had read about but never seen. He began to take overnight jaunts in the boat and camping out on the beach. One starry night, lying awake on a blanket, miles south of Hamelet, he realized the skiff was more than a toy. It was transportation, and a lot more.

At dawn he eagerly sailed back to the beach area, next to the old shed where he had hidden his three boxes of Cognac treasures, and lashed them on the skiff, well hidden under the blanket. From there it was a short row to the lighthouse. He ran upstairs and found Grover sitting up in bed, watching the gulls swoop and glide through space.

"Hi, Grove, I'm off as soon as I gather up some of my clothes and stuff."

"Off?"

"In the skiff. Got it all figured. Sail it around the bottom of the lake, keeping the shore in sight. Get to Chicago, sell the boat and, uh, some other things I've got. Get a job, maybe go to college part of the time, and get rich, who knows?"

Grover cocked his head, thinking. He stared at his brother and said, "You serious?"

"Damn right. You seem to be having fun working on this place. You don't need me anymore. In fact, once I get going over there, maybe I can send you money now and then. Do me a favor and tell Jere and Maddie not to worry." Ramsay

54

kept moving around the room as he talked, jamming clothes and things into an old duffle bag.

Grover sat still, watching him. "Well, I guess I get to be lord of the castle. So beat it, sailor. And by the way, what if there's no wind to push your schooner?"

"I've got oars."

Grover nodded, reached out and, perhaps for the first time, they shook hands.

Part Two ~ Chicago

1931-1933

JIGGS

CHAPTER 8

On her own in the illegal honky-tonk world of Chicago nightlife, Flora was dazzled right from the start. She found it to be a city where many working people struggled, while others cavorted, through the final quirky years of Prohibition. Good and bad, it was an exciting place to be. Without yearning at all for her previous years amid the whispering dunes of Hamelet, she quickly embraced the why-not attitude of her new life and discarded what little rural timidity she had brought to town.

Flora reasoned that she enjoyed working and kidding with most of the customers at Golden's where she was making many new friends, but Jiggs was another matter. She found him boorish, hard to like and, as she overheard female customers gossip about his arrogance and temper displays

FLORA'S MONEY

with the ladies, she became even more wary; before moving, she firmly decided that she would enjoy his fantastic offer for the free apartment, and the use of a dreamy car—but if he ever made any trouble she'd dump his deal and beat it, twenty-three skidoo. So, after three days of thinking over the possibilities of the apartment and car from Jiggs, she accepted his offer.

A week later she gathered up her belongings, mostly clothes, and moved in. And a week after that she added a throw-bolt to the front door of the apartment, to prevent any unwanted intrusions by a hard-drinking landlord.

Back home, in her early teens, years younger than her tall and developed body suggested, she had learned how to handle males when they verbally flirted, whether they were youths trying to act like grown men—or vice versa. But their banter was soda pop compared to the blatant pitches made by gin guzzlers at Golden's.

It was not unusual for blunt and crude propositions to be tossed across the bar at her by some of the customers, but she quickly learned how to defuse that kind of jazz with a laugh, a wisecrack or a comical wink—or sometimes just smiling and moving on.

Among many changes in her life, big and small, her whole relationship with cash also flip-flopped in Chicago. Before coming to the city, Flora had never personally owned more than a few coins or small bills at any one time in her whole life. But as she worked, she quickly improvised some unique ways to scoop up the currency and coins on the run, when affluent customers casually tossed them on the damp wood to pay a tab. Seeing greenbacks strewn among the iced

58

FLORA'S MONEY

glasses, with liquids clear or amber, and ashtrays that released sensual trails of gray smoke, Flora was energized and kept alert. Gliding back and forth grandly, with style, was easy and natural for her lithe body. She learned to make change quickly, palm all tips, and smoothly toss house cash into the hinged tin box under the bar. Her show time began at eight p.m. and sometimes lasted till dawn.

There were no receipts. She ran tabs in her head for the big spenders, or noted the numbers on disposable slips of paper; and she always swooped in to collect before the seersucker suit, or the checkered vest, left the scene. Flora also saw that these gents, with their slick center-parted hair and diamond stickpins in their neckties, took pride in over-tipping in front of their pals. This inspired her to add to their fun by taking the nabob's money, at settle-up times, and doing an underhand windmill circle with her long arm, just once, when sliding the change onto the bar in front of him. Then she would pucker-kiss the air in his direction and smile as she serenely slipped away to serve another customer.

Invariably, as Flora's choreography attracted ogles, the host plucked extra dollars from his change pile to put on the bar for her—and did it with a copycat flourish of the forearm and an airborne pucker-kiss back to her. Started as a joke, it eventually grew into a funny bit for customers, performed more than once during the evening, and sometimes causing other drinkers to toss a dollar on the bar and going pucker-pucker-kiss in her direction. Laughing and puckering, she would then swing around and glide as far as needed to sweep up the loot.

After a few months of learning the routines of her new world, financial temptations were thrust upon Flora one night that would be too much for many souls to resist. Supplies of

FLORA'S MONEY

bottle goods were regularly stored behind a sliding panel in a tiny backroom that Manny used as an office. It was located down the hall that led to the restrooms. Whenever she was at work, she saw that the day bartender, if he hadn't left yet, as well as Manny and Jiggs, freely grabbed bottles for restocking—and for pouring freebies for themselves and for their pals. Surprised at first, Flora watched them do it, then shrugged it off and learned to ignore the practice. She drank very little herself and only poured freebies if Manny or Jiggs said expansively, "Give him one on the house!"

Manny never worked behind the bar with Flora, unless they were very busy. At every closing, though, he would see that all the customers, and Flora, were out before he locked up. Once he was alone in the place, he took the cash from the tin box, hid the money in his office, switched off the lights and let himself out. Usually, the speakeasy closed four to six hours after midnight, or as soon as the last customer staggered, was pushed, or wobbled down the stairway. About noon the next day, Manny would reappear out front, grope through his pockets for keys and, looking pale and sour, reverse his routine. A little later, the part time day-bartender would wander up the stairs and start to work by sweeping out the place, and Golden's would then be ready for a new day.

One night, after Flora had worked at Golden's for several months, Manny surprised her by adding a new chore for her to handle. It was about two hours after twelve and, relaxed from drinking boilermakers with customer-friends, Manny showed Flora his closing-up routine. Between sips from a glass of rye-spiked beer, with periodic burps livening up their little tour around the nearly empty club, he showed her what to do to close the place by herself. Then he handed her two

FLORA'S MONEY

keys on a chain loop and told her to do the close-up that night on her own, both knowing that Golden's had to be kept open for several more hours.

As he staggered off to party elsewhere, he mumbled, "Keep those keys in a save—uh, safe place." From then on, closing up became part of her job, and Manny usually was gone long before she shut down.

Flora continued to learn more about the lax things the speakeasy guys allowed to happen. As far as she could tell, no one ever checked on the brands and number of bottled goods delivered by suppliers for stock, or the amount of cash taken in or paid out. She also saw that when boxes of booze were carried up the stairs by a delivery guy, Manny or Jiggs just grabbed a handful of bills out of the tin box and gave the well-dressed guy with the driver whatever amount of cash he asked for. Then the driver carried the boxes into the office, unpacked them and placed the bottles behind the sliding panel, sometimes not even bothering to close it afterwards.

Flora figured that these speakeasy guys just floated along, unconcerned about the law. "You'll never be paid anything by the house," Manny had told her bluntly when he hired her, "and don't expect any pay envelopes from us—we don't even want to know your last name. Work hard, grab your tips, and you should do okay if you move fast and smile a lot—or else you'll be no good for us either and you'll be out. Got it?"

Rhonda's yarns about the bootleggers, when she dropped in for a drink one night, earlier that same week, also bothered Flora when she heard her friend say, "Hey, Flora, look at all the cash flyin' across your bar. These guys really rake it in—and you know, I hear that they have to hide the loot they

FLORA'S MONEY

make, or spend it. They don't want to deposit money in a bank. The cops might find out and grab it for taxes, maybe kickbacks to private charities, like judges or who knows what! But still, the money rolls in, so they either hide it or blow it. That's what I hear." Flora thought about it a lot that night, especially since Manny had so recently piled the extra duty on her to lock up—and handed her the keys. Then she remembered Rhonda's chatter. That did it.

On her lock-up nights at the bar, Flora was careful to hide every dollar of house cash before leaving, and put it all in the secret place Manny told her about, when he said: "Unlock my office and look for a coffee can sitting in a drip pan under one of the three ice boxes in my office—where we keep the blocks of ice we chop up for the bar. There's always some melt water in the pans—I dump 'em myself when they get full. Put all the paper money in the can. We don't care about the coins. Be sure and snap the metal lid on tight to keep the water out and, uh—damn, you look great in that outfit—re-lock my office, then do the lights and lock the front door downstairs as you leave. Use the big key for that—see ya, babe."

After he left, Flora giggled and marveled that these big-money jerks hid their wads of cash in an empty can with a lid, just like she had always done with her meager coins as she grew up.

With her strong body she knew it would be easy for her to start a collection of new bottles of booze in the private storage locker that came with her apartment, and was located in the basement of the building. First, to protect her intended inventory, she replaced the cheap padlock on the door with a stronger one that she bought at a hardware store nearby.

A couple weeks after starting the lock-up chore at

FLORA'S MONEY

Golden's she worked out a plan for herself and began doing it every few nights. At closing time she locked the front door downstairs, took her oversized tote bag back to the locked office and let herself in. Then she would slide open the panel to gain access to the booze hiding place. Kneeling down in the windowless space, she made her selections from the mid-priced bottles of whisky, assuming they would be less likely to be missed than the top-shelf brands. She would then pack a dozen or so in her bag, turn out the lights, lock up and go home.

Once on the sidewalk, Flora stepped out into the dawn, standing tall and unafraid, easily toting the bag of loot with the canvas handles over one shoulder. Walking the few blocks of deserted streets to her apartment she let herself in the front hall, then went directly downstairs and added the bottles to her hiding place in the storeroom.

It was part of her plan that, since she had little interest in consuming any of the beverages, she would one day peddle the bottles to somebody—or maybe use them for stock if she ever opened a bar of her own. When she had about six dozen bottles, she decided that her collection in the storage room was big enough. "What the hell," she mused, looking at her loot one night before going back upstairs to her apartment, "these bums will never miss this much, but I don't want to take more than I can handle if I want to move out in a hurry."

Her success in taking the bottles from the closet at Golden's gave her a nibbling kind of elation and, to her surprise, aroused a feeling of achievement that was new and different. During the weeks she was bringing home the bottles of rye, bourbon, gin and scotch and champagne, she was careful to hide every dollar of the house cash in

FLORA'S MONEY

the secret place under the icebox, just as Manny had told her to do. Stealing actual money would be unthinkable, she believed, but swiping the booze was not the same thing. At least she thought that was how she felt—until the second big temptation came along.

CHAPTER 9

Late one night, after Manny had been sitting at the bar consuming his usual stream of drinks, periodically refreshed by Flora, he yawned, got up and went back to his office. She assumed he would soon be leaving, as usual. But this time he was back there for quite a while. When he came back most of the customers had straggled down the stairs, except for a couple of gents sitting at a table in the far corner of the room, still drinking and talking. Flora was behind the bar, rinsing a few glasses and puttering.

She heard Manny coming and glanced his way. He was carrying a bulging canvas rucksack by the shoulder straps and set it on the floor behind the bar, a few feet from Flora, and said, "Okay, kid—gonna blow now—oops, hafta go back and get my hat."

FLORA'S MONEY

Flora nodded and watched him return down the hall. Then she stared at the bag. She remembered seeing it before, hanging empty on the hall tree in the office. This was the first time she had ever seen it being used by anyone and it made her curious. As a rule, her boss usually wandered in and out empty-handed except for small things like an umbrella, a rolled-up copy of the Trib tucked under one arm, or maybe a small paper bag with a bottle cap sticking out the top.

She reached over and hefted the rucksack. Maybe ten pounds, or so, she guessed, gently putting it back down, thinking maybe it was bottles of booze. She glanced down the empty hall, then looked over the bar at the two customers at the table and made sure that they couldn't possibly see what she was doing. She squatted by the bag and pulled aside the loosely buckled flap to peek inside. Instead of bottles of booze, as she expected, looking back at her was the top row of two large cans, with more layers obviously underneath, all lying flat like fat cigars in a box—each with a commercial label with GOLDEN'S Gourmet COFFEE in big letters, and smaller lines of printing below that.

Eyes wide, Flora stared briefly, muffled a small giggle and let the flap fall back in place—just as she heard the office door slam, followed seconds later by the sounds of Manny's footsteps. She uncoiled herself at top speed and stood up, grabbing a glass and towel from a ledge on the way, and posed innocently polishing the glass as Manny came back behind the bar, picked up his bag and said, "Now we go. G'night again, baby."

Hoisting the bag straps to one shoulder, he swayed some, turned and made his way around to the front of the bar and walked over to the two guys in the corner. They got up. One of the men waved a ten spot at Flora and dropped it on the

FLORA'S MONEY

table.

She waved back and said, "Thanks boys. See ya' later!"

The three of them headed for the stairs and went down. A moment later, when Flora heard the main door squeal shut, she tossed the towel way down the bar. Laughing out loud, she skipped over to the steps and went down them two at a time to close the joint, officially, by locking herself in.

Within fifteen minutes she had tried shouldering aside the iceboxes in Manny's office and looking closely at the floor for a trapdoor that might have led to a hiding place for more cans, but there was nothing there. This is, after all, a tiny room, she thought, gazing around; it has a battered, empty desk, a gooseneck lamp, a sagging chair with squeaky casters, a wobbly hall-tree and three smelly iceboxes with drip pans underneath where she hid the money can, in one of them, each night. Finally, she looked up and realized that left only the crude drop-ceiling, made up of metal panels laid across a rack of wooden slats suspended on wires.

Flora reached up, pushed with the fingers of one hand and saw one of the panels rise up a few inches. Then she stepped up on the desk and easily pushed that panel, and the one next to it, up enough to slide them back out of the way so she could stick her head and shoulders through the open space. The desk light gave her enough light to see that there were board shelves reaching up about four feet into the space above the panels and lining two sides of the little attic space. Flora was astonished to see that dozens of Golden's coffee cans could be seen, nearly filling most of the shelves.

She picked four sample cans at random, each one from a different shelf, and sat down cross-legged on the desktop. One by one she pulled them open with her fingers and saw money—oodles of green paper, folded, wadded, in stacks

FLORA'S MONEY

and jammed loose inside the curved sides. She stared at each open can for a moment then carefully closed it, puffing soft whooshing sounds of amazement as she worked.

Well now, she thought, those two guys must come by to guard Manny as he pulls out a bunch of these cans to take to the big boss somewhere—and I can see that the cans are unevenly stashed, a few gaps here and there, many cans behind cans—imagine, all this loot! No records. Hell, somebody could steal these things! Flora laughed out loud, thinking I could take a few of these from time-to-time, and stop with the bottle goods. I could put the cans in the storeroom, maybe wrap them in bundles—maybe use Christmas paper! She giggled, then pondered some more: Maybe I could buy some more new cans at a grocery and switch 'em with some in the back—or maybe I'll just tap some cash off the top, here and there—this has to be done right—don't want to be too greedy.

She opened a few more and saw that all of them had cash jammed in right to the top. Then, inspired, she stood up again, put all the cans back and reached up to the top shelf to harvest six of the lovely cylinders and blow the dust off each one, thinking, I bet Manny can't reach that high—golly; he'd probably never miss 'em!

After checking that there was cash inside the six cans, and re-closing them, she placed them on the desktop, reached up, slipped the ceiling panel back in place, then stepped to the floor, excited and nervous. Her mind in a whirl, she grabbed the cans, fumbled, and dropped the keys on the floor. Frantic, she jammed the cans into her tote bag and quickly leaned over to pick up the key ring. Then she clicked off the desk light and made her way out of the little office—in the dark. In her hurry to lock the door, after she stepped into the hall,

68

FLORA'S MONEY

she didn't realize that she had only picked up five of the cans. She left, locking the doors as she went. The sixth can was left sitting in the dark, right in the middle of Manny's desk.

When Flora reached her apartment, she let herself in, set the tote bag on the small counter in the kitchenette and, deciding to make a quick sandwich and eat it as she took the money cans downstairs to lock them up, she pulled some bread and cheese out of the cupboard. To make room to fix the snack, she shoved the tote bag over a few inches, then concerned, she stopped and hefted it, looked inside and counted just five cans.

Breathing deeply, and swearing under her breath, she emptied the bag into the cupboard, took the bag, locked the apartment and walked rapidly down the empty streets to Golden's, doing her best not to run and attract attention at that hour. She scurried into the deserted entry room, leaped up the stairs three at a time, and let herself into Manny's office, hoping that she had left the can there, but not really sure—until she clicked on the desk light and saw the can right there in the middle of the desk, seeming to gaze at her like an amused owl. Almost in tears, Flora lifted the can to be sure it wasn't empty, hugged it, slipped into her tote bag and started to leave.

She had only gone as far as the top of the stairway when she heard the street door emit its familiar squeal; someone was apparently coming in. With no other choice to exit, Flora walked on tiptoe to a dark corner and slid down behind a row of tables to peek out, unseen. As she waited, she could hear footsteps climbing slowly up the hall stairs then coming down the short hall.

Flora was startled to see Jiggs walk in, apparently using his own set of keys. He appeared to be staggering and she

FLORA'S MONEY

could hear him humming to himself as he walked along the main aisle between the tables, bumping into chairs here and there in the dim light. She saw him go into Manny's office, after fumbling with the door lock, and then leave the door open as he turned on the desk light. Ten minutes later, he came out, slammed the office door, burped loudly, and began walking back past her hiding place, weaving as he went. Almost to the stairs, he stumbled and caught himself before falling. Flora heard thuds and rolling sounds, and saw one of the money cans roll right past her on the floor. Jiggs groped around, picking up a few other cans, wobbling as he went. Then he knocked over a chair, causing sharp clunks to echo through the room. Flora watched from the shadows as he made his way to the stairway and went down. Listening, she heard another can fall and slowly bounce, one step at a time, to somewhere near the bottom. Then the door squealed as he apparently went out.

Flora got up, retrieved the can on the floor near her corner, put it in her bag and went down the steps, looking for the can she heard go down the stairs and into the entry way. She didn't see it and decided he must have picked it up. When she pushed on the door she saw that he had forgotten to lock it. She paused, looked up and down the street, saw no one, went out, locked the door and left.

HECTOR

CHAPTER 10

Red-haired Rhonda continued to stop in regularly to see her young friend at work in the speakeasy, have a few drinks, and spend a sociable hour or two talking and joking with Flora and the other patrons. A lot of the men knew Rhonda; a few had dated her from time to time, and even taken her on long weekends to Wisconsin resorts.

Flora dated a few customers, too, after Rhonda fixed her up with bar acquaintances of hers, for early dinners, or to go see a movie at a matinee before it was time to go to work at Golden's. Other than those times, Flora spent her free hours by herself, walking or just riding streetcars around the city and sightseeing. That was until Rhonda introduced her to Hector.

Rhonda had the friendly knack of bringing Flora into

FLORA'S MONEY

her conversations with men she knew, as well as newcomers sitting near her at the bar, while Flora moved back and forth waiting on the customers. One night, Flora saw two men come in that she recognized as previous patrons during crowded times, when all she could do was serve them drinks and smile a lot. Both of the guys were likable gents, and somehow showed more class than most of the men frequenting the place.

One was rather short, about forty, strongly built and nice-looking in general; the other was much taller, but younger, with broad shoulders and a friendly carefree look that Flora noticed. She walked toward them as Rhonda said, "Hey, Flora, my friends the handsome twosome are here. You can have Hector, the big one. I'll take what's left—Quent!" That started a four-way round of jollity, with Flora joining in as she worked. When Hector joked with Flora that night, and watched her gliding behind the busy bar, reaching, bending and dispensing, he was attracted to her natural good looks, graceful moves and charming humor. He also admired her height, even though she was probably a few inches taller than he was, and felt they had a lot in common.

And, when Flora laughed at his wit that night and watched him standing tall on the other side of the strip—at least a head higher than anyone else in the long row of dumpy, slick-haired, stogie-chewing, hard-drinking city-dudes, she was *attracted to his natural good looks, graceful moves and charming humor.* She also admired his height, even though he was probably an inch or two shorter than she was—and she felt they had an uncommon lot in common, too.

An hour later, Quent looked at his watch and said, "Time to go, Hec, sorry. Got to go to work." Quent laid a twenty on the bar and said, "Goodnight, ladies. And remember,

72

FLORA'S MONEY

Rhonda, sometimes when you're hungry, left-overs are not too bad!"

Hector smiled warmly at Flora and said, "Hey, step over here a minute, okay?" She walked down to the end of the bar, out of earshot of the others where, in a gentle voice, he asked, "I was wondering—have you ever seen a bigtime baseball game?"

Flora gazed into his eyes, shaking her head.

"I know you work most nights," he said, "We can see the Cubs play tomorrow afternoon, maybe catch an early dinner. Want to?"

"Love to," she chirped quickly. She gave him her address; he mentioned the time he'd like to come by and pick her up. Then he winked at her and turned away.

After they had gone down the stairs, waving as they went, Rhonda turned and held on to Flora by the arm and said quietly, "Those guys are a couple of goodies. The word is they work for Gus, the guy what really owns this joint and a whole lot of others. But they're more than just a couple of goons, like most of these guys around the street. And I think big Hec really enjoyed your company. He'll be back to see you, I bet."

Flora smiled and said, "We're going to see the Cubs play tomorrow!"

Rhonda beamed, "And maybe an early dinner after?" In reply, Flora grinned and rapidly blinked her eyelids in a mock-flirting gesture that she had learned how to do so well.

They had a good time at the ballpark. Flora eventually learned that he was six years older than she was, came from a wealthy Chicago family that had gone broke when the stock market collapsed and his father's chain of banks failed; and that was when Hec's promising future as a banker

73

FLORA'S MONEY

evaporated.

Hector and Flora began seeing each other regularly after their first outing to the ball game. Since she worked practically every night, he began to take her to long lunches at Henrici's, and other popular restaurants, as well as to morning brunches and afternoon teas at some of the finer Michigan Avenue hotels—her first experiences in such grand establishments. One afternoon at lunch he asked where she was from and she said, laughing, "Oh I'm just a country girl from a place so small I'm sure you never heard of it." Before he could pursue the subject a waiter rolled up a two-tiered serving cart, full of dessert pastries, and distracted them. After that, the subject never happened to come up again. Within a few weeks their time together progressed to more informal socializing at her apartment in the pre-dawn hours, after they were both through work.

CHAPTER 11

1933 - Hamelet beach, 1 a.m. Barefooted, with bib overalls cut off at the knees and worn over her bathing suit, a grown-up Arie ran lightly up the two steps to the cottage porch. Perky, with pleasing contours and now barely eighteen, she crossed over to the raised bottom-half of the front window, and bent down from the waist to speak to her brother in the unlit room. She took a deep breath and said, "Carlos, you awake in there? I think the boat is here. You can hear the motor—out beyond the lighthouse."

He answered from inside, "Uh-huh, Sis, I'm coming."

"Lake's not rough, just kind of breathing heavy," she said, then glanced back over her shoulder and added, "all black out there. Hard to tell if there is anyone else on the beach. There's a little fog and the moon keeps hiding, off

FLORA'S MONEY

and on—still warm though. Ah, there's the light signal from the boat—three blinks."

"Be right with you, Arie. Just blink 'em back three times with your flashlight. Aim kind of up, not at the boat. They'll see it."

"Okay, oh, engine's off—real quiet now."

Carlos came out the front door, wearing a sleeveless shirt and old pants cut off at the knees. Tall and trim, in his late thirties, he eased the screen door shut so it wouldn't slam. He stepped out of his sandals, left them on the porch, and joined her on the sand at the bottom of the steps. "Hmm, I see the boat—hard to spot in the dark," he said quietly, then turned to Arie and asked, "Scared?"

"Gee, a little maybe, but I'm okay."

"And maybe you shouldn't be here," he said, touching her shoulder.

"I can't back out now, Carlos. We help stash one load of booze tonight, over in that shed, and then go back to town with enough cash to get the Chevy a new battery and buy some groceries. And we know a lot of folks around here have been secretly working with these guys for years. Anyway, your friend Quent said maybe he could use you as a pilot later on—though he hasn't given us too many details, has he?"

"No, but he will. Quent's okay. Everybody in the squadron liked him—and trusted him, too. Besides, we know he only offered us this chore tonight, this one time, because he saw we could use a few bucks."

"Well, we ready to go now?" she asked.

"Yes, stay close to me and be ready to skedaddle if anything goes haywire; let's head down to the water. Not much of a breeze—sounds carry when it's like this—they'll probably let the boat drift in close to shore so we can help them

76

FLORA'S MONEY

beach the front end and unload. Can you manage the cart for now?"

"Sure. You want a ride down to the water?" she asked with a little giggle, and then picked up the push-bar on the cart, a wooden crate mounted between two wheels from an old bicycle.

"No thanks," Carlos murmured, "go ahead, I'll be right behind you. And I'll help you push it back. If they have a very big load, we got a lot of haulin' to do to get it all ashore and stashed before daylight."

She led the way and began to stride across the dark beach, gripping the push-bar and peering ahead. As they neared the water she could feel the wet sand pack between her toes. A rippling wave foamed over her feet and then up around her ankles, unnoticed.

Carlos hesitated a few yards back from the water's edge, carefully looking around and staring into the darkness. A flitting memory surprised him: walking across a sandy field to his Nieuport fighter, prior to one of many pre-dawn combat patrols over France, sixteen years earlier. Just as quick, from habit, he shrugged the image away.

Arie stepped out into the shallows. Within seconds, wading up to her thighs, the cool water swirled and gently ballooned her along on tiptoe, her elbows bent and fingers just skimming the water's surface. As she moved forward and leaned into the caressing gel, pressing against her from the waist down, private thoughts returned from another night on this same beach. It was three months earlier at a beach picnic with her schoolmates at dusk, followed by a driftwood fire with sparks swirling in the wind.

She and Grover slipped away in the darkness, waded out into waist-deep water and began splashing each other

FLORA'S MONEY

and laughing. Then they came together, bare arms and legs entwining, for several silent minutes. But as usual, a furtive feeling overshadowed everything after that point in this special memory when her brother called out to her from the shore—making her break away and wade quickly back, with Grover trailing a few feet behind her.

But now, this night, a shout from Carlos came sharp and real, jolting her back to a full awareness with: "ARIE, WAIT! Something's wrong—COME BACK!"

Al Capone, the notorious bootlegger jailed in 1931 for income tax evasion, reportedly said in court: "You can't cure thirst by law."

CHAPTER 12

On the Chicago Northside one night earlier, Gus carried a crystal snifter of brandy from his dining room, cradled in one hand, with a long Cuban cigar already lit and clutched by the first two fingers of the same fist. He sat down at his carved walnut desk in the den of his townhouse to talk business with Jiggs, one of his key men, who had just been escorted in from the front hall by a uniformed maid. This was the same Jiggs, of course, who spent much of his own time in the speakeasy admiring Flora as she worked. He sank into a leather armchair opposite Gus and burped—unnoticed by him and ignored by his boss.

Gus set his drink on the desk, flicked a few cigar ashes off the sleeve of his tuxedo and came right to the point: "About two months ago, I'm sure you recall, we got

FLORA'S MONEY

hit with another phony raid on one of our trucks—out in the sticks near Whiting on a dead-end road, when you were supposed to be bringing in forty cases of scotch from Detroit. Right?"

"Right, Gus."

"And that was the third time somebody grabbed our stuff this spring, right?"

Jiggs nodded in reply, looking uncertain, not oozing confidence.

"You told me the truck engine just quit that night in Whiting, and before your driver could even get out to raise the hood, mugs trying to look like cops came out of the nearby woods, guns drawn, grabbed all four of our guys and tied 'em all to a big tree."

Jiggs nodded again, in silence.

"And," Gus snarled, "I asked what the hell they were doing on a road going nowhere? And who the hell were they tryin' to fool—the idiots! And you said, when you came and told me about it, that one of the fake cops just got in the driver's seat, turned the key and drove off with their guys hangin' on our rig—just like that! No engine problem, nothin' that needed to be fixed?"

"Right, that's what Mo told me when they finally got loose, hoofed it out of there and found a diner with a phone—I wasn't out there with 'em, you know," Jiggs mumbled, then sat straighter and said, in a louder voice: "But I found out which of our guys was bribed to set us up for that stupid heist. We took care of him! And two others we sort of convinced him to tell us about."

"Well, yeah," Gus replied, gazing for a moment at the foot-high porcelain nude that made up the base of his desk lamp, then said with a sigh, "you told me that before." He

FLORA'S MONEY

puffed, and played with his cigar, thinking, then announced: "Well, I've taken care of some things, too. Now, we're about ready to fly the loads in, using a special kind of plane I've been considering. But that's all I can tell you for now. Don't talk about it to anybody but Quent. Got it? I've put him in charge of this one. I'm only telling you now because working for me you'll be involved."

Relieved, Jiggs chortled and said, "Hot diggety, Gus— you did it again!" Standing up, he leaned across the desk, hand outstretched as if to offer an impulsive handshake. But by that time Gus was using his right hand to take a slow sip of his brandy and just stared at Jiggs, over the rim of his glass, then paused and held it in space in front of his chin; Jiggs straightened up, took an awkward step back, and managed to say, "Uh, when will we start using the plane?" He remained standing.

"Soon," Gus replied, and said, "but enough of that. I hear the cops have been asking you questions again. What's the latest?"

"Nothin' Gus. They're just makin' smoke. I'm still out in the fresh air, right?"

"You sure about that? I hear they're starting to snoop around some of our so-called friends in the business, too. For all I know, they could come knocking on my door any day now. Okay. That's it. Go on home. Don't come here unless I call you or send word through Quent." Then he got up and strode out of the room, without looking back. Jiggs turned, wiped his damp brow with his hand and walked toward the front hall.

CHAPTER 13

An hour later, Quent arrived at the townhouse and was promptly shown in. Gus, back at his desk, smiled warmly, gestured at the chair opposite and said, "Drink?"

"No thanks, Gus. Maybe later."

"Okay, Quent, tell me, what's happening with our new airplane, the Tin Goose?"

"Sure. As you know, we'll be slipping into Chi, way down on the south shore, tomorrow night—if all goes okay."

"Right. Great job. Fill me in. I want to be up on everything. I know that since last March, we've paid about forty-two thousand, plus spare parts and rush fees, for this Ford Tri-motor airplane, just like Admiral Byrd used when he flew over the South Pole back in twenty-nine—and he had three other guys and lots of supplies on board, so they took out

82

FLORA'S MONEY

the passenger seats to make room for their gear. And let's see, I know these are among the largest planes in the world, so they're quite roomy—and the wings are seventy-four feet from tip to tip. Right so far?"

"Yup, keep going, boss!" Quent loosened his necktie a little and sat back, attentive.

"Okay, it has three engines—one on each side under the wing, and one up on the nose. It can carry twelve to fifteen passengers, or the equivalent in freight, and a couple of our guys for guards, or whatever, along with the pilot and co-pilot up in the little cabin on the front end. Oh, and what did you find out about the sales for these planes, in general? Is it still a hot number?"

"Gus, the guys at the factory told me that operators are starting to buy them for use all over, to carry freight and passengers, in South America, Mexico, Alaska and other places. As you know, we had to lay on some extra cash to get ours in a hurry. Also, the factory guys said that the two former airmail pilots we hired, and sent out for training, did very well and should do a great job for us, one flyer as head pilot and the other as co-pilot. We've also got another man we may get to fly for us, too. Very good pilot; we were in the same squadron in the war.

"And Gus, your lawyer has nailed down all the special permits, licenses and things like that; no problem with your connections. We've also rented an old warehouse and dock, in an out of the way spot down on the south shore. To fool the locals, the building has a little office in a corner where we can pretend to sell tickets for people to fly to a few U.S. cities. If real customers show up, we just tell 'em sorry, no seats available—all sold out. Okay? Then, after flyin' to our pickup spot, and to Canada for loads if we want to, our guys

FLORA'S MONEY

unbolt some of the passenger seats, if they need more space, and stack 'em in a corner of the plane. After that we load up and take off. Now, I've got some answers to other things you asked about before we went to the factory."

Gus smiled and said, "Okay, now you keep going."

"Incidentally," Quent continued, "they said the nickname, the Tin Goose, has caught on because just about everything but the wings are made of shiny corrugated metal, as you've seen in the newspaper pictures. They also told me that there's another reason for the catchy name: pilots have raved about the wonderful way this plane handles in flight, but they claim it waddles somewhat like a goose when they taxi out across the field before take-off. But of course, that's not a problem at all."

"Now, our plane should be able to fly non-stop for over five-hundred miles at speeds up to ninety miles an hour, or more! We can fly it to Kansas City or Detroit and to a lot of Canadian spots up north—and make it to each of those places in one hop—or even to New York City or New Orleans, with only about two stops for gas—barring breakdowns or lousy weather that we have to expect now and then."

"Also, this first plane is mounted on pontoon floats, as you and I decided before. If we get a second one later, you may want to have that one with wheels. For now, though, we'll land on water wherever we want to. I think having the floats will work well. We can land lots of places, on remote waters, when we're going to and from Chi, and transfer the goods to small boats without needing a dock—and it's more private than trying to sneak in and out of busy airports. Being so big, it does attract a lot of gawkers wherever it goes, so I think the trick will be to stay away from crowded places as much as we can."

FLORA'S MONEY

Gus whistled softly and asked, "How much booze do you figure now, that we can carry on each trip?"

"Probably well over a ton—if a quart bottle of scotch weighs about two pounds, we can haul about fifty or more cases at a time. The plane can maybe do a couple flights on some days, and buzz right over the cops—or robbers." They exchanged smiles, and Quent continued, "Then, our trucks quietly make local deliveries to our customers all over town."

Gus finger-tapped a front tooth and said quietly, "Right. So, the first load is coming in from Canada, late tomorrow, to land near a quiet beach on the southeast side of the lake, unload out there this time, then fly back here empty?"

Quent nodded and said, "Yes, this is how we'll have to do it at first, until the boathouse—or goose house—is built, just south of here. Then we'll be able to land on the lake and taxi it right inside, like a big boat, and unload it without being seen. Anyhow, for this first trip in, I'll be over there on the other side of the lake, out of sight, when the plane brings in the first load, a biggie—to see that everything goes right."

Gus lit a cigar, let a few soft puffs drift away and said: "Like I mentioned before, good job! I'm also looking forward to taking a hop on the plane—and hey, maybe just between you and I, maybe we'll soon be able to call it our Golden Goose!"

"I sure hope so," Quent said chuckling, "and maybe I'll have that drink now!"

"Fine—and before you go, I also want to mention something else. I hear Jiggs is spending cash all over town, and I'm getting curious. Have one of your guys sniff around and get back to me—personally."

CHAPTER 14

Chicago Chinatown, later the same night, 3:25 a.m. Hector stared at his empty glass while he sat alone at a back table, near the swinging doors into the kitchen of a joint called the Tea Room, and waited for Quent to call. The drab establishment, named with a wink by its invisible owners because it was in a storefront on the edge of Chinatown, seldom closed and never served real tea. Instead, the only waiter dispensed bottles of unlabeled brew and shot glasses of whiskey, the drinks all imported from sources unknown and unquestioned. He also collected cash as he served each round, and carried the house money stuffed in his pockets—in case it became prudent to scram in a hurry.

Three burly guys at a table upfront were the only other people present. In shirtsleeves and still wearing shoulder-

FLORA'S MONEY

holstered pistols, they had draped their suit coats over their chair backs as they chatted and drank. They could have been off-duty detectives or hoods. Or maybe they were both. But either way, neither the management nor anyone else really cared.

The phone in the kitchen began ringing. Hector glanced around for the waiter and, thinking he might have gone down to the cellar for something, got up and went through the doors to answer the call.

"Yeah," he muttered into the mouthpiece.

"Hector, that you?"

"Yeah. Hi, Quent," he replied, yawning.

"I'll pick you up in about an hour in the alley behind your place. We have to go for a drive."

"Now? I was hopin' you were going to tell me you didn't need me anymore tonight. It'll be dawn pretty soon. Do we have to go out this late to get some of our customers to pay their bills?"

"Not this time. But we do need to get an early start. I met with Gus, earlier tonight. He wants us to take his car out of town before daylight and hide it, instead of driving my car, when we go out to check on the shipment coming in on our new plane tomorrow night. Anyhow, I'll tell you more about it on the way."

"We're leaving tonight? I was just going over to have a drink at Flora's before she closes. You never told me about this jaunt."

"Sorry, Gus insisted we keep it mum. Even Jiggs wasn't told. But now that it's time for us to go, I'm telling you."

"And Gus wants us to hide his car? Why? Which one? What's going on, Quent?"

"Later, Hector."

FLORA'S MONEY

"C'mon, gimme a clue!"

"Okay—Gus got a tip. Feds may pick him up, anytime now, for questioning or worse. He wants us to take his elegant car and stow it in a barn or someplace, out in the sticks."

"So the cops can't impound it for evidence or whatever?"

"Naw. Just so his current babe, or any of his other guys won't run off with it in case they keep him inside for awhile."

"Quent, are you talking about his new customized, four-door touring car?"

"Right. The model J Duesenberg, a LeGrande Phaeton, kind of like Gary Cooper drives, out in Hollywood—to make palookas like us drool and all the dames get the hots. But you've seen it."

"Yeah, I've seen it—and so have half the people in town; that fire-red paint job is hard to miss. Damn, will Gus really let you drive it? Or, even better, will I finally get a ride in it? They say it'll do a hundred! And he wants us to hide that beautiful thing? Why not have Bernard do it, the fawncy chauffeur he hired when he got the doosey?"

"Well, it seems Jiggs had a blow-out this week with Bernard over some lady he's been after himself. So Bernie left town in a hurry, or maybe he had a little accident. I didn't ask. But anyway, Gus doesn't give a damn about his chauffeur's love life. When he heard that Bernard had left he told Jiggs not to replace him—because for now he doesn't need a driver since we're going to hide the car. Gus said he feels his wagon will be safe with us because he remembered I used to be a relief driver in Indy and know how to handle all that horsepower—and he also told me that Jiggs isn't to know anything about this whole hide-the-limo project; it's

FLORA'S MONEY

to be our secret."

"Or else?"

"You got it! And bring some old clothes for the beach. I've already picked up some sandwiches and a few things. This trip may take a few days."

"Okay, but I'll miss seeing Flora tonight."

"Hey, save it till you get back. Get going, man!"

Right after hanging up the phone, Hector went out the front door to leave the Tea Room and go to his rooming house. Just outside he met Manny, the manager from Goldens, rushing up the sidewalk; he stopped in front of Hector, grabbed him by the arm and, breathing hard, blurted: "Hector! There you are! Where's Flora? Have you seen her in the last couple days?"

"No—what's wrong?"

"She didn't show up for work. I can't find her!"

"Hey, Manny, the kid's entitled to a night off once in a while."

"Yeah, yeah. But there's something screwy going on. Flora's missing and our collection guys came in a couple hours ago and had me shut the joint down. Said they had to check up on the cash we've been taking in—and they told me they're pulling in loot from all over town, for some reason, and they think somebody has been into mine—they say a lot of dough seems to be missing! They're over there now, raisin' hell! They only let me out to look for Flora. But you know me, Hector—I've always played fair with the bosses."

Hector said, calmly, "Flora couldn't have anything to do with this. The cops are pushing everybody, Manny; it's in the newspapers and there's rumors all over the street. You know

89

FLORA'S MONEY

that. Maybe she's just afraid to come in for now because of all the talk about some of speaks being shut down. But never mind—I have to go." With that he brushed past Manny and left.

When Hector got to his rooming house, he tried to call Flora at her apartment, in spite of the late hour. After letting it ring seven times he hung up.

CHAPTER 15

Headed around the south shore of Lake Michigan, the next afternoon, Quent and Hector were enthroned in the front seat of the Duesenberg, a four-door blood-red touring sedan, and felt like they were on a royal outing. With the convertible top down and glistening spoke wheels twinkling in the sun, they sported along the unpaved roads and through desolate areas of piney woods and sand dunes, mile after mile.

Quent drove with an intense concentration, reliving his days skidding on dirt racetracks in rural areas around Indianapolis. Hector perched next to him, enthralled at seeing the speedometer needle waver so high up on the dial— and by watching Quent's adroit handling of the large and stately vehicle.

It had been an exhilarating trip, in spite of several wrong

FLORA'S MONEY

turns and a stop to change a flat tire for one of the white-walled spares encased and strapped on both running boards. Hector, easily a third heavier and a foot taller than his boss, wrestled with the tire change, while Quent took some tools from the boxy trunk, mounted over the rear bumper, and respectfully fiddled around under the hood. Then they climbed back into the leather seats and sped on, chins raised, backs straight.

Each man sported a bow tie, a fashionable-striped seersucker suit, and a well-chewed cigar jammed into one corner of the mouth, unlit in the windswept car. Hector held onto the dashboard with one hand and gripped the stiff brim of his round, straw skimmer with the fingertips of the other. Quent drove all the way, wearing a visored cap backwards on his head, racing-style, and peering through owlish goggles left over from his Indy years.

The Duesenberg, doing close to forty, sped toward an intersection with another dirt road where they passed Grover sitting and sketching wild flowers, back from the road, by a small pond. Eyes wide, he stared at this dazzling intrusion into his sleepy world, turning his head and shoulders to follow the royal vehicle as it glided past.

At the corner, Quent spun the wheel into a right turn and immediately saw that the lane dead-ended a few hundred feet ahead. Without slowing down, he used an open patch of weeds and sand to jounce around in a circle and head back the other way.

Once on the other side of the cross-over, he reduced the car's speed to a crawl and headed down the dirt lane. Through the trees, and past the sand-dune cliffs, they could see far out on the cobalt waters of the lake where sunlight succumbed to haze and little gray clouds cluttered the horizon. He wondered if they would be in for a thunderstorm later that afternoon.

They passed two lonely shacks, then a sagging boat house with dock wreckage half-submerged in the still water of a small cove. A short distance further on, the road ended. He stopped the car and turned off the throaty tickety-ticks of the engine. Quent removed his goggles and gazed around silently at the lonely view. Hector spoke first, "So. Here we are. Lost, I assume."

"No, I think we're there," Quent replied, removing his cap and wiping one palm over his balding head. Then he opened his door and stood up on the running board to look around. "Remember that sign we saw way back before we got on this road, Hector? It said Town of Hamelet. Right?"

"Yeah, the only one we saw for miles, but I didn't see any town, did you?"

"No, but even though I've been up and down these roads a few times before, it's always confusing when you leave the main highway—yet, as I recall we're probably inside the boundary line of Hamelet. The populated part is supposed to be on up the shore a mile or two. I remember, to get here, you follow the roads along the lake down through Gary, past all the steel mills and go right out into the scrubby beach country, as we just did, and play left-right-left-right with the lake for about twenty miles or so. Then you find the outlying areas of Hamelet village. And it seems to have worked."

"What's this left-right stuff? What are we, dancing?"

"No, when you have a big hunk of geography like a lake to follow in a car—and you can see water, on your left, way off in the distance, just keep turning left toward the lake and when it looks like you're getting too close to the water you grab a road to the right, then later go left—and keep doing

93

FLORA'S MONEY

that till you wind up, way down the line, on the last road runnin' parallel to the lake, approximately where you guess you want to be and—"

"You're puttin' me on, Quent. We've been chasing our tail all morning, seems like. Now you're telling me this Hamelet place is a town, but there ain't no town—there's a village somewhere else!" Both men stepped out on the sand, lit cigarettes and leaned against the Duesenberg. Quent kept talking: "Never mind. I admit we got twisted a few times, but I'm pretty sure we're in the right place now. At least, this is where we should find Carlos, the guy we're meeting down here. He and his sister just came out here yesterday for this project. Her name's Arie, short for Yarinet. Spanish, I think. Anyway, look down the beach. See the first cottage, it's all by itself. From the way he talked, I think that's the one."

"Sure—if you say so, Quent. Do they live in that cottage all year round?"

"No, actually they were staying in Chi, but they used to live over in Hamelet. In fact his sister grew up there, and he's lived there too, off and on over the years. But they don't have the family house anymore."

"And his name is Carlos?"

"Right, a friend of mine I haven't seen since the war. A good man. He was one of our best pilots."

"How did you find each other now?"

"Well, I saw his name on a list in a reunion letter, along with his postmaster-hold address in Hamelet, which turned out to be his hometown and near to a place that we decided to use as our drop. I sent him a note and luckily they were in town at their usual rooming house, so he went to a phone and called me. We had a friendly chat and, as I hoped, he needs a pilot job. He was flying the mail and got laid off months

FLORA'S MONEY

ago. So I told him we might have a regular job for him later on, not right now—maybe flying for us, but I didn't let on much about that. And as we talked I realized that he was just about broke. So I offered him a chance to grab a few bucks tonight for helping us handle the booze coming in, this one time.

"This area serves our purpose, as you can see, only deserted cottages. They say most of them were repossessed by the banks in recent years, or bought up by absentee land-speculators. They just board em up these days—not many people can afford to rent vacation cottages—so if the locals living in Hamelet, or folks from anywhere else, want to come out and play or take care of some business, they just pick a place, pry some boards off a few windows, jimmy the door and move on in. Nobody cares and the owners probably don't even know it.

"And because of the size of the load expected tonight, I also hired two guys that you already know, Morrie and Jake, to come over from Chicago in their boat to help make the transfer, and do some hauling, too."

Hector asked, "So where do we stash this gorgeous machine later, for storage, and how do we get back home? It would be a long swim."

"We'll figure that out after tonight. Right now we're going back up this road a little way and see if we can pull off behind a dune, or a shed, and find a temporary hide-away for tonight. We should try to stay out of sight this afternoon, and especially tonight." They got back in the car. Quent started the engine and drove back inshore for about a hundred yards, past the old boathouse on the left, then went in behind a dense thicket of greenery and parked. "This'll do, I think," Quent said, "and maybe we can cut some more bushy stuff

95

FLORA'S MONEY

to kind of pile up around the car, too."

"Okay, Quent. Then, after that, maybe I'll have a sandwich and take a break."

"Sure. And there's something else you should know. Before we left, Gus gave me some expense money in case we need it for payoffs or whatever—it's in two coffee cans; I've got them wedged in under the back seat."

"Really, Quent. Big bills or little bills?"

"Big. Should be five thousand in each can."

"Whew—well, when we get the car parked and all, I'll stretch out on the back seat for a quick nap. Anyone comes around they'll see me and beat it. After that I'll keep an eye on things, okay?"

"Good idea, Hec. Never know who might be sneaking around out here. I need to wander around a bit and touch base with Carlos. But I won't be gone long." They stepped out of the car, slipped off their hats, ties and suit coats, then halted and looked at each other, mortified. Quent verbalized their thoughts: "Hey, did you bring any other clothes, like I said?"

"Nope. Damn. And it's getting hotter now that we've stopped riding. Did you?"

"No. Forgot all about it. Well, let's stick this stuff in the trunk. I guess we can get by in our undershorts here in the woods, and maybe tonight down on the beach. For now, I'll keep my pants on to go visiting."

Quent stopped behind a one-story wooden shed, near the rear of the tiny cottage, where the tangled undergrowth was thick and he could peek around the corner without being seen. The summer heat was building up as the afternoon wore on; it was humid and becoming more overcast. He stood and watched for a few moments.

96

FLORA'S MONEY

Deserted, run-down place, he thought, except for one give away: some wide boards had been pried off a few windows, for ventilation, and dumped on the ground. Quent stepped forward, walked along the side of the house up to the dilapidated front porch and looked out at the wide view of the dunes, sand flats and lonely lakefront—then jerked his head around as the screen door suddenly squeaked open and he heard, "Well, I'll be damned! It looks like ol' Quent himself! Welcome!"

"Hi there, lieutenant!" Quent replied.

A well-tanned Carlos, in swim trunks, came across to the rail. He grinned and reached down to shake Quent's hand. At the same time, Arie stepped out on the porch and stopped, a friendly expression on her face.

"Hey, Carlos! Haven't seen you since the war. You look great. And this must be your sister, Arie," Quent said.

"Right, and Arie meet Quent, the best airplane fixer the army ever had!" For a few minutes, with Arie perched on the top step listening, the two men swapped some army memories as they stood on the empty porch—then briefly discussed what Quent wanted them to do that night. He never mentioned the arrival of the plane; they'd find out about that later, he reasoned.

Quent pinched off the smoldering tip of his cigarette, flicked the butt over the porch railing and said, "Now then, let's play the game and keep it all vague, okay? Better you don't know too much. But I will say this: be prepared for surprises, sometimes these transfers get fouled up and we have to make quick changes. There's always a lot of small-boat traffic on the lake after dark, as everybody knows—booze coming down from Canada by water, or from back east by truck, to these wide-open beaches for shipment to speakeasies and runners

97

FLORA'S MONEY

all over the Midwest. And it's hard to know who's bribing who, or which cops out here are owned by which big guys in the city. Anyhow, I'm only here to watch from a distance to make sure our plan works and everybody stays honest—and you two are here to help move the goods on this beach, that's all. The set-up looks fine, the unpopulated beach and all, and you have a handy shed for storage out back I see. You ready for tonight?" Carlos and Arie both nodded.

Then Quent said, "Now, I'm going back to the car and get some rest. I have a man with me, name's Hector. You may meet him later. Maybe not. In fact you might not see us at all, but we'll be out there ready to help you two if anything gets sticky. And if anybody asks, you don't know me and are just bystanders—but I'll have some cash for you both after it's all over tonight, or tomorrow morning, latest—and we'll talk some more about maybe getting you back in a cockpit again. Okay?" Carlos grinned, reached out to shake hands and said, "Ready when you are, general!"

"Man, that's a nice promotion for an ol' sarge!" Quent said, with a laugh. Then he went down the steps and around the house, to return through the woods to the car.

GORK I

CHAPTER 16

Two hours later, a flatbed truck, with a framed-canvas enclosure covering the back came along the same road to the place where Grover was drawing and slowed to a halt with the motor still chugging. The driver leaned out his window, spat at the road, looked over at the youth and called out: "Hey friend, seen any strangers around here or down by the beach today?"

Eager to gossip with anyone about the flashy car, Grover walked over to the truck and tried to describe the strangers he had, indeed, recently seen. Then he said: "And near as I could tell, no one seemed to be after 'em to make 'em go so fast. The only thing chasing them was a mammoth cloud of dust they was stirring up themselves. Wooo-ee!"

"Which way did they go?"

FLORA'S MONEY

"Well, that's another thing—they made the right-hand turn onto the old road down there at the corner, just skidding all the way round, then all that dust had barely settled and they come flyin' back, cause that road dead-ends a few hundred feet along by the marshes. They buzzed right over and went tearing down the other way. Ain't been anyone else come by since."

"Did they come back?" asked the trucker, scratching his days-old black whiskers.

"No, and that way only goes less than a mile to where the road ends at the lake. Weird, ain't it? Nothing down that way except mostly boarded up cottages on the beach, empty sheds and dunes."

"Thanks, kid. Live around here?" the driver asked.

"Down the shore some. Where you from?"

"Up north. What's your name?"

"Grover. Are you in the haulin' business?"

"Name's Gorki. Haulin'? Yeah, you could say that. Right now I'm just cruisin' around lookin' for pick-up loads, or whatever. Never know what you might find out here along the beaches."

"I guess so. Most days it's pretty quiet, but other times whenever I walk anywhere on the beach, I see cars and boats coming and going—especially at night. Are you into that, or maybe you'd rather not say."

"Hey, kid. Like they say, ask me no questions, I'll tell you no lies!" Gorki replied with a quick wink. "You still in school, Grover?"

"No. I graduated this year."

"Okay, Grove. Maybe we can do a little business now and then, if I need a strong back. How can I find you?"

"You know the old lighthouse—out on the point, down

FLORA'S MONEY

the beach, a little south of here?"

"Sure, I've seen it from a distance."

"I live in the tower. If I'm not there, maybe you could leave a note on the door," Grover said.

"You live in the place? Really? I thought it was all shut down."

"Yes, it was deactivated years ago; belongs to my brother and me now. He moved to Chicago a while back and found a job out there. So I have the place all to myself."

"Hey, Grove, sounds like a nice set-up. You have folks around here?" Gorki asked.

"Yes, my uncle and aunt. They have a cottage on the beach, near town. He's the town cop."

"Oh, really!" Gorki chuckled, his mind rapidly sorting potentials. "Is there a way to drive out to the lighthouse?"

"There's a path from the lane through the trees, out to the lighthouse. Never tried to get a car beyond the lane; might be possible."

"Well, have to go now. So long, kid." Grover nodded and stepped back from the truck. Revving the engine, Gorki waved, drove to the crossing, swung the truck wide, turned it left toward the lake and disappeared from Grover's view. After a few hundred feet, he impulsively turned the truck into a lane with little more than wheel ruts leading into a dense growth of brush and pine thickets. When the branches began to whip and claw at the canvas enclosure he stopped, turned off the engine and glanced around.

"Perfect," he thought. "Almost like parking in a big cave." To open his door, he pushed hard to press back the pine boughs so he could slip out and stand on the running board. He lifted up one corner of the canvas, tied it off to let in some air, and slipped inside the cargo space.

101

FLORA'S MONEY

The gloomy area was empty except for a blanket roll, a small box of canned food, a bag of donuts and a half-empty quart of whiskey. Weary from the long night of man-handling the truck, he sprawled on a blanket and yawned, glad that he didn't plan to venture down to the beach until well after dark—and went to sleep, soothed by the pine-scented air and the boughs crackling in the soft breezes off the lake.

Two miles south of Gorki's chosen spot for a nap, a caravan of nine enclosed wagons, each pulled by one or two horses, swayed and creaked along on wooden spoke wheels, passing through miles of desolate dunes and pine woods. Though called Gypsies by most strangers, the name they used among themselves was *Rom* and their native language *Romani*. This day, as usual, they stayed away from populated areas whenever possible.

Twenty-two Rom adults and children, from tots to grandparents, rode in the quaint cabin-wagons, or trudged alongside on foot. They were well aware that they were not welcome by most of the *gaje,* or Americans, and that they were often so feared by farmers and townspeople that some communities, including Hamelet, had passed ordinances against Roms settling in, getting regular jobs, or owning property. By need, Roms lived by their wits, using what skills they had. Eight of the high, narrow wagons held family possessions and provided meager living and sleeping space for this wandering group. The ninth wagon carried the extra supplies used in making handmade metal tools, as well as brooms, baskets and woven mats—all produced from trees, plants and reeds taken from forests and marshes along the way.

This group was descended from nomadic bands that had

FLORA'S MONEY

spread across large areas of Europe from northern India since the fourteenth century, and started coming to America, via Canada, hundreds of years later. The Roms were often misunderstood, mistreated and even enslaved in some countries by officials pressured by bigoted citizens. As Roms trekked into the U.S. from Canada, over many years, they often met rejection by citizens who resented the Gypsies' roaming lifestyles, their indifferences to local mores and their refusals to change their ways to suit other societies. Many Roms did not like to send their children to local schools, for fear they would be exposed to the craziness of *gadzikanime,* or Americanization, and then might grow up not learning the traditions of their own culture.

On this sultry day in July, Ivan, the caravan elder, sat on the board seat of the first wagon, next to his twenty-year-old grandson who lightly held the reins of a lumbering mare pulling their wagon. Ivan wiped a cloth across his forehead and said quietly, in Romani, "Are we near that camp we stayed in last time through here—by the dark tower on the lake?" His grandson looked at him and nodded.

"Can you find it again, Peri?" Ivan asked. The young man nodded again, and flicked the reins lightly to encourage the tired horse. "Go there," Ivan said, "after dark tonight we can all walk through the woods to the lake for a soak. No one will see us or make trouble. Hot night. The water will cool us. We all need it." His grandson grinned and pretended to beat the horse rapidly with an imaginary whip.

CHAPTER 17

Soon after Grover had watched Gorki pull away in his truck and turn the corner, right after their chat about the Duesenberg, he decided to do some exploring down toward the beach on his way home, and see if he could spot that fancy car. He tucked his drawing tablet under his arm and walked about fifty feet past the crossroads, then angled into the denser woods, heading for the shore area.

There was no real path to follow, but he didn't need one—after wandering in the area all his life, he could easily find his way, even at night. This time, within a few minutes, he glimpsed something red and shiny through a small opening in the boughs and branches ahead. He pushed on and soon had a better view: it was, for sure, the mighty automobile, hidden there, in his woods!

FLORA'S MONEY

Golly, this is really keen, he marveled to himself, then moved slower, automatically ducking his head down between his raised shoulders—the useless way many animals do to make themselves at least feel less visible—and finally stooped down and crawled behind clumps of underbrush, careful not to make noise by breaking any brittle twigs. He instinctively sensed that stealth seemed appropriate, and was quite sure this car had something to do with bootleggers—and well aware that they could do bad things to snoopers messing around in their dealings.

But this time he couldn't resist the temptation to sneak a look and perhaps see some titillating secrets he could share with his friend Millie—perhaps bring her out later, on their date that night, to see the car and maybe even sit in it for awhile.

He began to fantasize, and got a little careless. Since he had seen no one around as he drew closer, he rose up to a half-crouch and boldly reached out to touch the gleaming fender with his left hand—but stopped it in mid-air when he looked up and spotted the soles of two very large, white, wing-tipped shoes obviously holding feet, with ankles resting on the top edge of the rear passenger door, right in front of him, and slanting inside.

Startled, Grover ducked and silently backed away, thinking, "one of those guys must be in there—maybe asleep, maybe not—and where's the other one?" He moved back among the trees and kept going down to the sandy stretches at the edge of the water, and went on home, thinking most of the way about his late date with Millie after she finished her shift as a waitress at the diner in town.

~

FLORA'S MONEY

Millie, an elfin blond divorcee from Chicago, new to town earlier that summer and eager for friendship, was almost six years older than Grover. Due to his limited cash he didn't go to the diner very often, but late one night before going to bed he decided to stop in, spend a nickel, and have a doughnut. He perched on a counter stool to eat it. There were no other customers. Millie admired his looks, steady manner and the nicely filled polo shirt he wore, and began chatting with him as she worked, asking questions and telling him a little about herself. After a while, wiping down the counter she said quietly, with a little smile, "We'll be closing soon. Maybe, if you want, you could walk me home—not far, just a room. I stay with a couple. They have two little kids." Surprised and pleased at her offer, Grover smiled back and nodded, not sure what to say.

"Okay," Millie said quietly, "You want to wait outside? Won't be long. The boss will be locking up pretty soon." Grover nodded again, handed her the nickel and went outside.

Millie came out about fifteen minutes later. They fell in step on the board sidewalk built on the sand along the street in front of the diner. On the way, they spoke little, though partway there she slipped her hand inside his arm, just above the elbow as they walked. Her warm fingers felt pleasant on his skin. She let go in front of the house, looked up at him and said, "Well, goodnight, Grover. Sorry I can't invite you in, the place is so small and they all go to bed early."

He nodded and said, "So long—uh, goodnight."

Grover started to turn away when she said softly, "Hey, maybe tomorrow night we could take a walk on the beach— you could maybe show me around."

"Sure!" He said, "We could wade in the shallows to cool

106

FLORA'S MONEY

off—if we dress for it. And maybe we could count some stars," he added, suddenly feeling bold.

"My, aren't you the ol' wolf, though," she teased.

The next night, Grover waited for her in back of the diner until almost midnight because some customers hung around, slow-eating after regular closing time. Inside, she changed from her work clothes and came out dressed for a hot night on the beach, in shorts, a blue halter tied at neck and waist, and nothing else—practical for walking and splashing she figured, or maybe lolling on the sand among the sparsely populated dunes. He wore bathing trunks and an undershirt. Both of them were barefooted.

They started walking, hand in hand, after she gave him a quick kiss on the cheek. The beach area, even near town, was deserted. As they strolled, Grover said, "Millie, I've got something special for you to see tonight." Then he told her about the classy car with the two men, probably big-city bootleggers, and added, "Come on, we'll take a peek!"

When they neared the wooded area where he had seen the Duesenberg that afternoon, he said, "We can go through here—keep hold of my hand and follow behind me, it's even darker in there."

"Are you sure this is the way?" she asked quietly, after several minutes.

"Don't worry," he whispered, squeezing her hand a little more, "we're getting close—better not talk now. Those guys might be around—duck under this branch, look through there." She stared, took several steps to get closer and reached out with both hands to touch a smooth fender. Entranced, she made a low moan of delight.

Grover circled the car and looked in it as best he could in the dark, to be sure no one was napping in the back this

107

time. Millie gingerly stepped up on the running board on the right-hand side, giggled, opened a front door and slipped in. Breathless, she slid across to the driver's side. The convertible top was now up, with side window-curtains in place in the back. She caressed the cool leather upholstery with her hands, enjoying the heady aroma and the silken touch. Then she placed her hands on the wheel, like she was driving and murmured, "Heavenly."

Grover slipped into the passenger seat, paused and waited, peering at her in the darkness. She reached her right hand out to touch his bare knee, saying, "Hey, c'mon!" Laughing, she twisted her body, squirmed toward him to push out from under the steering wheel and openly groped and climbed on him to slip over to the backseat, tugging at his shoulder as she went. He twisted quickly and also slid over to sprawl awkwardly across her lap.

Gorki had fallen into a heavy sleep in the back of his truck that afternoon and didn't wake up until it was quite dark. Using his flashlight, he pulled out some of his grocery cache and ate it while sitting up front in the driver's seat. Then he went for a long walk in the dark woods and looked out over parts of the open beach. He saw no one.

But as he was headed back to his truck, and moving silently through the trees, he thought he heard some human squeals and a few spoken words, too quiet to be understood. Following the sounds he found a fancy car that had to be the one Grover had told him about that afternoon. It was just a shadowy shape at first, but as he got closer he could see dull glimmers of some of the silvery trim. He sneaked nearer and realized from the muted voices, one of them female, and the

FLORA'S MONEY

gentle car-squeaks, what was going on. A couple, maybe his young friend Grover and a gal, were busy inside—but hey, he wondered, where were the two gents that brought this car in here? An obvious scheme came quickly to mind; he knew he had to move fast.

From what he could see of the automobile sitting there in the dark, partly covered in brush, he knew it could bring him a lot of cash. He slowly stepped back a dozen feet, stood behind a tree, put his hand partly over his mouth, and bawled in a harsh voice that he doubted Grover, or anyone else, would recognize at a time like this: "HEY, YOU KIDS, WHAT THE HELL'S GOING ON HERE? GET OUTTA MY CAR!"

That did it. There was a sudden stop of all sounds, except for the squeaks, for just a moment, then some thuds and bumps caused by people making a fast exit out of a rear door on the other side—followed by a few polite squeaks, slowing to a stop, from the swaying springs of the grand auto.

Gorki listened to sounds of cracking branches fade very fast off into the dark woods, then went over, opened a front door, poked his head in and flicked on his flashlight for a quick look around inside. He smiled when the light beam spotted two articles of clothing on the floor in front; he picked them up with two fingers, saw what they were, and then quickly dropped them: a pair of men's walking shorts, and a blue triangle of cloth complete with tie strings dangling from each corner.

Chuckling, he saw that the rear door on the other side of the car had been left wide-open; he climbed into the front and, stretching over, closed it. Then he settled back into the driver's seat and began to feel for wires under the dashboard. Head tilted back, a private grin fixed on his face, he took a deep breath and started the engine as quietly as he could, not revving it up, in case the two men might be near enough to hear it. Without turning on the headlights, he eased the machine back out of the thicket, slowly shifted it out of reverse and steered it back to the dirt lane. "Damn, feel this baby," he muttered to himself. "Snug as new boots and ready to fly! I need to hold it down for now and sneak her out onto the main road where I can open her up and scram."

While he drove slowly through the trees, Gorki lightly steered with one hand and kept twisting his head, side to side, eyes wary, trying to peer into the darkness—until he gasped, grabbed the wheel with both hands and smacked the brake pedal with his foot; three or four shadowy shapes of animals or men blocked the narrow lane ahead. Reflexes told him to pour on the power and to turn or plow ahead blindly, but dense trees and brush on both sides made him hesitate for seconds. "BACK UP!" he hissed to himself, jerking his head

FLORA'S MONEY

to instinctively look over his left shoulder and at the same time snatching for the gear shift with his right hand to jam it in reverse—but he saw that more figures suddenly appeared in the lane behind him.

When he swiveled his head back toward the front, someone jumped on his running board. Gorki had a whiff of gasoline through his open window, saw the glow from a red-tipped ember curl into a yellow flame as it ignited a soaked rag, apparently tied to a hefty stick. The torch flared inches away from his face.

"Hey! Gorki, that you?" the attacker asked in a deep rumble, speaking in Romani.

"Ivanovitch, dear uncle. How the hell did you get here?" Gorki whispered in relief.

"How you think? Our wagons are back in the woods." Ivan replied, then raised his voice and spoke to the other men stepping closer to the small flickering flame: "HEY, LOOK! We caught a really big fish in this fancy boat. GORKI! Our wandering brother. He takes off in our old truck, months ago. Now, look how rich he is!" Someone lit another torch, illuminating leering faces and more of the car.

Gorki sat back, letting the motor idle, took a deep breath and said, "Ivan, Peri. How did you get down here from Canada so fast? I have the truck hidden and I need to move this fancy wagon out of here, now. I'll come back and find you in a couple days."

"Yes, I see you got business that has nothing to do with us. We're all going down to enjoy the lake. You go ahead," Ivan said, as he stepped down from the running board and motioned the others to move back. Gorki reached out to touch Ivan's fingertips, and then drove slowly forward along the dark lane.

FLORA'S MONEY

Ivan turned quickly, pulled aside Bruno, Peri's older brother who was standing nearby, and whispered briefly in his ear, "Jump on back. Don't let Gorki see you. Bring it back if he leaves it somewhere. Hide it near here." By then, the Duesenberg was only about ten yards along the way and it was still possible for Bruno to sprint after it, grab the handles of the trunk mounted on the rear and leap, twist and sit, legs dangling, on the back bumpers, unseen or heard by Gorki. Ivan watched the car fade into the darkness and said to Peri, "Good. Bruno knows horseless buggies."

Part Three ~ The Raid

1933

CHAPTER 18

Back in town, Grover's uncle Jerry sat in his office with two federal agents, talking over their plans for later that night. The Seth Thomas pendulum-clock, on the wall over his desk, showed the time as just past twelve.

Located in the same building as the only firehouse in town, on Grant Street but down a short alley on the side, the Hamelet police station was not easy to find. But it had been in the same place since 1889, and all the residents knew where it was, though hardly anyone ever had much of a reason to go there.

Outside, over the door, bolted flat against the weathered bricks, was a foot-high wooden panel, painted black with peeling gold-leaf letters reading POLICE. Inside headquarters, as some town wits called it, there was one large room,

FLORA'S MONEY

with a short counter across the front end, and an open space where there once had been a gate.

Jerry was officially just a town cop, but he was usually called chief by everyone in town, even though he was the only full-time peacekeeper they had. All the locals knew that in case of emergency if the chief wasn't in his office, and the front door was locked, they could walk over to his cottage or look for him around town; keeping the office always open was unheard of in Hamlet.

His roll-top desk dominated the back wall, six oaken captains' chairs were scattered around the room and two filing cabinets leaned toward each other in a corner. There was also a long table in the middle of the room, in front of Jerry's desk, handy for small meetings and feet propping-up during the chief's think sessions. A doorway next to the desk led to a toilet room. The windowless space at the end of the hall had been made into a small jail-cell of sorts, walled in with metal-mesh fencing rather than more costly bars.

Other than booking a Saturday night drunk or listening to anxious citizens, reporting now and then that they had seen Gypsy peddlers near their land, nothing much happened at the police station—except for the federal agents who sometimes came in to plan and launch raids against bootleggers operating in that area of the lake.

"Okay," Jerry announced as the meeting with the feds ended, "I guess we're ready. If we leave now, we'll have plenty of time to drive out, park on the town road and walk in through the woods without being spotted, then hook up with the action when it all starts."

"Fine," Frank, the agent-in-charge replied, slipping bullets into the chamber of his pistol, "And if our tip is right, we should be able to grab some contraband, make arrests,

FLORA'S MONEY

wave the flag and do our job. Never know how these raids will turn out—at least we'll have surprise on our side, I hope." They all stood up. Jerry strapped on a doughboy helmet, purchased from an army surplus store years before, and settled his holstered pistol with his right hand as they went out.

A few hundred feet out in the lake, not far from the point, Morrie and Jake stood up in their boat and peered toward the shore. It was only visible to them as a lighter band between the black woods and equally opaque water. When they had turned off the motor of the modified fishing-boat, a twenty-footer with a small cabin in front, it drifted slowly toward the beach. Jake stood on the duckboards back of the cabin and gently poled the boat through the shallows, pushing with one oar. He was tense and still, waiting.

After a few moments, Morrie pointed his flashlight at the shore and clicked it on and off three times. A little later, he said in a low voice: "See that, they've answered. Three blinks. Somebody should be out to meet us soon."

"Right." Jake quietly replied. "Soon as the bow nudges sand, hop in the cabin and be ready to pop back out and surprise any trouble makers if anything goes wrong."

"Righto. I know the routine. And while I'm in there I might just have a dose of medicine. Want a quick one before the fun starts?"

"No, maybe later. Morrie, I've been doing some heavy thinking. How come we're pickin' up a load, instead of us loading up in Chicago and dropping it off to the locals out here, like Quent has us do most of the time? And where's the stuff coming from tonight? And what about the cash for us to pay for it?"

FLORA'S MONEY

"Well, you said before that Quent told you that part is already taken care of. 'Don't worry about it,' he said."

"Yeah. But usually, when we get out here and unload we're done for the night. Then we just amble back to the city, ease into the river and put the boat away—then go on home, real innocent-like. This time it's all backwards."

"Ah, Jake, we're here. Nuts. Maybe they're tryin' somepin' new. Let's see what happens." He pulled open the cabin door and went inside.

While the two boatmen were talking, out on their boat, a single file of nineteen Gypsies, led by Ivan and Peri, walked unheard and unseen out of the woods and on to the dark beach, about two hundred yards behind and to the north of Arie and Carlos. The Gypsies couldn't hear them at that distance, or see them either, in the dark.

Ivan's people followed each other, headed in a loose line for the water. They assumed they would have the beach to themselves at night but, from habit, they were still cautious and kept their voices low. All of the Rom looked forward to a private outing, wading and diving in the lake, without harassment from the police for using a public beach, as sometimes happened in their travels.

The women and girls had on simple shifts; the men and boys, shirtless, wore only shorts or cut-off pants. Several of the elders, including Ivan, slowed down at the edge of the wet sand and stepped carefully into the low, slowing waves. Others in the group began to walk a little faster, eager to splash and dive; joined by Peri, they silently ran into the water and made shallow dives. After his first plunge, Peri stood up, stretched his arms over his head to dive again, then stalled,

FLORA'S MONEY

shook the wet hair back from his face and peered down the quiet shore, listening.

Thirty minutes after midnight, Quent and Hector walked out of the wooded area behind the cottage Carlos had borrowed, then circled around the buildings and crossed the beach in the deep darkness. Near the water they slipped off their shoes and carried them along as they moved down the shoreline. They found a low place where storms had scooped out the sand, sat down, and began to wait. For a while they were lulled by the moist softness of the warm air and eventually became indifferent to the smell of dead fish and soggy driftwood. Only intermittent gurgling from the calm expanse of black waters dominating their view marred the silence.

Quent spotted Arie twice, pacing nearby, but she apparently never saw them. When they heard the idling motor of the boat, as it eased around the point, they both got up on all fours and, in a few minutes, saw the exchange of triple blinks—and a little later they could just make out Arie and her brother with a cart, a little way along the shore, hurrying toward the water.

"Is that Carlos and his sister?" Hector whispered. "Shhh—yes." Quent hissed in reply. Then, to their surprise they heard Carlos call out: "Arie, wait! Something's wrong. COME BACK! Leave the cart, head for the shed—run!" From out on the lake, a rumbling big-engine sound began rolling across the beach, getting louder fast.

At the same time, over in the woods: Grover and Millie had—barely—started to run from Gorki. Given the scanty clothes they

FLORA'S MONEY

had left after they fled the big car, trying to hurry through the prickly weeds and low-hanging tree branches left them scratched and breathless. Grover pulled her along by the hand, as gently as he could, slowing down and stopping a few times so he could listen for any give-away sounds that they were being chased. When they reached the edge of the woods where the beach began, Millie stopped, gasping: "Grover, wait, I can't run out there in the open like this! You dragged me out so fast. And look at you! What'll we do?" she wheezed, in a tearful voice. "What if someone sees us?"

"I know. Sorry, Millie." Grover replied, "We can't stay here in the woods. I don't think that guy from the car is chasing us, but I'm not sure. He must be a bootlegger, and there might be more of them around. They can get rough. Maybe, we could—oh-oh!" Before he could finish, the shrill whine of the siren, coming at them from the lake, shocked them both. Then Grover almost shouted, "Millie, c'mon, we have to get out of here! It must be the cops are makin' a raid! And we're right in the middle of it!" Grabbing her hand he pulled her out of the trees to where the beach started. The siren kept howling as they began to run across the sand, back toward town.

Near the woods, a shout: "Grover! What the hell are you two doing out here? Where are your clothes?"

Uncle Jere

CHAPTER 19

A few seconds later, a sharp-edged bolt of intense light flared and sliced through the darkness. Its beam streaked across the water and swept back and forth in a wide arc over the beach, glaring from a searchlight on a powerful launch coming around the point at high speed. The howling whoops of the siren, and the increasing growl from the craft's engine, produced an echoing din all across the area. All of the Gypsies began to run, splashing from the water or jumping up from where they sat on the sand and dashing for the safety of the woods, this time not in single file.

The blinding light was still making its first sweeps, when it came their way, moving swiftly until it spotted the unexpected crowd of hurrying people. The beam hesitated just long enough to provide a stark glimpse of running adults

FLORA'S MONEY

grabbing children and helping older people hurry along. Then the beam flicked away, but returned immediately for another quick look; apparently the operator was stunned with disbelief at the appearance of such a big flock of citizens. Finally, the beam swerved away.

As the searchlight skipped over other people, scattered and transfixed elsewhere on the beach, the craft drew closer. The siren gave way to a few distant echoes and then stopped. Immediately, a strident voice, harsh with authority and doom, echoed over the water, mightily aided by a huge megaphone: "HOLD IT! You people jus' stay where YOU ARE! WE ARE FEDERAL AGENTS, DAMMIT, AND YOU ARE SURROUNDED—ounded—unded. WE ALREADY HAVE MEN ON THE BEACH—each—ch."

Confused tableaus popped on and off as the light moved, showing panicky people either frozen in place or trying to hide by dashing in and out of elusive shadows. Shouts, curses and muffled voices provided background sound-affects, here and there:

From Jake's boat, already beached: "Morrie! Come on outta there. Time to scram!" Jake hollered as he scrambled over one side of their boat and landed, feet first in the waist-deep water. Elbows and hands pumping back and forth, in a futile effort to speed things up, he waded and splashed toward shore.

At the same time, Morrie stumbled from the cabin and threw himself over the other side of the boat in a flat-out stomach-smacking want-to-be dive. He hit water, sank, got up and, for a man with a four-quart beer-belly bulging out in front, ran quite swiftly up onto the sand and kept going—with Jake angry and dripping, close behind him.

FLORA'S MONEY

The fed's launch reduced speed and, cutting the engine a few hundred revs too late, scraped to a jarring stop parallel to Jake's boat, about twenty feet away, but with the bow farther up on the beach than might be expected of an official craft.

One agent, named Ernie, a new trainee, had been assigned to stay on board the government boat and handle the big searchlight mounted on a deck post near the bow. Eager to please, he swung it jerkily this way and that, like a drunken stagehand on a vaudeville balcony, not at all sure which stars of the show should be illuminated and in what order.

Five more agents jumped from the launch, down onto the beach, and began to spread out. Two of them ran to the smaller boat, the back half still afloat, and hopped aboard, waving rifles, ready for action. One of the men landed on the deck of the assumed smuggler's boat, tripped, dropped his rifle onto the floorboards and scrambled after it.

The other man poked open the unlatched cabin door with the barrel of his gun, stuck his head in for a quick look, then shouted "Empty!" Both men vaulted back over the side and landed with all four of their feet encumbered in sopping sand—just long enough to make them stumble into a jumble amid an unusually large wave that arrived at the same time they did. Disgusted and drenched they got up and ran down the beach, shaking the water off their weapons as they ran, still looking for smugglers.

At that moment, the moving beam of light spotted Jerry and the two agents running across the back of the beach, up where the trees started. Ernie swung his light ahead, in the same direction they were going, and saw two more guys that they were apparently chasing, running into the woods.

FLORA'S MONEY

As Ernie jerked the spotlight about, he could see that the pair of fugitives were only wearing trunks of some kind, not unusual for a beach—but what he couldn't see was that these two, apparently the bad guys, were garbed only in white BVD undershorts.

He kept poking around until the beam displayed two other people running on the sand, parallel to the woods, in the direction of town. He glanced, started to pass them over—and then jerked the light back, his wits yelling at him: Hey? Is that a topless woman? He held the light directly on them. They came to an awkward stop, like jittery statues, and stared directly into the glare—until there was a single, echoing *CA-RACK-ETY!*

A gunshot had brought back the darkness and ended the revealing light show. Someone on shore had fired only once and managed to blow out the searchlight.

Stupefied, but unhurt, Ernie's natural reactions took over. He let go of the light-grip and slid to the deck, face up, on top of another agent, face down, cowering there with both arms helmeting his head; his megaphone, tall as a trash can, bounced across the deck, then neatly spun over the side and disappeared.

For a few seconds there was silence all over the beach—then shouts, commands, squeals and swear words could be heard in the dark, coming from various directions:

On the government boat, a loud, disgusted command: "Ernie! Get off my back. The war's over! Watch out for broken glass from your damn light, it's all over—ouch—the deck. And dammit, where's my horn?"

FLORA'S MONEY

Near the woods, a shout: "Grover! What the hell are you two doing out here? Where are your clothes? Never mind. Frank—it's my nephew—turn off your flashlight, please! They can't be part of this. Beat it, kids. Find some big leaves, or something, and hide!"

Behind Carlos's cottage, a gasping mutter: "Hector, let's wait here for a bit, behind this shed. I think those two cops gave up. We'll go back to the car after things calm down. Damn, I left my shoes back where we were sitting, but I see you have yours."

At the same time, in the sandy washout used by Quent and Hector, a fed with a flashlight, speaks softly to himself: "What the hell's this? A pair of classy white shoes someone dropped. Screwy, they're both for the right foot!"

Minutes later, in the harsh light of a lantern, near the beached launch: "Okay, men; anyone get hurt?" Frank asked his agents. Negative head shakes, all around. "Did anyone find a stash of booze anyplace?" Agents exchange glances, shrugs, head-shakes. Then Frank asked: "Any arrests?"

One of the agents replied: "We caught the two boot-leggers off the little boat, if that's what they are—got 'em handcuffed back-to-back, over there."

"So where's their load, Hank?"

"Not on their boat, Frank."

"As I guessed. Anybody find alcohol—anyplace?"

More shrugs, feet shuffling. Jerry spoke up, "I was with

FLORA'S MONEY

you, Frank."

"Yeah, of course. So where did this tip for a booze drop come from, Jere?"

"Dunno, I first heard about it from your Chicago office when someone called me."

"Someone? Who?" Frank asked. "Dunno. I just assumed—" Jerry said, softly.

"Oh? Jerry, I think we've been had—again. Phony tips—or maybe some runners are laughing at us, up in the dunes, after sampling their wares, and right now are sleeping it off—or they're pulling a drop somewhere else while we're down here running around in the dark. Cripes! "

"Uh, one other thing," Jerry said. "What about the shot that blew the searchlight?"

"Yeah, I was comin' to that," Frank said, heaving a big sigh: "What about it, guys?" More shrugs. "Well, I think it might have come from one of those guys Jerry and I were after. We lost 'em in the dark. Helluva shot. One thing, if we ever catch the shooter we can nail him for firing at us, but don't hold your breath. What a night. Let's go home. Hank, take the cuffs off those fishermen. Turn 'em loose." As soon as the handcuffs were off, Morrie and Jake hustled right over to their boat and began to shove it into the water; two of the agents shrugged at each other and went over to help them push.

"There they go. Good riddance," Hank's partner whispered, watching the little boat leave, then said, "Boy, if Frank ever found out you tripped, when we were chasing those characters, and accidentally fired that amazing shot."

"Hah. He knows one of us might have screwed up, but his version will sound better back in Chicago."

~

FLORA'S MONEY

Meanwhile, back in the woods: "GEE-SUZZ! Hector! Where's the goddam car? This is the place, ain't it?"

"Quent, it's so dark, but this seems right. That's the old boathouse over there, I think. We weren't gone very long. Who could have—ouch! I just stepped on another sharp stone."

"Son-of-a-bitch, Hector. We're screwed if somebody has snatched that wagon—and all our stuff, the stash of dough in the back, our clothes—come on, we better start lookin' around. He must have jumped the wires or—damn, I left the key in my pants and we put it all in the trunk. Maybe they simply found the key and used it. Let's go! We must find that car—I hope they just moved it to some other place around here. If not, we've had it! You still have your gun, don't you?"

"Yeah. I've been carrying it tucked into one of my shoes since we left the beach, makes a swell holster. Here, you might as well wear 'em—probably too big, but better then nothin' on the sharp stones. I'll carry the gun. Oh-oh. That's weird."

"What the hell you talking about, Hector? Let's go!"

"It's one of your shoes. I must have grabbed one of yours and one of mine back there. Both are white, and in the dark I didn't notice till now. Maybe you can wear them anyhow. Mine might be a little big—oops. They're both for the left foot. Sorry."

"Aw shut up! Keep 'em. We can't go back to the beach now. We gotta check around, then go and see if Carlos is back at his place and has a car we can borrow—maybe some clothes—and some cash. Damn! What a screw-up. C'mon!"

~

126

FLORA'S MONEY

At the same time, a few miles south of the beach: The Duesenberg, with motor idling and headlights turned off, was rolling to a stop in front of a sagging barn, deep in a pine woods behind the junk-filled foundation of a burned-out farmhouse. Just before it came to a halt, Bruno, still clinging to the rear bumper, tensed, slipped himself off on the muddy lane, landed silently and scuttled unseen into the nearby trees. Feeling his way through the soaked and totally dark underbrush, he managed to hunker down across the lane from the old barn, thankful that even though there were dank and dripping branches it was still a warm night. With the patience of a prowling predator, he began what he assumed would be a long vigil, at least till dawn, or whenever his prey would leave the scene; if he left in the car, Bruno figured he could hop back on; if Gorki left on foot, Bruno had other plans.

Gorki stepped out of the car and quickly beamed his flashlight about, ignoring the lightly falling rain and thinking hard: Looks just about the way I left it the last time I stored some goods here. I'll run this wagon inside, take a nap, and then in daylight I'll pile some of the old timbers and junk in front of the doors to discourage anybody from getting nosy. He yawned and reached for the rusty latch holding the barn doors shut, wondering how much cash this royal wagon would bring.

After he had the car inside, and shut down, he closed the barn doors, got into the rear seat, laid back and turned off his flashlight. He interlocked his fingers behind his head and, knees bent, propped his feet on the leather armrest under the opposite window. He continued to think about a plan: Tomorrow, I'll hike back to the beach. I don't have to hide, no one but Ivan and the boys know I have this buggy—and even they don't know where I've taken it. I'll look up my

FLORA'S MONEY

young friend Grover, out at that deserted lighthouse, and check on the old sheds or whatever other hiding places there might be out there. Those guys must have already searched that area by now—and maybe they've already left and are looking for it out on the roads back to Chi—if they have another car.

Anyway, when it seems okay, and I've found a better place to hide this thing, I'll drive my truck back here and rig up a ramp. Just before daylight I'll drive the truck back to the shore with the car under the canvas in back—and move the car closer to the shore. It'll be hidden near to where they left it—the area they're least likely to search again, then when I've found a buyer, maybe I can take it entirely out of the area by boat. Maybe.

He dozed off and a few hours later woke up refreshed, though it was still before dawn; turning on his flashlight, he climbed out of the car, opened the trunk and looked inside. After pushing some loose clothing out of the way he saw that they were rumpled coats and trousers from two suits; he ran his hand through all the pockets and found loose change, two wallets, a cigar lighter, a pencil stub, a bottle opener, a stick of Wrigley's chewing gum, and an empty pocket flask. To his special glee, there also was a single key. He slipped it into his pocket.

Without stopping to carefully count the money in the wallets, he pulled the bills out, fanned them quickly, whistled softly and stuffed them all in his pants pocket. Everything else from the suits he slipped back into one of the coat pockets to look at later. A flat-topped straw skimmer in the trunk caught his attention. He tried it on; it fit, so he kept the jaunty hat perched on his head and closed the trunk. Then he stepped around to the front seat and climbed in to try the

FLORA'S MONEY

key. It worked. Delighted, he let the engine idle for a moment before shutting it down, but just before he switched off the key he heard the engine sputter and begin to make uneven sounds; the car swayed slightly—and the motor stopped. Silence. Gorki frowned, tried to start it again. Nothing. He wondered if he should try cranking it, not sure that the car had a crank, or even needed one. Then he looked at the gas gauge on the walnut dashboard. It read empty. With key on, he pressed the starter several times, making it growl, but it still wouldn't start.

Since he had a few gallons of gas in a can on his truck, and could have gone after it last night, he was angry that he had not paid more attention to the Duesenberg when he first started it. He put the key in his pocket, got out of the car and slid back one of the barn doors just enough to slip out into the darkness. Then he jerked the door shut, piled a few charred boards in front of it, settled the skimmer snugly on his head and began walking down the lane toward the road.

Across from the barn, Bruno was roused by the engine sounds, heard it cough and, to his surprise, not start. Then he saw Gorki come out, block the doors and leave. After waiting for a few minutes, to be sure he had left, Bruno stood up, stretched, and hurried across to the barn, flexing his stiffened back and wind-milling his arms as he went. He stopped at the doors, faced with a quick decision, thinking—Gorki couldn't start the car. No gas? So dark in the barn, hard to see things. No light. I go in to check, I lose him. Best I follow now. Car won't move without him, or maybe me. He turned and went down the lane knowing he had to stay back out of sight, yet keep up, like stalking a wounded bear.

At dawn, Bruno hurried back through the woods to

FLORA'S MONEY

the caravan camp. Everyone was up and getting ready to get back on the dirt road to leave the area. During the night, Ivan had sent Peri back to the beach to make sure the cops had left the scene. On his return, it was decided that all the commotion was not about them and they should just move on as early as possible.

Bruno found Ivan, sitting on a stump, drinking tea and watching his people hitching up the horses and preparing to go. Ivan looked at Bruno standing there, breathing heavily, and said, "Well?"

"The rich car is in a barn, maybe one hour from here. I hid outside. Way before daylight, I heard Gorki try to start car."

"Try?"

"Last night, it run. This morning it was out of gas, I think. I followed him back, almost to beach. He had truck hidden in the woods, got in and drove out. I ran to jump on and slipped. Maybe he went back to car. Maybe had gas for car. Don't know. Sorry."

Ivan stared at Bruno, thinking, and finally said, "Okay. Get in wagon. Sleep. You did your best. Gorki promised to come find us. Maybe, maybe not." He sipped his tea and nodded as Bruno sighed and walked to his wagon.

CHAPTER 20

Later, the same morning, down on the beach, Arie opened her eyes and gazed around the bare room when first light began to show inside the unfurnished cottage. Still wearing the same clothes from the night before, she slipped out of her makeshift bed, a folded quilt spread on the floor. Through the screen door she saw Carlos coming up on the porch and went out to join him. A gentle rain was falling from a gloomy sky.

"Sleep well?" he asked.

She shrugged and said, "Yeah, good while it lasted. What's going on?"

"We have some action down on the beach. Take a look out there."

"Jeepers! Is that real?"

FLORA'S MONEY

"Yup, Arie. It's a Ford Tri-motor, one of the famous Tin Goose airplanes, mounted on floats so it can land right on the water, as it did last night. Came in just before daylight. I was half awake and trying to sleep and when I heard the engine they were using to taxi in, I looked out and saw it. They brought her into the shallows and ran some lines to those scrub trees down there. Incredible."

Down on the beach, the pattering raindrops were easing up, though still creating tiny pockmarks scattered over the leaden surfaces of the lake. But even with the dismal overcast, the silvery airplane gleamed, swaying lightly and looking majestic on the drab water.

"It's so big. What's it doing here? Can we go out for a closer look?" Arie asked.

"Pretty soon. Apparently it was supposed to come in last night, in time to transfer part of its load to the boat we were trying to meet. Quent also intended for us to store some of it temporarily in our shed for other buyers, as you know, but engine trouble delayed the plane. Quent and Hector were trying to get a little sleep on our porch and heard the engine noise, same as I did."

"Golly, I must have slept through the whole thing." Arie said.

"Anyhow, sleepy head," he continued, "we took the old skiff and oars from the shed, and lugged it all down there, so they could go out to talk to the pilots. Hector came back ashore in the skiff to keep outsiders away, in case too many spectators came along. And he told me they had expected the plane last night—and first they were worried when it was late and then they were glad it wasn't here when the feds showed up. The engine start-up they did to test-run their repairs is what woke you up, I guess. Quent's helping them work out

FLORA'S MONEY

the problem; remember, he used to be an airplane mechanic. And Arie, Hector also said that the flying job they have for me will be that plane or one like it, and Quent will talk to us about it when he comes back in."

"Really! You know how to fly that kind of plane?"

"Well, I've only flown single-engine up to now, but I could learn."

Arie continued to gaze at the plane, a grim look on her face. "Are you sure you really want to work for them? Seems so risky. You could go to jail."

"Hey, last night, since the plane was running so late, everything just got out of whack. It doesn't always work like that. And as soon as we can afford it, we'll get you located in a decent place—maybe here. Whatever you want."

Meanwhile, up the beach toward Hamelet, Jerry's wife Madge turned from the window, leaned over the bed and said, softly, "Jerry—Jere, wake up," then repeated it again. She placed her hand on his bare chest to gently rouse him. It worked.

His eyes blinked, and then he stared at her for a second and mumbled, "What? I just got to sleep—I think."

"Sorry, hon, but you better see this—there's a great big airplane down toward the point." She was standing in the narrow space between their bed and the window, without nightclothes except for the skimpy shift she held in her left hand.

"You woke me to see an airplane? I don't hear anything. Did it land on the beach?"

"No, it's on the water, just floatin' there. I woke up, and heard something. Maybe it was the engine noise that woke me, but it's not doing it now—or maybe I just woke up because

133

FLORA'S MONEY

it's so warm in here, and—"

"Maddie, what's happening?" Jerry interrupted, yawning.

"I can't tell. Take a look yourself!"

Jerry groaned, crawled to her side of the bed, sat up, leaned over to the window with one hand on the sill, the other on her bare rump and said, "Damn, lookit that! It's huge!"

"What is? You mean the airplane?" Madge asked, giggling. She sat down next to him and added, "You used to say I was sleek."

"Huh? What? Oh yeah," he said, raising the shade a little more and staring out: "Cripes, it's just getting light. What a night." Still sitting on the bed he leaned toward the window, placed his left forearm and hand flat on the sill, and rested his chin on top of the arm. He peered out the window, muttering, "Cheez, I 'spose I should go down there—dunno why, though. Feds are gone. Seems to be just a few people movin' around. Still rainin' some." As he spoke he let his right hand wander around her back. "Maybe I should go check on Grover, huh?"

"Up to you, Jerry. When you came home last night, or whenever it was, you said that you spoke to Grover in the middle of the raid and he was doing okay then."

Jerry grunted, and said, "Yeah, he sure was!"

Chuckling, he pulled himself back and flopped back on his side of the bed. She turned and slid in beside him.

"Still awful early, Jere," she said, "we were up most of the night—I think we need another lil' nap."

Back at the plane, thirty minutes later, Quent motioned

FLORA'S MONEY

Hector to come out in the skiff and pick him up. They came ashore and walked up to the cottage in the lingering drizzle—two weary guys, soaked, straggling hair dispersed and stuck flat on their heads. They were still barefoot and wearing clinging-wet undershorts; Carlos's sagging-wet sweater covered Quent's torso, and a rain-spattered piece of oilcloth tablecover was knotted and hanging loosely around Hector's shoulders.

When they stepped up on the porch, Carlos handed each of them a faded towel and said, "Hey, love your outfits. And Quent, you've got grease on your hands, just like the old days back in the squadron." Before they could do more than just growl back, the screen door opened and Arie came out carrying two glass jars for cups and a blackened pot of coffee that she had boiled up on the woodstove in the kitchen. Under her arm she had a Colonial Bread wrapper with some apples and hardened doughnuts inside. She kept her eyes averted from their scanty outfits as she poured.

"Oh, darlin'. Coffee! Give us a bunch, please!" Hector said, as he sat down on the floor and leaned against the wall.

"Careful, gents, hot stuff," Arie said, "go to it. We already had ours—used grampa's old recipe: an eggshell in the bottom of the pot to settle the grounds."

"Carlos," Quent said, chewing on a doughnut, "the plane getting here late might work out okay, after all, in spite of all the screw-ups last night. I couldn't tell you about our new plane yesterday afternoon, but I can now—but we still want to keep it a secret as long as we can. Anyhow, the first thing will be to get you whatever training you need, and then checked out in the Goose—and you'll be paid starting from today. Okay?"

135

FLORA'S MONEY

"Hah! Of course," Carlos said, with a grin.

"And I can just stay here in Hamelet," Arie said, happily, "Maybe find a job in town. I could stay in the rooms we've rented in town. Right here with all my old friends."

"Okay, great." Quent replied, smiling at Arie. Then he said: "Let me fill you both in. That Goose, of course, belongs to my boss. It's brand new; the pilots just picked it up from Ford yesterday. We're kinda'starting a little airline to fly in and out of Chicago. Carlos, I think we can use you as a back-up pilot, and Jed will show you whatever you don't already know about flying this baby. If everything clicks we'll probably add another plane later on. By the way, our guys just finished up the special training they needed from Ford to fly the Goose. And yesterday they gassed her up and took off for Canada to pick up our first load. That done, they refueled and took off from over the border at dusk. The plan was for them to land here around one a.m. this morning and unload, putting some of it in your shed and the rest on Jake's boat. But after the plane got well out over the lake they started having some stalls on that port engine and set her down on the water offshore, somewhere north of here. The lake was calm, fortunately, even though there was a little rain and haze last night."

"Quent, couldn't they fly it with just two engines?" Hector asked.

"In theory, yes. But they haven't had that much experience yet, especially with a heavy load on board. Anyhow, they decided to play it safe. They set her down on the lake and taxied the rest of the way here on the surface, like a boat, watching for the old lighthouse over there that I'd told them about, as they came down the coast. It was slow going and almost daylight by the time they got here. So then Jed and

FLORA'S MONEY

I went to work on the mechanical problem and I think we fixed it. As soon as we get back on board we're going to rev it up and take off if everything checks out okay. We need to move fast, and get out of here before any local lawmen get nosey. Carlos, I'd like you to ride back with us now, if you can." Carlos nodded and glanced at Arie, giving her a little smile.

"Unless we get a better idea," Quent continued, "we're going to fly on to Chi and unload it all there, this time. We'll anchor on the lake in the quiet spot we have set up and unload the booze. Grab the clothes you want to take along, Carlos, and here's a hundred bucks, some of the money I borrowed from Jed. I know we said forty, but you'll need to leave enough with Arie to tide her over for a while. Consider it an advance. And I'd like to pay off the repairs on your car and borrow it for a few days. I want Hector to stay here for now and take care of a few matters. He has some cash now, and will pay the garage for you."

"Right, Quent. Then I'll buy some duds and a big breakfast," Hector said.

"Okay, kids, let's take off, each in our own way!" Quent announced with a laugh, and hurried down the porch steps. The others stood up, eager to get going as Carlos said, "Hey, here we go! I'll run back to our rooms in town, grab some clothes and come right back. Arie, maybe you could fetch our blankets and stuff from the cottage and take Hector over to get the car. And here's some cash for your expenses. Okay?"

About five-hundred feet down the shore from the Goose, Grover lay full-length on the lofty walkway that encircled the

FLORA'S MONEY

top of his lighthouse. The night before, he had hurried Millie along, with her arms crossed over her bare breasts, and taken her back to her rooms in town. He had decided it was better than risk taking her across the beach to his place, in case the cops stopped them, or if Uncle Jerry decided to show up at the tower later to check up on him, in spite of the hour.

They approached her rooming house from the rear, staying in the deep shadows. There were no lights showing inside or out. The noise on the beach apparently had not aroused anyone there, or perhaps, based on previous late-night disturbances by other bootlegger chases, the family she lived with was just staying out of sight by hiding in bed. Before she ran on in, Grover whispered in her ear: "Pants? Anything!"

Millie nodded and scurried on to the back door. He hid behind two trashcans till she quickly came back out, wearing a robe. Ducking down behind the cans, next to Grover, she handed him a small bundle, and whispered: "Go now. Don't come around anymore—I'm gonna leave this town, maybe tomorrow!" Then she stood up, pulled her robe close and ran towards the house before he could speak. He heard her make low whimpering sounds as she went.

Grover sighed, looked at the closed door for a moment, then held up the little bundle, shook it out and, difficult as it was in the dark, he realized he was holding a very frilly pair of pajama pants. He stepped into the petite trousers and found them tight, very short and only able to cover him from calves to a place low on his hips. The waist was too small for him to connect all the buttons, but the garment worked as long as he used one hand to keep hitching the thing up.

Quick visions kept running through his mind as he started for his tower: poor Millie, practically nude, in motion, holding his hand so tightly as they ran; and the sensations he

138

FLORA'S MONEY

felt, from her—and from his own exposure, wearing just a shirt, with his free hand trying to provide cover and support for himself. "Wild. A nightmare. Is this really happening?" he whispered to himself, almost running, dazed, yet chuckling softly.

On the way to the tower, he skirted the open beach. Going through the edge of the woods most of the way, he came to the narrow path that led him to the lighthouse door. He went in and, as usual, ran all the way up the winding steps, two or three at a time. Without lighting a candle, he dropped his sweaty shirt and girlish pants on the floor to sprawl on his cot and quickly fall asleep.

Just before dawn, he too was roused by the sounds of the arriving Ford Tri-Motor. He jumped up and took a quick look through a window. Curious and excited, he slipped into a poncho and went outside through the doorway to the observation gallery. Then he dropped down on his stomach and stretched his neck to peer out over the edge, eyes perplexed like a bemused gargoyle. Unnoticed by the people down on the beach near the plane, the scene reminded him of Lilliputians walking around and crawling onto the tied-down Gulliver. Eventually, he pulled back a little, cushioned his head on one arm and, ignoring the drizzling rain, soon dozed until the engine start-ups of the departing plane woke him again.

Without moving, he watched it taxi out to the open water. He heard the blast of motor sounds as the pilot increased power and guided the pontoon plane straight out across the lake. It gained speed, lifted off, dripping some foaming water, and kept going west.

Daylight was arriving, and he saw that patches of blue, edged with the fire preceding the full glare of the sun, had

FLORA'S MONEY

started to appear through the separating gray clouds, low down in the east. He glanced lazily back and forth at the plane disappearing into the cobalt sky to the west, and then he looked back to the east and squinted at the deep-orange ball. He sat up, still drowsy, leaned back against the wall below the lighthouse windows and admired the panorama, dreamily gazing at the color show.

Down on the beach, Arie stood alone, staring across the lake, watching the departing plane. Hector had already walked back to the cottage, after helping with the tether ropes before take off. As he passed Arie he said, "Maybe I'll grab a little nap up on the porch," then added with a yawn, "been a busy night, please give me a holler in an hour or three." He winked at Arie and pretended to stagger for a few steps.

After he was gone, Arie turned away from the lake, unsure what she was going to do next. Once again she peered along the shore to the top of the lighthouse, at the figure lying on the balcony. She was sure it was Grover she had spotted lying up there when she first came out on the porch, but said nothing about him to Carlos. Since then she had privately looked over at Grover, several times, in spite of all the distractions about the plane and the discussions with Quent. Now, Grover seemed to be sitting up, though it was too far away for her to know if he was awake, or even if he had seen her. She wondered if he knew she was back in town.

Wrists crossed, and holding an upper arm in each hand, she began to slowly walk toward the tower. A few gulls gliding about the lonely beach made the only sounds, a few shrill calls, now and then. For a few moments she hesitated, thinking: should I do this? I haven't seen him for months.

Then she resumed walking, her bare feet operating on their own, until she stood on the rocky outcropping at the

FLORA'S MONEY

base of the lighthouse. "Grover, you awake up there. Hi, wake up," she called gently, so close she had to tilt her head way back to look straight up the tower wall. "Hoo, up there, good morning," she tried again, louder. Grover's tousled head and bare shoulders appeared against the sky, peering down from the lofty edge of the gallery. His voice floated down to her: "Arie! Golly. Hey, what's up?"

"You are, I guess. Joke; did I wake you?"

"No, uh, I guess so. But I was awake before, I mean—"

Arie laughed and said, "Never mind. Maybe you dozed off. Be careful up there!" she added, seeing him sway outward a little, supported by one arm hooked over the middle railing. "Can I come up? Or do you want to sleep some more?"

"No, no, I'm awake. C'mon up. Great to see you again. Door's not locked. Just follow the steps."

She laughed again, leaned way back, waved and said, "Follow the steps. Seems logical. Here I come!"

CHAPTER 21

Arie walked into the ground-level door of the lighthouse as Grover hurried in from the gallery up above, thinking: Arie! Here! Holy smokes!

Groggy from sleep, he worked at groping his way back to reality, still weary after his busy night with Millie, the surprise raid—and then the coming and going of the huge airplane. Yanking the poncho over his head and tossing it aside, he felt the cool air on his skin and realized the need to put something on, quickly! He reached into a bushel-basket of rumpled clothes, found some work pants and stepped into them. Fumbling with the fly-buttons, he sidled awkwardly over to the stairway, looked down, and hollered happily, "Arie! You comin' along okay?"

"Okay—ay, ay!" echoed up from the depths, followed

FLORA'S MONEY

by, "come—ing—ing!"

Grover hovered at the stairwell, waiting for her. His glance, flitting around the room, focused on the little pile of Millie's pants and his undershirt, dropped to the floor on the way to bed the night before—then, he heard, "Almost there—I see day—light—ite!'

Grover gulped, hopped sideways, scooped up the pajama pants and sent them winging out an open window, legs a-flail. Arie's head appeared in the stairway a moment later as she came up around the final curve and stopped, two steps from the top. Puffing and laughing, she lolled her head back and blew a heavy whoosh of air straight up. He reached out to grasp her outstretched hands, pulled her up the last step and wrapped his arms around her shoulders.

"Arie—welcome," he said in a hearty voice, then added more quietly, "and hey, you know we're practically in the same position as the last time we were together—except then we were underwater, remember?" They remained standing. His hands slid down to her waist. She placed one of hers on each of his bare shoulders and nodded, her shyness melting away. "I remember, Grove," she replied softly, "our graduation picnic on the beach—we went for a dip, after dark."

"And your brother called you in and took you home."

She sighed and said, "Yes, and the next morning, early, he had to drive our flivver to Chicago so he could see about a possible job, as a conductor on a trolley car—and he didn't want to leave me here, because he wasn't sure when he'd get back. He didn't get that job, by the way, and so he had to keep looking. Before we left, I did run out here to say goodbye that morning, and called to you from down below. I thought maybe you were still asleep, and I didn't think I should just walk in. So—I just left. Sorry."

FLORA'S MONEY

"Gee I'm sorry, too." Grover replied, "I did run over to your place, first thing to see you off and you had already gone. I wondered if you were mad at me. Or if maybe your brother was. I knew you planned to leave sometime that day, but I didn't know what time or when you were coming back. Then, weeks later, I got your postcard, but your address wasn't on it." They slowly stepped apart.

"Don't worry, Grover, he wasn't mad. He likes you. I'm sorry, but we moved around Chicago so much—some nights we even had to find a deserted alley, or a vacant lot, and sleep in the car. I kept hoping we'd be back here long before now, at least for a visit."

He took her hand and guided her around the end of a bench to sit down, in front of one of the windows facing out at the lake. He sat down next to her and said, "Well, now you're back, and I'm glad. And here we are up in this funny ol' castle, enjoying the view."

"Yes and it really is beautiful. Almost breath-taking, you might say," she said, and then laughed when he let the tip of his tongue show, squinted at her and replied, "Hah! Sorry about that climb, Arie. You know, I'm been thinking about putting an elevator of some kind in here. I've even made some sketches of how a rope and pulley arrangement might make it work, up and down the open core of the stairwell. And we'd have a small cage, or something to ride in, just big enough for two people at a time."

"Sounds cozy."

"True, and once we're up here it can be quite cozy too." As he spoke, he made a sweeping gesture with his right hand, partway around the circle of windows, and added, "Especially when it gets stormy and those mammoth gray clouds come in low, so close you can reach out to touch

FLORA'S MONEY

the scary stuff—and then you realize, hey, it's only a lot of puffy pillows, putting on an act—pretending. Maybe because clouds get bored just being white and misty, floating around on sunny afternoons."

Arie smiled and said in a quiet voice, "Yes, but that can't be too bad. On those happy days the big white clouds get to make themselves in to all kinds of animal shapes, dancing elves and lots of other things."

Grover reached over, patted her cheek and said, "I guess we've had cloud-chats before."

"You know we have. The first time when we were maybe about five or six," Arie said, eyes twinkling.

"Right; like I said, welcome back. And, another thing, anytime you come out here, from now on, you can yoo-hoo me by yelling up the speaking tube I just put in a few weeks ago. Too bad I didn't have it that morning you came out to say goodbye; I would have heard you, for sure."

"You put it in yourself? How does it work?"

"I'll show you when we go down, Arie. I got some old tubing from Oren, over at the Emporium, and two funnels, one for up here and one that goes outside near the door downstairs. He also threw in some connectors and so on, all for free, sort of—I owe him some sweeping time at his store, but that's easy. Oren said all the gear for this was salvaged from a wrecked lake-steamer, years ago. Since then it has just been piled in the junk by the old blacksmith shop he used to operate out back of his store—you remember, where we used to go watch them pump the forge and hammer on red-hot horseshoes, hinges, and other things for his customers—anyway," Grover continued, "when I asked him what I could make the tube out of, he showed me the parts and told me he figured the old tower was a good place for

145

FLORA'S MONEY

it to be."

"Of course. From one historic place to another. How did you know how to put it all together?"

"Well, it was pretty obvious. I just pretended like I was putting it back on the ship, and hooking it up between the captain in the wheelhouse and the guy running the engines, several decks below. It's not electric or anything, and it really works, as long as you speak up, LOUD."

"I'm sure it does, Grove. This place seems ideal for you—full of challenges and wonderful things to do. Really different, like having your own little world—as long as you don't mind climbing steps, and apparently you don't—but you're even dreaming up a way to beat that with an elevator." She gazed out the window for a moment and said, "Gosh, you can almost see Hamelet from up here. How can you ever get to sleep with so much to look at out there? I bet you must sleep with one eye open. That wouldn't surprise me, either."

"Wait till you see it on a starry night, or when the moon is full," he said. They exchanged glances, sitting quietly and looking out over the lake for a long moment. He spoke first, "Arie, you know this is the first time you and I were ever up here alone."

"I know. You used to say that your uncle was very strict about that sort of thing, didn't you?"

"That was a long time ago, back when Ramsay and I first moved in. But he pretty much leaves me alone now. For one thing, I think all the steps are getting to him sometimes. But enough of that. Tell me, when did you get back and what are your plans? Are you back for good, or what?"

"I'm not sure yet. I hope I'll be here the rest of the summer, at least. But Carlos just got a flying job again and,

FLORA'S MONEY

well—but maybe I shouldn't talk about that yet."

"Hey, that's right. That big plane this morning, I saw—uh, some people get on it. It took off and went west, maybe to Chicago, maybe somewhere else. I don't need to know." He leaned toward her, their faces inches apart, and Grover added, "All the excitement last night—maybe we should talk about it or maybe not. I mean we both know why there was a Fed raid last night, why that plane came in here and what your brother is up to. Never mind, I've run errands for those guys, too, and never told anyone, especially Uncle Jere—and you must know I won't say anything now about anyone else doing it."

"Golly, Grove. I think what you're saying is that we can have a personal conversation about all this without having to say anything out loud. Is that how you feel, too?"

"Yes, you're right. Hey, we've known each forever. Seems like all we have to do is be together and listen to the silence. Is that possible?"

"Apparently. We seem to be almost doing it right now," Arie whispered, watching his face closely.

"Well, I'm thinking, silently you'll notice, of several things," he said, "like we don't have to mention that we're worried about your brother's safety, even though he may be into something dangerous. And we both are thinking that what he's doing may be only temporary if they change the dumb law and Prohibition is abolished—like some newspapers say it could happen, this year or next. Then, we can all stop trying to exist under twisted rules of what's right and what's wrong."

"Grover?"

"What?"

She leaned forward and gave him a slow kiss on the

FLORA'S MONEY

cheek. He began to slip his arms around her. Their lips lined up for contact—but jerked apart when a short, shrill whistle engulfed the air around them, followed by a voice that they both realized must be coming out of the tube over by the steps: "GROVER, YOU UP THERE—ERE? CAN YOU HEAR ME—E—E?"

Wide-eyed, Grover said, "Damn, sounds like Uncle Jere's down there!" For a long moment Grover frowned and bared his teeth, thinking hard. Then he winked at Arie, turned to-ward the funnel and shouted, "HEY JERE. I'LL BE RIGHT DOWN." After a short pause, they heard, "OKAY. I'LL BE OUTSIDE—IDE."

Startled, Arie sat straighter, staring wide-eyed at Grover.

CHAPTER 22

"Arie, don't worry. I'll go down and talk to him. I think it's best to let him know you're up here with me. He probably won't want to climb the steps and come up. Wait a couple minutes till I get down there, then go out on the gallery and wave when I call you. Say hi, but be brief." He went over to the basket as he talked, pulled out an undershirt, slipped it on and headed for the steps.

"Grover, won't he be mad at you for letting me come up here?"

"No. He used to have rules—a long time ago. We've never given him any trouble. I'll handle it. Has he seen you or your brother since you came back this time?" She shook her head and said, "I don't think so. He probably has no idea that Carlos was even here."

FLORA'S MONEY

"Good. Enjoy the view. I'll be back as soon as he leaves." He threw her a kiss and disappeared down the steps. At the bottom he walked outside. Jerry sat on one of the ledge outcroppings near the door, smoking a cigarette. He looked at Grover and said, "Well, that voice thing works pretty good."

Grover smiled, sat down next to him, and said, "Yeah, Jere. Comes in handy. And now I'm working on some sketches for a manual elevator, you know, with ropes and muscle power. "

"Really? Hey, that'll be the first elevator in Hamelet."

"I guess that's right—if I get it to work."

"You will, Grove. Just like all the painting and other fix-ups you've done out here."

"So, you had a busy night," Grover commented evenly, a little surprised at himself for bringing it up, but anxious to get through it.

Jerry nodded and said, "Boy, and how. Quite a crowd out there, all over the place. And did you know anything about that plane that came in?"

"No, it woke me up, coming and going. I watched it from up top. A great machine."

"You didn't come down?"

"No. The view from up there was great."

Jerry gazed out at the lake, for a moment, then ground out his cigarette with his heel and said, "I bet."

Grover watched him and again plunged ahead: "By the way, Arie stopped by to see me." He leaned out from the tower wall, looked straight up, waved and said, "Hey, there she is. Watching the birds."

Surprised, Jerry leaned back to look up. He saw her out on the balcony, leaning against the rail and called out: "HEY,

FLORA'S MONEY

ARIE. HOW'S THE SCENERY FROM UP THERE?" He stretched out his left arm and wiggled his fingers at her.

"HI JERRY. VIEW'S GREAT! I'M FLYING!" She waved again and strolled slowly around out of sight. Jerry watched her go, and then asked quietly, "Uh, she's been away for awhile, hasn't she?"

"Yes."

"Sweet kid. I always liked Arie."

"Me too," Grover grinned. Jerry gave a short laugh, cleared his throat and went on; "You two grew up together. Nice. Well, everything okay, then?"

"Sure."

"Hey, fine." Jerry said, absently, "that's right, I did see you last night, didn't I? Pretty dark out there when the spotlight went out. I guess you were, uh, enjoying the beach, huh? Havin a dip on a hot night—then all hell broke loose!" Grover nodded and shrugged, rolling his eyes.

"So. You got your girl back to her house okay? And, nobody else saw you, right?"

Again, Grover answered with a couple nods, then looked away, puckered his lips, and exhaled.

"Well, time to check things in town. Got in so late last night I'm afraid I overslept some this morning. Almost missed seeing that big plane. Maddie heard it, woke me up. We saw it pull out. Beautiful sight." He got up, yawned and started along the path toward town. Grover stood and watched him stroll across the sand. He looked back, raised his arm straight up and waved once, then continued. Grover wasn't sure if the wave was for him, or maybe Arie if she was still out on the gallery. But since he couldn't see her from where he stood by the ledge, he waved at Jerry anyway before going back inside to begin to do the steps, two at a time.

151

FLORA'S MONEY

Arie and Grover returned to the bench where they were sitting when Jerry stopped by, and chatted until she said she had to leave for a while and do an errand for Carlos.

"Coming back later?" Grover asked.

"Yes, okay?"

"Sure, I'll be here. I'll walk you down. Back in a couple hours?"

"Probably. When I get back I'll yodel up the tube!" They both laughed and began walking down the spiraling, narrow steps, single file, with her leading. Outside, he clasped her hands in both of his and said, "Hey, I'm really glad you're back." She let him hold her hands for a long moment.

"See you soon," she whispered. Then she turned to walk back to the cottage to rouse Hector and go with him to get her brother's truck for him to use.

Out on the beach, in the hot sun, small waves bubbled and flowed in the shallows. A few yards away, on the drier sand, an easy breeze fluttered a cloth thing, blue and frilly, and nudged it aimlessly toward the water.

CHAPTER 23

Mid-morning, the same day, downtown Hamelet. Flora lugged a large valise in each hand as she came striding toward the Emporium, one of the oldest shops in the six-block area of stores and offices in the business area. She had just parked the Packard roadster, angled into the curb in small-town fashion, got out, unlocked the rumble seat and removed the two bags, then carefully relocked it and started out.

She came to a halt in front of the store, glanced at the dusty jugs, washboards, fly papers, horse collars, pitchforks and old magazines in the two store windows, and sailed through the entry area between them. This brought her to the two side-by-side glassed front doors. To unload one hand, so she could push the door to her right, she quickly tucked one of the cases under her left arm, poked out the freed

FLORA'S MONEY

hand and straight-armed the push-panel on the right door. Bad choice; that was the locked one.

A ricochet effect off the immovable door propelled her, left-shoulder and bulging valises first, against the unlocked door. It flew open with a bang as the case under her arm slipped and sailed inside the store on its own, making an upside-down crash-landing on the floor—with very loud crunching and clinking sounds.

Flora gasped. Silhouetted for a moment against the bright sky behind her, she stumbled on through the doorway, her short bolero jacket flapping open and revealing a lacy blouse swelled with the outline of a full-bosomed lady. Her cloche hat, snug atop her blond hair, was knocked askew in the collision.

Once inside, she put the other valise down, straightened up and stared down the dismal center aisle, past the sparsely loaded counters and shelves of the old Emporium. For the first minute or two she saw no sign of life in the gloomy place.

No customers or clerks, and no hangers-on sitting on the two benches back where the wood stove glowed in winter—until a shadowy figure edged slowly through a door, about fifty feet away in the back of the store. The dusty plank flooring squeaked when he started to shuffle up to the front.

Flora knew it was her uncle Oren and started to call out to him, but was interrupted when the elderly man had come partway up the aisle, stopped, peered in her direction and demanded: "Now you hold it. Right there! We got ya' covered. What's the big idea—why'd you come crashin' in here like that?"

She stared, then giggled when she saw his weapon, an

FLORA'S MONEY

old croquet mallet, and called out, "Hey, you ol' sweetie, it's me, Flora. You're my Uncle Orangie—remember?"

Flora's first thrill of watching moving shadows on the wall didn't come along until she moved into Chicago, where she managed to take in a movie matinee at least twice a week. And Flora enjoyed the apartment in Jiggs's building for quite a while. He still watched her at work behind the bar and had knocked on her apartment door a few times at odd hours after a long night of boozing. And sometimes he would give himself away by calling out to her by name. Since she hardly ever had any visitors, it wasn't hard to figure out that Jiggs was on the prowl again. Flora simply never answered the door when she suspected it was him, and tip-toed around till he had left, glad that she had installed the throw bolt on the door when she moved in.

Flora continued to work hard during the hours when Golden's was open, and slowly enlarged her collection of coffee cans until the summer of 1933 when her lifestyle changed abruptly. It all started when Jiggs told Bernard, the suave gent he had hired to chauffeur the boss around in the Duesenberg, to give Flora some driving lessons in the Packard during his time off. After the first lesson, without bothering to mention it to Jiggs, Flora invited Rhonda to go along too, thinking she'd enjoy the fancy car—as well as meeting the chauffeur, a gent about Rhonda's forty-something age.

Then one afternoon, the outings came to an end. Jiggs happened to be walking toward the apartment building where Flora lived and, from about a block away, he thought he saw Bernie going in the front door. He wasn't sure from that distance, but Jiggs thought the chauffeur was holding

FLORA'S MONEY

the door for someone else just before he went in too. Jiggs stopped, stared and frowned. Then he yanked out a pocket flask, downed a big gulp and began muttering to himself. He took a second swallow, turned around and began shuffling away from his building, taking sips from the flask as he went. Twice he rudely bumped shoulders with other people on the sidewalk, but he paid no attention.

After trudging for several blocks, he abruptly turned around and began striding back to his building and then went up the stairs to Flora's door. For the first and only time he decided to use his owner's passkey, but after rummaging through his pockets he couldn't find it. Instead, he resorted to wood-splintering kicks until the wrecked door flew open and he stumbled in—to see a very riled Rhonda in the bed with Bernie.

"Rhonda! Damn!"

"Jiggs! Double damn, you clown!"

"Where's Flora?"

"Who knows? Walking in the park, maybe, or gone to the moon. She came up here to unlock the door for us and left right after. What the hell's the problem?" Throughout this exchange Bernard, bare-chested, sat up in the bed, wide-eyed and scared speechless. Rhonda sprawled next to him, angry and uncovered, glaring at Jiggs.

"What's going on?" Jiggs shouted.

"What do you think, fatso? Nice place you got here—lot nicer then mine. Got any more free apartments?" Rhonda hollered back. Jiggs pulled out a pistol.

Terrified, Bernie jumped out of bed, his bum showing. Snatching clothes up into a tangled ball, he ran out of the apartment. A puffing Jiggs went over to a window, yanked it up, stuck the gun out and fired three times, straight up. Then

FLORA'S MONEY

he pulled the weapon back inside, waved it in the air a few seconds and put it back in his pocket. He glared at Rhonda. Meanwhile, the chauffeur startled pedestrians and motorists as he was seen running down Clark Street barefooted, hugging clothes, and his pale legs glistening in the summer sun.

Red faced and breathing hard, Jiggs smashed a ceramic table lamp—forgetting in his frenzy that he owned all the furnishings in the place. Then he stomped out of the apartment and tried to slam the door as he went—but the damaged frame he created going in wouldn't let the door close; instead, it gave Jiggs a final frustration by just making mild crunching sounds.

Jiggs ran down to the street to flag down a taxi but, having heard the shots, an approaching cabbie was already squealing his wheels around the next corner by the time Jiggs arrived at the curb. He hailed another cab just coming along and jumped in the minute it was slowed down enough. As it pulled away, Jiggs saw his Packard roadster parked in the lot next door to his building and thought, I gotta get that Flora out of my apartment, and grab my Packard, too, maybe tonight.

An hour later, Flora returned from her walk, saw the gaping door and pushed it slowly open, unsure what she would find. She stepped inside, walked across the room and saw a note on the neatly made bed:

Flo—I hate that toad Jiggsy—but poor Bernie. Had a little moustache, same as Dougie Fairbanks! But Jiggsy barges in right after we hit the bed, runs Bernie out at gunpoint and spoils everything. Hey! Time for you to move the hell outta here! Sorry about the lamp—your landlord did it. What a temper—hope the lamp belonged to him. And thanks anyhow. Ta-ta ~ Rhonda.

FLORA'S MONEY

Flora looked in the mirror over the dresser—and grinned at herself, remembering that the keys to the Packard were still in her pocket. Elated, she looked at the keys and said to herself, Okay! It's time to leave, to load up and go hide for a while, to be rid of Jiggs and scram before any of the mugs at Golden's connects her with the shrinking pile of money cans.

Then she remembered Hector and remained standing, thinking and nibbling on a thumbnail. Golly, maybe I shouldn't try to talk to him right now; maybe Rhonda can help me reach him later, after I go—where? Hamelet? Drive out and drop in on Uncle Oren for a while—see how he's doing with his store? She looked at herself in the mirror again, smacked a balled fist into the flat of her other hand, and said aloud, "That's it!"

She drove the regal Packard around to the alley behind the apartment building and parked near the back door. From there she could use the back stairs to go up to her apartment, or down to the basement. She piled her personal things in the front of the car in the space behind the two seats, on the passenger seat, and in the spacious trunk permanently strapped on the rear bumper. Then she decided that due to lack of enough space she would leave most of the bottles behind on the hall floor. Using a bushel basket, she made several trips to transfer just the money cans into the rumble seat.

After an hour of packing and carrying, she was ready to go. By then she had also decided to just go and never return to the club again. It could be too dangerous, especially, she thought, if those bums ever got wise to what she had done. By late afternoon she drove out of the alley, looking forward to her first visit back to Hamelet since moving to Chicago.

FLORA'S MONEY

On her way out of town she got lost a few times, followed by swift u-turns, like Bernie had shown her how to do. Once out on the country roads, in the dark, she had more trouble finding her way but kept going by asking directions, once at a remote farm house, and then from a leering gent in the office of a row of five tourist cabins, just shutting down for the night. Some time before dawn she stopped for an hour's rest, slouching back in the driver's seat as much as she could with her long legs. Later, she stopped again at an all-night diner for breakfast. She finally arrived in front of the Emporium by mid-morning, eager to see familiar faces.

At least on this trip, she remembered more than once during the night, she wasn't returning home as a grubby, very poor hitchhiker disguised as a tall tramp.

Frank, the agent in charge of the raid in Hamelet, drove himself back home late that same night, arriving back at his rooming house in Chicago well after dawn. After sleeping a few hours he finally made it into his office about noon, tossed his suit coat on a side chair and sat down at his rolltop desk, still wearing his shoulder holster and gun over his shirt. He shoved up the lid of the desk and yawned, removed a bottle of scotch from a drawer, unscrewed the cap, swallowed a mouthful, winced and put the bottle back. Then he started to look over the papers scattered loosely around on his blotter. A scrawl on a piece of notepaper from one of his agents caught his attention: *Frank - Turned up another tip about Jiggs. Bringing him in for a chat, if we can find him. Noon now, back SAP – JM.*

159

CHAPTER 24

Gus was still asleep, in the spacious bedroom of his town-house, when the ringing of the French phone woke him up. Next to him, from under the top sheet, protruded the head of another sleeper, face buried in a pillow, with tufts of yellow hair in curlers, rising and falling a little as she snored, oblivious to the strident sounds.

He reached out from the tangled sheets with his hairy arm and snatched the phone off its high cradle. Still on his back, he mumbled, "Yeh—Quent?" into the mouthpiece. He listened, then said: "So, the plane is back—okay! So, how'd they do—A RAID?" He sat up and said, "HUH—oh; our Goose was late and the cops had already left? Chee! So you had 'em fly the plane here and land down at the lake dock—with the booze still on it! They're unloading it all,

FLORA'S MONEY

into a rowboat—NOW? IN BROAD DAYLIGHT? You what? Oh—you hid all the bottles in suitcases that you had the boys take out to the plane—where the hell did you get that many bags? Never mind. Makes sense. Great."

He looked over at his table clock, yawned and said, "Lessee, it's almost noon. Tell Jiggs to get my Hudson and pick me up in two hours. I want to go see that airplane and have the pilot take us on a little hop around the lake, see what it's like to fly like a birdie. Huh? Sure you should go with us. Why not? And Jiggs, too. What—he's never been up? I know that, so what, neither have I. Hey, set it up. And take some champagne along. We'll have a toast—up in the sky!" Then he hung up.

Gus glanced over at the sheet-covered mounds next to him, yawned again and smacked the biggest hump with the flat of his hand, causing only a little movement, though the snoring stopped. He lay back down.

Quent stood on the dock watching his guys bring the last rowboat full of suitcases in and helped them carry that load into the warehouse. He saw Jiggs drive Gus into the parking area, walked over to meet them by the office door, and said, "Hi, what do you think of our flying machine out there?"

"Uh, beautiful," Gus replied, "but before we go out, there's a phone in there, right? I need to make a couple calls." Quent nodded, pulled the door open for him and stepped back; Gus went inside, the door closed behind him.

Jiggs stood in silence, frowning at the plane and absently unwrapping a fresh cigar without looking at it.

"Is Gus in a good mood this morning?" Quent asked.

"Guess so. He told me on the way down here that we're

161

FLORA'S MONEY

going to have champagne and wants to have a toast up there to celebrate. I dunno. He wants me to go up with him—I'm not sure I want to do that. But it's old stuff to you, huh? Flew in the war, and all."

"Hey, don't worry, once you're up, you'll love it," Quent said, then added, "Well, I better check with the pilot and see if we're ready for the hop when Gus comes out."

"Uh-huh—do you have to say 'hop?' Anyway, off the record, tell the pilot we want a short trip, not too long," Jiggs said, scowling, "and do you have a life jacket I can wear?"

"Sure, Jiggs. Good idea, it'll make you feel safer. I'll get you one when we get on board." Jiggs frowned and grunted, "Yeah. I'm a lousy swimmer."

The pervasive roaring and lurching involved in the lift-off run across frisky waves abruptly lessened as the pontoon-mounted plane became airborne. For Gus, it was scary and exhilarating, all at once. During the minutes following, he gawked out the window by his seat in the first row of the passenger cabin and tried to adjust to the remarkable experience. Swaddled in the bulky life jacket, Jiggs huddled in the seat directly behind Gus—rigid, gasping, and staring at the floor.

At Quent's request Carlos rode as an observer, sitting on the edge of the steps behind Arnie the co-pilot, with his feet in the step-well leading up front to the pilot's small cabin. When the plane leveled off some and began a more controlled, though normally bumpy, cruising, Quent brought Gus a dripping glass of sloshing champagne. Gus rolled his eyes, smiling. Quent turned and headed back toward the rear of the plane, intending to pour another glass for Jiggs

FLORA'S MONEY

from the open bottle he had wedged in a locker to avoid spilling—but Jiggs panicked, jumped to his feet and lurched awkwardly after Quent, grabbing the seat tops as he went.

Moments later, the whine and roar of the three engines, from just the other side of the thin, unlined metal walls, suddenly ratcheted to an even higher level. Jolted and startled, Gus dropped his almost-empty champagne glass, grabbed the metal arms of his seat, his eyes fixed on the bulkhead in front of him as it vibrated upwards, then tilted and pitched. At the same time there was a startling flash of sunlight, let in to the cabin for seconds, and the usual noise level of the three engines screamed briefly higher, before a loud thud reduced the sounds and eliminated the bouncing streaks of the sun.

Jed, the chief pilot, barked over his right shoulder: "Check on the people in back!" as he and Arnie struggled with the controls. Carlos jumped up and stepped down and through the door into the main cabin.

At the same time, Quent made his way forward, hanging on to the seat tops until he could flop down in the empty place across the narrow aisle from Gus. "QUENT! WHAT THE HELL HAPPENED BACK THERE?" Gus shouted.

"I CAN'T BELIEVE IT," Quent hollered back, "IT WAS JIGGS. HE'S GONE! WENT RIGHT OUT THE DAMN DOOR!"

Gus and Carlos stared and strained to hear as Quent shouted, breathing fast, sometimes repeating himself to be heard: "Jiggs came wobbling back from his seat right behind you there—pushed past me in the aisle—pale, confused—airsick—hand over his mouth. I pointed at the storage door, straight back, where we have the bucket and yelled at him to go in—didn't hear me, or didn't understand—just turned

163

FLORA'S MONEY

and lunged at the exit door!"

Quent shook his head, frowning. "I tried to grab him—not quick enough—somehow the door opened and he stumbled out! I—almost went with him! Jiggs disappeared—the wind slammed the door shut. AND HE WAS GONE!"

Jiggs had left the cabin, headfirst into hard blasts of cold air that took his breath and tore at his clothes as he fainted—and slammed belly first over the plump starboard pontoon, one of the two canoe-shapes suspended with sturdy struts below each of the two lower engines. On his way out and down his feet tangled in the bottom steps of the permanently mounted passenger ladder that angled down from the outside sill of the cabin door to the top of the float. His upper body, arms, and head drooped down the outside of it and, for a moment, he looked like a floppy rag doll tossed at a stepladder by a bored child.

He sprawled on the pontoon for only a few seconds, till his feet slipped down off the ladder and his body swiveled and begin sliding aft along the last few feet of the float—until a strap on his life jacket caught on a metal bracket on the pontoon. That stopped his launch into about four hundred feet of nothing. If anyone inside the plane had looked quickly out and down, from one of the windows on that side of the cabin, they might have seen him. But no one did.

He was still unconscious, minutes later, when the pilot put the plane into a glide that let the pontoons touch the lake's surface with a feathery splash, followed by a lunging bounce, and the dazzling creation of awesome spray, spewing cobalt-and-white torrents of water. From where Jiggs was riding the aquatic view would have been spectacular; but he

FLORA'S MONEY

missed all that as well as seeing the big waves, churned up in the landing, wash over him, lift him off, and leave him floating astern—on his back. The pilots taxied the plane toward their buoy and cut the engines in time to drift up to the floating tie-off ring, leaving Jiggs, still afloat, almost a quarter-mile away.

Arnie stepped out on a pontoon, snared the buoy, tied off and pulled in their empty rowboat, still tied to the buoy from their trip out, and positioned it for Gus, Quent, Carlos, Jed and himself to get in. The sun was beginning to slant from the west, casting long shadows from the run-down buildings, trees and boathouses along the shore. There were only a few other boats, all of modest size and empty of people, tied to other buoys in the area.

As Arnie rowed them in, he sat facing the rear of the boat, as rowers do, but he kept looking inland over his shoulder to guide the boat. No one spoke during the short ride to the dock. Quent and the others hunched in their seats, gazing ashore, looking glum.

Just before they reached the dock, Carlos peered way down the shore and noticed two men, who seemed to be looking their way as they strolled. Maybe they were just curious about the arrival of such a large plane, he thought—but anyway he nudged Quent and nodded in their direction. Quent looked over at them, shrugged, yawned and paid no further attention.

At the dock, they all climbed out of the boat and Quent led them into the office, closed the door, took a bottle of scotch from a desk drawer, removed the cap and passed it to Gus. He swallowed a mouthful, handed the scotch back to Quent and gestured for him to pass it around, and said: "Well, so the poor bastard got sick. Airsick, you call it? He

165

FLORA'S MONEY

panics, pushes at the wrong door, hits the latches or whatever, and he's gone. Sucked out or fell out, or maybe both." Then he asked Jed, "Where were we then, do you think?"

"About three or four miles offshore," he replied quietly, "and five or six-hundred feet altitude. I don't think there were any boaters or ships in sight, none that we could see anyway. Surely, no one could have survived a drop like that one—and since we were already on the way back, and were about to descend for landing, I just kept the glide angle going. It would have been hopeless to circle back and look for him—and it just seemed best to leave the area."

"Yeah, I guess you're right," Gus replied, then stuck a cigar in his mouth, lit up, took a puff, shook his head slowly and said: "Well, that was quite a ride and, uh, we're going to miss him. Quent, have a better lock put on that door, okay? And clam up everybody, we can't report this even though it was an accident, right?" He looked around, collecting nods, and then said, "Okay, I guess it's time to go home. I'll drive myself back. Quent, you look like you need some sleep. Call me later. We got some loose ends to clean up."

Standing at the water's edge, the two men Carlos had seen remained where they were, staring out over the water and occasionally taking quick looks at the tethered plane.

"So what the hell's going on, Morrie," Jake mused out loud, "that was Quent we just saw come ashore with those guys, wasn't it?"

"Yeah. Dunno if he spotted us or not. But he did ask us last week to check in with him down here after the job last night, didn't he? He does owe us for a trip, I guess, even though his project kinda flopped. But the big question here is

FLORA'S MONEY

what fell off that flyin' monster when it was landing? Did they toss somebody out, do you think? Seems to be something floatin' over there, for sure—first I see it, then I don't. Must be it bobs a little, now and then, from the chop of the wake the plane left behind. If it's a body, I'm outta here. Let's go back to the truck and go home, Jake."

"Doesn't make sense, Morrie, to dump anybody after they land, so near in. Why not do it way out over the lake? And whatever it is, it looks like they fixed it so it would float. Maybe they mean to get it later. Strange. And that sure looked like Quent coming in with those guys, but how did he get mixed up with a plane like this one? Anyhow, they all seem to have left. We'll have to catch him later about our money. It'll be dark soon. Maybe we should just row out to our boat and take it over for a closer look at whatever that's floatin' out there—hey, I just saw it again. Seems closer, Morrie. What d'you think?"

"Dunno, Jake. I've got a bad feelin' about this. But we have to go look; could be somebody's still alive."

CHAPTER 25

Noon, earlier the same day, in Hamelet. Right after literally dropping in on her uncle, Flora sat down with Oren in his cluttered office in the rear of the Emporium, and had a friendly chat. She patiently explained in very general terms that she had gone to Chicago, found work in a kind of restaurant, and now she was back to spend more time with him and maybe help him with his store. He listened, nodding slightly, and then took off his spectacles and began wiping them with a bandana from his pocket.

"Yes, I got your postcards and knew you were over there. And I'm glad you came back—Flory—really." Then he blew his nose, and managed to smile in spite of a shiny tear running down one cheek. Flora reached over and patted his shoulder, smiled and said, "And I'm glad to be back, Uncle

168

FLORA'S MONEY

Orangie. Now I need to unload the car, and go say hello to my old friends, Grover and Ramsay. Okay?"

"Yes, do that. You know they live in the old lighthouse now, at least Grover does. Ramsay used to, but he went off a while after you did. Some say he went to Chicago, too. Did you ever see him?"

"No, Unc, Chicago is really a big place. So, Grover lives in the lighthouse! And Ramsay has gone off to the big city. Golly, I've really been out of touch."

A few minutes later, after driving the Packard around to the back of the store, she carried her personal things upstairs to her old room and changed into shorts, an old sweater and sandals. Before unloading any of the money cans, she visited the stack of burlap bags, still where she remembered them in the storeroom, then went back out to the car and began putting the containers in the bags and knotting them closed.

She was just packing in the last few cans when Uncle Oren wandered out. There were six bags piled on the ground and she was just finishing the seventh. He leaned on his cane, stared at the Packard for several moments and reached out to lightly touch one of the massive headlights, saying in a rambling fashion: "Flora! Whose car is this? And what have you got there? Oh, coffee, three cans—you must really like that stuff. And what's in all these bags? But hey, this fancy car—wow!"

"Never mind, Uncle. These bags? Just things I got. Souvenirs, like. Car is nice, isn't it? Remember when you let me drive you around in the truck?"

He nodded, touched the headlight again, carefully with one finger, like it was a live thing, and said slowly, "I remember. Sold that truck, while back. Had to. No matter, I can't

FLORA'S MONEY

see well enough to drive anyhow. Yeah, you got pretty good at wheeling that ol' Ford—you were just a kid then—a big kid, but—"

Flora laughed. "Right. Just a big kid! Still am, Uncle. Still the same Flory."

Oren nodded, smiling at first, and then squinting at her, he lowered his voice and said, "Flory. This car—you didn't steal it, did you?"

"Goodness, no! Belongs to a friend back in Chicago. Don't worry. Tell you what. Why don't you sit down over there on that shady bench while I tote these things inside and run the car into your old blacksmith shop, out of the way, okay? Then I'll make you a cold drink, one you'll really like. After that I want to go down and see if Grover is home."

Oren sat down and said, "Right, Flory. Go see your old friends."

Back upstairs, she chipped some ice from the dwindling chunk in the ice box in Oren's kitchen, put it in a tall glass, poured in a couple inches of bourbon from one of her valise bottles, added water, and took the glass outside. Oren was leaning back against the wall, resting, and smiled as she handed him the drink.

"Thanks, Flory. Ah, a little ice water will be nice."

"Right, but this is better than plain ice water. You'll see. Sip it slow." She grinned, patted him on the shoulder and started walking across the beach.

"Hey—Grover, Hi!" Flora called and waved both of her long arms as she trotted across the beach to the tower. "What are you doing up there?"

Grover, dangling shirtless from long ropes tied to the

FLORA'S MONEY

gallery railing up above, sat on a board-seat while slapping white paint on the curved wall. He held the wide brush in one hand. A gallon-size paint can was hooked to his board by a loop of wire. At that moment he was about twenty feet above the foundation stones and twisted his neck to look down at her, smiling over his right shoulder and shouting: "Flora! Welcome back! Where you been?"

"Across there somewhere." She laughed and pointed out to the west. "There's a big town out that way called Chicago!"

"So I've heard. Gosh, you look great—wait a minute. I'm coming down." He tossed his brush into the nearly empty bucket and began to fuss with the ropes.

"Grover, come on, jump, I'll catch you!"

"Tempting offer. But stand clear." With that he swung himself off the seat with a separate line that reached the ground, and nimbly began stepping down the wall, backwards, lowering himself hand-under-hand and landing on his feet, almost in front of her. She stepped toward him with arms outspread.

"Hey, watch out, Flo. There's paint all over this hand."

"Who cares? Gimme a hug!"

Breathless, after being lifted a foot off the ground and squeezed for joyful seconds against her momentous breasts, until she set him down, Grover blinked, gasped and said, "So. Where the hell you been? Are you real, or just a ghost? No wait, I got it!" Baring his teeth to suppress a chuckle, he sputtered, "You're not a ghost—you're just a big ol' high-spirited, very high, in fact, lady!"

"That'll do, you little, uh—no wait. You're not so little anymore. My, you must be what, pushing six-foot?"

"Guess so, if I stand up straight."

FLORA'S MONEY

"So, you're getting this place all fixed up?"

"Some. Still a lot to do. I'll give you a tour, later."

"Great. So, Oren told me Ramsay's left."

"Yup. Went to Chicago. Didn't you see him over there?"

"Hah. Oren just asked me the same thing. Don't you hicks know what a big place that is? Do you ever hear from him? What's he doing?"

"He's been back a couple times; did odd jobs at first. Drove an elevator for a while, in a six-story building; imagine. He bragged about it at first, till I reminded him that our lighthouse is about that tall! After the elevator job he found a better deal in a bank; started as an office clerk, filing and things like that. But since then he's been promoted a couple times. Now he's some kind of assistant, works directly for one of the managers."

"Sounds like your brother. Always thinking, like you; couple of smart guys."

"Well, last time he was here, he said that when he went back he had an evening job lined up as cashier in a movie house—and will get to see the pictures free. Guess he's doing okay. But what have you been up to?"

"Quite a lot, actually. I want to talk to you about that, and some ideas I've got, now that I'm back."

"Okay, let's sit down and—oh, here comes somebody you know. Arie's back in town, too. See, she's comin' across the beach right now."

"Flora! My goodness," Arie shouted when she got close enough to the lighthouse to recognize her. They both broke into a sprint and ran towards each other.

"Hey, Arie baby. Golly, we're all starting to look like grown-ups," Flora replied, laughing and reaching out to her

FLORA'S MONEY

lifelong friend. They gave each other a big hug, then stepped apart and turned to walk back toward Grover. Flora slipped her arm over Arie's shoulder as they walked.

"What a place you have here, Grover. I can't believe you live up there," Flora said.

"Have you seen the view, yet?" Arie asked.

"No, but I'd love to go up."

Later, after Grover had slipped his shirt back on, he led them up the winding stairs, through the top room and out on the gallery. They strolled slowly, clear around the gallery twice, spotting places they recognized around Hamelet and laughing at the shrill screeches of the gulls as they flowed effortlessly past, wings flared out.

"You two have a wonderful thing here—but you know that, don't you," Flora said, "a place like this to watch the world. Peaceful. Beautiful. You know, I left here so bored with dull ol' Hamelet, but when I was driving out here yesterday I could hardly wait to get back."

"Are you going to stay for good, now?" Arie asked.

"For good? Maybe. At least I've got enough saved up to make this home base. Right now, there are so many things I want to do here, and I also want to do some traveling—I just don't know where to start. I want to re-do the Emporium, from top to bottom. Clean it up. Bring it up to date and sell modern things people need, like radios, electric iceboxes and washing machines. And I'd like to make part of it into a restaurant, and add a bar as soon as they make them legal. Booze will be legal again, they say, maybe in a few months, maybe longer, but changing the law is coming."

"Flora, do you think the folks around here can afford to spend much money in a place like that?" Grover asked.

"They say more work and better-paying jobs are coming,

173

FLORA'S MONEY

too. President Roosevelt talks about it on the radio a lot, from what I've heard from customers back in Chicago. And folks around here have always talked about business being better in this area, once we start getting more summer vacationers to come enjoy the beach."

Grover sat quietly for a few minutes, thinking, while Arie and Flora continued to chat about new clothing styles they had seen in the movie fan magazines, and the marvels of the new kitchen stoves that don't need burning wood, and all those ashes. Then he said, "Flora, your ideas are exciting. But it takes money to do all those things," Grover said.

"Well, I may have enough money saved up to get us started. We'll talk about this some more."

"Get us—started, Flora?" Grover asked.

"Sure. What I have in mind, I can't do all by myself—you two could fit in, maybe work with me as special assistants, maybe partners. We'll talk about it some more, soon." Grover and Arie exchanged quick glances, surprised by what she was saying.

Flora smiled and said, "Shall we go down now? I should go back to town. Uncle Oren may want someone to cook him a real meal for a change."

As they went down the winding stairs, single file, Flora saw a metal door on the level just below the tower room. It apparently led into a built-in room, suspended in the core area of the tower, at the top of the open stairwell. Flora stopped and asked, "What's in there?"

"Kind of a junk shop now. It used to house some of the machinery of the revolving light set-up they took out years ago. I use the room mostly to store my art stuff."

"Can I see inside?"

"Sure." Grover lifted the old-style thumb-latch and

FLORA'S MONEY

swung the metal door in. "Kind of gloomy. It only has one little window for light, but it opens for air. When Ramsay and I were kids, and sneaked into the tower to play knights, this was our tower dungeon!"

Flora looked around inside the enclosure, about the size of a very big closet, she thought, not bad—easier place to guard up here than over at Oren's. A couple dozen unframed paintings, in various sizes on canvass-stretched panels, were stacked on one side. There was also an easel and a small table holding brushes and other gear. She turned to him and asked, "Can a better lock be put on this door?"

Grover laughed. "Probably. Why, do you want to lock your crown jewels up in here?"

"Well, not exactly. But, hey, would you let me rent say, half the room, to store some things I brought down with me from Chicago? You could leave your artwork right there."

"Sure, Flora, but you wouldn't have to pay me, you know that."

"Whatever you say. But could we bring the stuff down soon, maybe later today?"

At the same time, back in Chicago Rhonda was flicking a feather duster over a display rack in the hat shop where she worked, when two men came in. She glanced at them, grunted and said, "Manny! Never thought I'd see you in here. Want to buy yourself a bonnet?"

"Where's Flora?" he growled, ignoring her sarcasm.

"Probably home sleepin'. She works pretty late; you ought to know that! Who's your friend?"

Again he disregarded the question and blurted: "She hasn't shown up at work. You know her address? Maybe

FLORA'S MONEY

she's sick."

"So, are you her doctor?"

"Come on, Rhonda. Maybe somebody should check on her. Do you know where she is? "

"Not off hand."

"Damn you. We need to talk to her." She yawned and kept on dusting; the two men stalked out of the shop. Manny slammed the door.

Two hours later, Rhonda answered the telephone in the shop and heard Flora say, "Rhonda! I'm glad you're still in the shop."

"Hey, Flory, what's going on? Manny and a goon came in here this afternoon lookin for you."

"Oh! Really? They wanted me? What'd he say?"

"He's having a fit. Says he needs to talk to you—told me you haven't been coming to work, and asked did I know where you were."

"Did you tell him anything?"

"Naw, I wouldn't, you know that, and besides, how could I? Actually, I told him the truth—I didn't know where you were. I tried to sell him a bonnet, as a joke, and they left mad."

"Gee, they're really looking for me?"

"Yup. But wild things are going on around here. I heard this morning that some of the bigtime boots are getting hustled by the cops and the Feds are putting on the pressure too. Are you okay? I hope you left town."

"I'm fine—and far away, kinda' far anyway."

"Gotcha. Stay there. And I got more to tell you. I heard a rumor this morning, over at the coffee joint where I have breakfast sometimes—they say that a guy identified as Jiggs was fished out of the lake, yesterday maybe, and nobody

176

FLORA'S MONEY

knows if he fell in or got pushed."

Flora gasped and said, "Is he still alive?"

"Nobody knew this morning. Probably not."

"That's awful."

"Yeah. Some of those boys play rough. Anyway, I hope you moved out of his place."

"Yes, completely. And I got your note. I never saw Jiggs after you did—or heard anything about him until right now. What a shock."

"Well, I never saw Jiggs after he crashed into your apartment that day—and poor ol' Bernie and I were just getting to know each other, if you get my meaning, when the bozo storms in, fires his gun out the window and scares our chauffeur pal so bad he ran out carrying his clothes in a bundle."

"Is Bernie okay?"

"Oh yeah, but he may still be runnin' somewhere! Poor guy."

"So that's what happened—I saw the busted door, and got your note."

"Flora, did you tell Hector about your leaving, or where you were going?"

"No. I couldn't get him on the phone, and I had to pack up and leave. Things are so mixed up. I'm going to miss him. Maybe if you see Hec around anywhere, tell him I'll call him again soon."

"Sure, Flora, we'll all get together again one of these days. Give me a call here anytime. I really know the name of your hometown. I remember you told me onetime that it rhymes with omelet. Right?"

Flora laughed and said, "You got it. And what goes with eggs if you—let it?"

"Aha! That's our secret, kiddo."

CHAPTER 26

Two days after the raid. "Harrumph. Hull-low."

"Hello, sir. This is the long distance operator. I have a collect call for a Mr. Quent from a Mr. Hector. Will you accept—"

"Uh, sure, yeah."

"—the collect charges?"

"Yeah. This is a Mr. Quent."

"Quent! Sorry to call you so early—out here in the jungles of Indiana, or maybe it's Michigan. Wanted to catch you before you left your place—"

"Yeah, you did? Cheez, only five aye-em. What's up? Find that red limo yet?" Quent asked. He sat up in bed and leaned back against the uncomfortable pipes of the brass bed-frame to listen, eyes half-closed.

FLORA'S MONEY

"No, not quite."

"Huh?"

"Well, I've been lookin' now, what—going on two days, I guess. Seems longer. Anyhow, I've been drivin' Carlos's truck up and down all the back roads around here—in fact, they're all back roads, seems like. I been doing like you said. Bought some workpants, a cheap shirt and some work boots the first morning, so I'd kinda look like I belong in this burg—had to wait in the woods till Arie walked to a store in town, bought the pants and brought them back to me, so I wouldn't get arrested for being in public in my bee-vee-dees. Anyway, the duds are stiff and new so at least I look like a neat hick. Then we walked over and bailed out their Chevy. Arie drove me the few blocks to their flat, gave me the car key, and went in the house. I plan to sleep nights in the Chevy, or back at that empty cottage, till we're done. I drove around for a while, then stopped downtown, if you can call it that, and walked around some—snooping, and chatting with a few folks in the diner."

"And?" Quent asked.

"Nothing, at least at first. I mean, how do you walk up to a stranger and say, 'Pardon me. Have you noticed any convertible fire engines around here that look stolen?' Then I decided to go to the only gas station in town, far as I know—fill the tank and get a free map."

"So?"

"First I took the main road back west, maybe three miles or so, figured out where I thought I was on the map and started cruisin' back and forth, up and down, stopping and poking around on foot in woodsy places lookin' for the car, and in any kind of hiding place, like a barn or whatever. Got chased by dogs twice, almost got lost among the dunes a

FLORA'S MONEY

couple times, stepped into a pond in a marshy place—soaked my new boots and—"

"Hector!"

"What?"

"So?"

"So? Huh?"

"That's it? Two days and all you've done is get your new booties wet?" Quent growled.

"Well, there was that guy with the skimmer—"

"Skimmer?"

"Yeah, like my straw hat. I saw a guy wearing one, maybe the same one I left in the Duesey. He was walking across a field, out near the main road that you and I drove in on the other day—Y'know, when we were playing that left-right, right-left dancin' game." Hector added.

"Oh?"

"Yeah. I see this guy, wearing grungy clothes and the fancy hat, walking straight into the woods on the lake side of the road. Don't know if he even noticed me, or not. I drove partway across the sandy ground thinking I could head him off and talk turkey to the guy, but it was soft ground, and I got—"

"Stuck!" Quent shouted.

"Uh, yeah."

"So you got out, chased him and he got away? Right? Then you spent the rest of the day sneaking around in the woods and couldn't find him? Right? And you didn't see his face and won't recognize him if you find him again, except maybe for the hat? Good you spotted that thing—gosh knows how many other straws are walkin around out there, especially now, in the summer!" Quent intoned softly, restrained, but with a metallic edge to his voice as he increased

FLORA'S MONEY

the volume toward the end of his comments.

"You got it, Quent. That's what's happening. In fact, I searched all through that area. It's really not too far from where we parked the Duesey when we got here. Walked and drove all around there, even after dark. Only slept for a couple hours, in the Chevy, till dawn. Then I drove into Hamelet and found this phone booth to call you before I go back out again. But hell, we know the car was moved, but how far, and to where? Anyway, I'll keep goin' till you say stop."

"Or until you find that car! Okay, Hector? Keep in touch. If I'm not home, try the Tea Room. Don't leave any messages, especially about where you are, or what you're doing. If I'm not there, just say goodbye. Keep trying every couple hours or so, both places if you have to, until we connect. And when you do find the car, don't bring it here. Hide it someplace new, out there, then call me. Be careful."

CHAPTER 27

Arie had just come out on the front steps of the house where she and her brother had rooms, to begin walking back to revisit Grover, when Hector happened to drive by in the borrowed truck. He rolled to a stop and called out, "C'mon, I'll give you a lift."

Arie smiled and came over to the Chevy as he reached over to unlatch and shove open the passenger door. Just then, Gorki's flatbed truck, with the canvas enclosure on the back, approached from the opposite direction and rumbled by, stirring up a cloud of dirt as it passed.

Hector looked closely at the driver, as he had been doing with every vehicle he passed since he started searching. This time he sat up straighter, stared after the truck and said loud enough for Arie to hear as she was getting in, "Damn!

FLORA'S MONEY

THERE GOES MY HAT!"

Arie got in and said, "Your hat?"

"That guy!" Hector pointed down the road, "He's wearing my hat, I bet you anything he's the one!"

Mystified, Arie asked again, quietly, "Your hat?"

"Well, yes. I don't know the man, but I saw him once before. I've been thinking right along that he's the one who stole Quent's car from us the night of the raid. Hope you don't mind going along—don't want to lose him, and I may need you to drive your truck back if—well, never mind. I'll explain later." Hector jammed the idling Chevy into gear and they took off. She could see that he was unusually tense as he spun the wheel and made a squealing u-turn.

Hector stayed way back and followed the truck without being spotted by Gorki. It was not too hard to do, since it was a straight dirt road, with few crossing roads, typical of the country byways around Hamelet. Within a few minutes, Hector saw the truck slow down and turn right.

About a hundred feet from where the flatbed truck had just turned off, Hector pulled the Chevy to the side of the dirt road, turned off the engine and said, "Wait here, Arie. That looks like an old driveway, or farm lane—hard to tell with all the bushes and trees in the way—wait a sec."

Moving quickly, he opened his door and stood up on the fender, listening. "Aha, I hear his truck." A few moments later, he added, "Now I don't. He must have stopped; can't have gone very far down that lane." He stepped down to the road, reached in, handed the key to Arie and said, "If you see or hear the truck coming out, duck down so he can't see you. After he makes the turn onto the road and leaves, start 'er up. Don't wait for me to show. Whichever way he goes, wait till he's out of sight and drive on in. I'll be waitin' for

183

FLORA'S MONEY

you, or on my way out on that lane."

"Gee, you're not going to walk back in there are you?" she asked.

"Not just walk, sneak might be a better word. Best you wait here. Won't be long." He winked at her, got out of the Chevy and headed into the thick brush and piney woods next to the road they were on. Worried, Arie watched him disappear in among the trees, and then slipped down in the seat, her eyes barely peeking over the dashboard.

Hector hurried into the woods until he saw the truck parked just past a dilapidated barn. En route he took the pistol from his bulging front pocket, checked it at a glance for readiness, and slipped it into the belt on his pants, at the back, easy to grab. Then, from across the lane, he peeked through the tangle of branches and looked around the area outside the barn as he crept closer.

The sliding doors on the barn were open and Hector could see the gorgeous reds, whites and shiny chromes of the rear view of the Duesenberg, and the driver moving around next to it on the right. Delighted, Hec doubled both fists, made a one-two jab in the air and grinned. He moved on past the open door, far enough to cross the lane unseen, and crept along the barn wall. At the edge of the open door he stopped and waited, his back to the wall.

Gorki had spent the first minutes after arrival raising the hood to check for anything he could spot that was loose. Then he moved to the side of the car, located the spout for the gas tank, removed the cap and began pouring from the large jerrycan he had brought. At that moment, Hector stepped around the edge of the door, held his gun waist high and said, "Okay, put the can down. If I shoot now that gas—and that dandy machine—will make a hell of a fire." Startled, Gorki

FLORA'S MONEY

jerked his head to look, saw the gun, and reacted. He swung around, splashing some gas as he let the can slip to the floor, its weight keeping it upright; he lunged impulsively—and ran into black—as Hector hit him with the butt of the gun, just above the left ear, and down he went.

It was all over in minutes, but the time dragged for Arie. Right after Hector went into the woods, she had slipped over to the driver's seat and put the key in the ignition, ready for it to be turned on in a hurry. Parked in the sun, the Chevy was already getting hot inside. She considered going over to the nearby woods to hide in the cool shade, but thought better of it and stayed in the truck. A wasp floated through the open window, zigzagged silently around and finally hovered inches away from her sweaty face.

Distracted, she started to wave the creature aside—but a sharp bang echoed from the direction of the lane, followed by an echoing fa-boom that made her jerk back and impulsively tip herself over. This put her upper body almost flat on the passenger side of the double cushion, her feet bumping into the floor pedals and steering post.

CHAPTER 28

Horrified and confused, Arie peeked over the dash and saw a column of black smoke curling up over the woods, vivid against the sunny sky—about in the direction Hector had gone. She sat up, staring, dumfounded and too shocked to make a sensible decision: run, wait, or what? That was when she heard the emerging sound of a powerful engine, apparently coming from the lane. Then she saw the completely unexpected sight of the elegant Duesenberg touring car lunge into view, swing wide into the road and turn in her direction, with a smiling Hector at the wheel, waving his long right arm. Trying hard not to shed tears of relief, Arie watched as Hector let the red machine roll to a stop next to the Chevy, heading the opposite way.

"Hey, kid! Look! I got my hat," he called out as he popped

FLORA'S MONEY

the straw skimmer on his head at a jaunty angle.

"You okay?" he asked.

Relieved, Arie laughed and nodded.

"Ready to go, Arie?"

"Yes—what was that explosion? Did I hear a shot first? What happened to that man?"

'He's okay, taking a little snooze. Worst he'll have is a bad headache."

"But that explosion?"

"Well, as I started driving out the lane, I stopped and fired once to maybe blow a tire so he couldn't follow us." Then Hector laughed and said, "Hit the gas tank instead, I guess, my, my. Tell you the rest later. Best we beat it now. All that smoke will attract people. Anyhow, turn around and follow me. I'll wait. Let's go back out to the beach."

Minutes later, when Gorki regained his senses and got up off the barn floor, the acrid fumes from the fire made his eyes smart. The Duesenberg was gone. He stepped out the door and saw his truck, still ablaze and giving off black smoke. Angry and groggy, he held one hand to the side of his aching head and began trudging down the lane to the road. When he looked back in the direction of the fire he could see the column of smoke rising well above the treetops. Disgusted, he stepped into the woods to follow along the main road toward town, yet be out of sight to anyone who might be driving out to see what was burning.

Jerry had just come out of his police office, and started to jaywalk across the intersection at the corner to visit Oscar's drug store, when he spotted the grand Duesenberg touring

FLORA'S MONEY

car majestically heading his way. He stopped and stared. Now, whose car is that, he wondered—and who's driving it? Then he was distracted for a few seconds by the elegant, silver radiator cap that was gliding past him at eye level—until he caught sight of a second vehicle following directly behind the red Duesenberg and realized that the second machine was the battered Chevy truck that belonged to Carlos—and Arie was driving it! There were no other cars in sight, or people on the sidewalk, not unusual mid-day in Hamelet.

The little parade kept coming and was past Jerry before he could decide if he wanted to call out for her to stop, so he could ask some questions: was she with that guy? If so, why? Where were they going, where had they been and where did that fancy car come from?

Puzzled, Jerry stood on the curb watching the rear ends of the mismatched vehicles move on down the street. Does Grover know about this, he wondered, does it matter and—oops, where's that black smoke coming from, back over there, in the general direction those two just came from?

His head swiveled back and forth, between the smoke and the departing vehicles, like someone watching a kid playing toss-and-catch with a rubber ball on the side of a barn, until both vehicles turned right and drove from his sight.

Jerry hurried to his police car, parked in front of his office, opting to check out the smoke source first—then maybe go talk to Grover. He followed the rising cloud in the distance and soon drove into the lane leading to the smoldering ruins of a truck, too far gone for him to try to identify—or to tell if there were any human remains in the tangled metal. He parked near the deserted barn, well back from the wreck, got out, looked in the barn and behind it, and then walked down the lane a little way to where it ended in the woods.

FLORA'S MONEY

Well acquainted with the old farm as just another one of the abandoned homesteads around the countryside, he saw nothing unusual but the fire, and perhaps that had been an unwanted junker lit by a prankster. By then he could hear the clanging bell on Hamelet's ancient fire truck and figured that since someone had raised an alarm, the volunteers would take care of the fading blaze; he got back in his car and left.

On his way through town, not far from his office, he pulled over and parked to think about what he had seen Arie doing. He lit a cigarette, tossed the burnt match out the car window, and decided to just cruise on out to the beach and snoop around before talking to anyone.

CHAPTER 29

Hector knew the area around Hamelet quite well by now, so it was easy for him to drive out toward the wooded area near the lighthouse, with Arie following. On the way he drove past the abandoned and lop-sided boathouse near where Quent had parked the Duesenberg the night of the raid, and knew he was in the area he wanted; it had lots of thickets dense with pines, brush and tall weeds. When he reached the open sand of the beach he slowed down, put the elegant car in low gear, and drove to the more wooded stretch that led toward the lighthouse.

Arie stopped at the edge of the beach, turned off the Chevy and stepped out on the sands, watching. Other than three young boys playing down by the water, who didn't notice the vehicles, and a sleeping person on a blanket, farther up

FLORA'S MONEY

the beach, there was no one else about. Hector maneuvered the limo in among the pines until the car was well screened from the open sands on the beach. He was about fifty feet from the tower, and could see the top part of it when he looked up. In a few minutes he came walking back into Arie's view and waved.

Grover, up in the tower, heard the car motors, looked down and was startled by what he saw: the canvas roof of what looked like the fantastic Duesenberg, parked there in his nearby woods. He was also surprised to see Arie standing by the Chevy, parked in the open up by the back of the beach. Curious and excited, he ran down the tower steps and hurried out the front door, then slowed down when he saw Arie and a stranger walking towards him across the sand. "Hi, Grover, this is Hector, one of Carlos's friends," Arie said as the three of them met on the beach. Hector smiled, held out his hand and said, "Hello, Grover."

"Hi—Hector." Grover said, shaking his hand and then glancing at Arie.

"Is it okay if he leaves his car back in there for a few days?" she asked.

"Yeah, sure. I guess so. You say he knows Carlos?"

"Yes."

"Oh, I see," Grover said, though Arie knew he had no clear idea what was going on. Since she and Grover had agreed not to discuss what her brother was actually doing, she hadn't yet mentioned anything to Grover about helping Hector at her brother's request. There was an awkward silence for a few moments before Hector said, "Thank you. It'll just be there until my boss gets back."

Though she wanted desperately to tell Grover about her adventures earlier that afternoon, she just said quietly, "Don't

FLORA'S MONEY

worry, Grove, I'll tell you more about this later." As she talked, they all began strolling toward the lighthouse.

Hector smiled and remarked, "Just a guess, but I bet you two have been friends for maybe a long time."

Arie said, "You could say that."

Grover grinned and added, "Only since we were little kids." Then Hector gazed up at the tower and asked, "Does someone live up there?"

Arie chuckled and said, "Yes, Grover does."

"Really? Fantastic." Hector said.

"Would you like to go up to see the view sometime?" Grover asked.

"I sure would, but I've got a couple errands to do. Maybe later, okay?"

"Sure, anytime." By then they were at the base of the lighthouse. Hector smiled politely, waved a palm and walked away. They sat down on the ledges. Grover took Arie's hand and said, "Hector. Interesting name. Seems like a friendly kind of guy."

"He's got an easy-going manner," Arie said. "I have a good feeling about him, though we just met a couple days ago. He works for Carlos's new boss, but I'm not sure what he does. Anyhow, before they took off in the plane, Carlos said that Hector could borrow our truck." She shrugged and added, "I hope you don't mind?"

"Arie, if you say he's okay that's good enough for me." He was tempted to ask about the Duesenberg that Hector appeared to have acquired somehow, but decided it was probably best not to. Instead he said, "Now I should go over and help Flora bring down whatever it is she wants to store in the tower."

"Okay, Grove, maybe I'll just sit here and admire the

FLORA'S MONEY

sunset till you both come back—this has been a busy couple of days."

Grover watched as Flora closed the front door of the Emporium and heard her say, "Must be about closing time— sun's going down. Oren will be locking up soon and going out for his evening walk around town. You say you have a cart out back? We can load my stuff in and push it down to meet Arie at your place, okay? I have it all ready in my room upstairs. Let's bring 'em down."

Earlier, when she carried the burlap bags in from the Packard she piled them temporarily on the floor. Then, thinking ahead, she decided to pull three of the cans out of one of the big bags, slip them into a shoulder-strap tote bag, and shove the tote under her bed.

Grover followed her up the stairs. When he saw the pile of burlap bags he stopped, laughed, and said, "Jeepers, Flora, what's all this?"

"You'll find out. I'll explain it all to you and Arie after we get down to the lighthouse and stash them in your storeroom, okay?" He nodded, picked up three of the bags and started back down the hall to the stairs. After he was out of the room, she took the tote-bag from under the bed, hung it over one shoulder by the strap, then scooped up the other four bags and followed him.

By the time the sun had slipped below the lake's horizon, and a few bright stars were beginning to show through the twilight, Grover and Flora had walked to the lighthouse. He pushed the cart, loaded with bulging burlap bags, while she walked alongside, one hand steadying the pile.

Arie sat on the ledge by the lighthouse door, waiting

FLORA'S MONEY

for them. She was surprised to see the size of the cargo they brought along, but before she could comment, Grover grinned and said, "Want to give us a hand? These are Flora's crown jewels, or something—she's promised to tell us all about them after we stash the bags upstairs." Arie shrugged, stepped forward and picked up one of the bags.

They were able to carry the load into the tower and up to the storeroom in one trip, then pile them on the floor and shut the door. Flora said, "I know you both must think I'm nuts—all this secret stuff, but let's go on up and I'll explain." She still had the tote bag on her shoulder as they went up the few remaining steps.

Hector went back to the Duesenberg, after talking to Arie and meeting Grover. He decided that before it got too dark he would make a closer check on Quent's money cans hidden in the car. Making sure there was no one around he slid the rear seat cushion forward, pulled the two cans out, set them on the floor, pushed the seat back and sat down on it. He removed the lids and saw that each container seemed to be loosely filled with fifty and hundred dollar-bills. He sorted all the money from the first can into two little piles on the seat and, as the daylight faded, he counted it and found it totaled five thousand dollars even. The second can proved to have the same amount. He put all the cash into little stacks and tossed the empty cans on the floor. Next, he began stowing the bills in a way he thought would be safer than carrying the awkward cans around under his arm—and better than leaving the money in the car.

He started by unrolling the long sleeves of the work shirt he had on. Next he carefully picked up a flat stack of the

FLORA'S MONEY

bills and balanced them on his arm, putting the stack on top of the unbuttoned cuff; then he turned the cuff back over the flat stack of bills and laid another stack on top of the exposed underside of the sleeve. He continued to balance a little stack on top, and roll the cloth one turn at a time, until that sleeve was loaded and rolled up above his elbow; then he did the same with the sleeve on his other arm. For a large man like Hector, the thick roll-ups appeared normal. Finished with the project he leaned back for a moment, chuckling and thinking, damn, this two-dollar shirt is now worth ten thousand bucks!

Reluctant to leave the car unguarded for longer than necessary, on the wild chance that the trucker or any other troublemaker might turn up, he decided to hurry over to the phone booth on foot and call Quent; he'd give him the good news, see if he had any more instructions and then come right back.

Quent answered the call, and was delighted to hear Hector gleefully announcing, in a loud voice, "Good news! Man, what an afternoon. I spotted the guy with my skimmer and I got the Duesenberg, our clothes and the cans of dough! There's ten thousand bucks in those two cans."

"Wow, Hec! Are you sober? Really, you got it all? The car, everything?"

"Yup—happened to be giving Arie a lift and saw him go by in a truck. We whipped around and tailed him."

"Damn good, Hector. I love ya! Save the rest of the story. I want to hear it, but things are happening here."

"What's going on?"

"Not sure, yet. Big changes. Gus may get arrested, and maybe some of us. We don't know. Guard that fancy car— and all that cash. We're going to need it. Stay out of sight,

FLORA'S MONEY

but let Arie know where to find you."

"No problem. She's right here with me. I had to clue her in a little about the Duesey. I'll tell you why later, okay?"

"Yeah. Fine. Uh, before I hang up. Where's our red wagon now?"

"Hidden in the woods behind the lighthouse."

"Perfect. We may come out there by plane late tonight, before dawn, I hope. Maybe the time has come for us to get some clean jobs—like we've talked about. So watch the lake by the lighthouse. Carlos may be with us, too. See you soon."

Hector returned to the Duesenberg. It was completely dark in the woods. Before deciding what to do next he leaned against a fender, glanced at the nearby lighthouse and realized he could see a soft glow in the windows up top. The light was dim, but he thought he could see people moving about up there—must be Arie and her boyfriend, Grover. He sat down on the running board, leaned back and tried to relax.

CHAPTER 30

When Flora, Arie and Grover got to the room up top he arranged two of the benches to face each other in front of the open windows, put the old card table between them, then lit a candle and placed it on the table. Flora looked seriously at her two friends, took a deep breath, and started to talk. At first, she was hesitant, and spoke slowly, not sure how she could tell her friends what she had done to acquire the cans. But once started, the telling got easier. The soft light of the candle helped.

She told them about first arriving in the city, working in the diner, and then finding a good job at Golden's where she had to learn how to make drinks and handle the brash customers—and she explained how and why she had started taking the bottles of booze. Then she stopped talking and

FLORA'S MONEY

reached for her tote bag sitting on the floor by her feet. She took out the three Golden's cans, lined them up on the table, and proceeded to tell them briefly how Manny's rucksack led her to find the hiding place in the ceiling. Arie, leaning close, stared at the cans, then reached out and, glancing at Flora, hefted one can carefully, put it back down and asked, "Can we open one?"

Flora nodded and said, "Sure, pry the top off, but hold it over the table. It's kind of full." Grover pried the lid off with his fingers, tipped the can and poured a jumbled wad of greenbacks into the center of the table. Several bills, some folded, some rolled up, fell loosely around the impressive little heap. He tipped the can again and held it so he could look inside, then poked his fingers in and raked out the last of the bills. Arie gasped and whispered, "Are they real?"

"They sure look it," Grover replied, "it's just that we've never seen so much of it at one time before."

Flora sighed, took a deep breath and dragged a fingertip under one eye to wipe away a tear, and said, "Scary, isn't it? They're real, all right."

"My gosh," Grover said, "How much money is in this can?"

"I dunno," Flora replied.

"How many cans are there?"

"I'm not sure. You saw the seven bags down there."

"They're all full of these cans?"

"Well, yes. Every night when we closed, cans like these were used to hide the cash. They apparently had been doing it for years. Anyhow, my boss told me to put the cash in one of the cans at closing time, so I did. I assumed Manny took the bills out the next day, and put the can back for the next load, though later I found out he just took the can with the

198

FLORA'S MONEY

money and hid it—and put a different can under the icebox for the next batch. And the night he showed me his hiding routine of the daily can he didn't say anything about what happened to them after that. So, finding all the cash in the ceiling made me realize that they probably never bothered to count the money, or put it in bundles, or organize it in any way. At least not while they kept it up there—and, well, it seemed so easy to start taking a few cans every few nights at closing, instead of the booze, so I did.

"And you know, when Manny first showed me what they were using to hold their money, it made me laugh, because I used to save my pennies and trinkets in a cocoa can with the same kind of re-closeable lid."

"So did I," Arie said, smiling.

Grover toyed with the little pile on the table, poking it with one finger as he said, "And as far as you know, the amounts are not the same in every can?"

"Well, I checked four or five of the cans, when I first found them, and they all had different amounts of cash. What I need to do soon is open each can and count it all up."

"I'm surprised you didn't do that before now. Weren't you curious?" Arie asked.

"Well, once I got them back to my basement, maybe I was too scared—or maybe it was guilt on my part. Golly, this was my first time doing anything like this. You must know that. First it was snitching a few bottles of booze from Manny's hidden closet, because everyone else was, and then this opportunity with the cash came along. And it was well known out there that bootleggers never wanted any of their take recorded in banks—or any place else. It's no secret these guys broke the law to get all this money. The cash rolled in so fast they had to hide it wherever they could. This has to be only a

199

FLORA'S MONEY

small part of what they must have grabbed since Prohibition started about a dozen years ago. So how wrong is it for me to take money from these crooks when they got it by breaking the law—and think about it—when it's not practical to return it to anybody, why can't I use it for honest things?"

Flora rubbed her forehead with one finger and continued, "When I realized where they were hiding their loot up in the ceiling, I don't know, maybe I just got greedy so I started helping myself. And after a few months, I knew it was time to scram—everybody back in the city was talking about Repeal and saying the bootleggers will be out of business when it happens, and a lot of them will go to jail, maybe. So, kids, what do I do with it all?"

"Well," Grover said, slowly, "Maybe you should talk to the Judge sometime, and see what he suggests. He knows all the legal stuff, and he's an old friend. Your problem is, you've got the money, you can't return it—now what?"

Flora said, "You're right, I guess. But I want to count all the money first. Finding a safe way to store it in the future is going to be a real problem, I imagine, since the only bank we ever had in Hamelet closed years ago. Your room is perfect for now, anyway, if it's okay by you."

"Of course it is," Grover said, " and Flora, nobody locks doors around here, very often, but I see why you asked about it. We'll get two sets of locks with two keys. Then we can keep the storeroom locked and use the other lock on the main door downstairs, whenever I leave the tower area. I'll keep one of each of the keys, if that's okay, and you keep the two other keys."

Flora nodded as he spoke, and said, "Fine, let's do it." The three of them then went to work to get a total on the money in just the three cans, for starters. Flora made stacks of

FLORA'S MONEY

the currency on the table, by denomination, while the others counted. When they finished, Grover said, "Golly, we have an astounding total of seven thousand seven hundred and forty dollars."

All three of them sat in silence, looking wide-eyed at each other, until Flora said, "For now, let's put the money back in the cans. I'll take them with me tonight, in my tote bag, and hide the cash at Oren's so I can use it for paying up some of his bills, and have the rest handy to live on for a while. We should get rid of the empty cans right away, too."

As they talked, Grover took an old envelope from his pocket, turned it over, began to scribble numbers on the back and said, "Flora have you ever tried to estimate, just roughly, how much money you've got all together in the bags?"

"No, not really. I just know it must be a terrible lot—how much do you think it is?"

"Very roughly, let's see. The three cans we just counted came to seven thousand seven hundred forty. Divide that by three and you get twenty-five hundred and eighty per can. But, as you said, the cans are all going to be different amounts. So let's just guess for now that, conservatively, each can has an average of only two thousand dollars. We have seven bags of cans down there, with maybe twenty cans per bag—that's forty thousand dollars per bag, I think."

Arie and Flora stared and listened intently as Grover continued, "So, for a total, seven times forty is—Arie, how much?"

She whispered, "Twenty-eight thousand, no! Gracious, can it be two-hundred and, uh, eighty thousand—dollars?"

"That's what I get," Grover said, "but until we count it all, who knows, it could be less or more, maybe a lot more, maybe closer to five-hundred thousand—and that'd be a half

FLORA'S MONEY

million wouldn't it?"

Flora gasped, crossed her arms on the table, put her head down on them and squealed, "My God! Is that—possible?" Arie put one hand on Flora's heaving shoulders and waited, unable to say anything. Flora sat up, shaking her head; tears had left streaks on her cheeks and made her eyes red.

Grover stood up and then sat back down, trying to keep calm and, on impulse, he joked, "Flora, don't worry, maybe when we do a real count it'll be a lot less." Arie and Flora hugged each other, laughing and crying at the same time.

Grover sat back and said, "Flora, I do have a serious question—if we're ready, there is something else that bothers me. Is it possible that any of the people at that bar, Golden's, or the bosses, can connect you with all this cash being missing? Are they likely to come looking for you?"

Flora hesitated, and said slowly, "It's possible, but I don't really know. For one thing, Manny and the rest never knew where I was from, and besides, I know for a fact that I wasn't the only one who got into that money. I'll have to be careful of strangers, I know, and get rid of those cans as soon as possible; they can be trouble if anybody from over there sees them somehow." After that, Grover and Arie sat in silence, wondering.

"Okay, Flora," Grover said, moments later, "if you're ready, I have one other question. What about the car you drove down here in—or shouldn't I ask?"

"Sure you should. I can't keep any secrets from you two, now," she sniffed, and added, "A guy I worked for at the saloon actually loaned the car to me, no strings attached, he kept saying, so I used it and he even had a chauffeur guy teach me how to drive in city traffic."

"What kind of car is it?" Grover asked.

FLORA'S MONEY

"A Packard roadster, fairly new, I think. Really quite nice."

"Wow. Does it have a rumble seat?"

"Yes. I used that to haul the money cans. And I put two valises with some of the booze bottles in there also. By the way, I didn't bring all the bottles I had. Not enough room, so I just left them in the basement hall. Whoever found them could throw quite a nice party."

"Just left them? In the hall?" Grover asked, amazed.

"Yup. I started to leave them in the storage room, but changed my mind. I heard that according to the law, it's illegal for a person to have more liquor than they need for their personal use—but come to think of it, when it comes to breaking the law—" Flora stopped and giggled. She looked at her friends, saw them smiling and laughed louder. They joined in, chuckling, then suddenly all three let it out, laughing in relief with unexpected merriment.

"Anyway," Flora finally said, catching her breath, "back to the Packard. Where were we?"

"I was just going to ask you," Arie said, still giggling, "is the car yours to keep, Flora?"

"I'm trying to work that out. It's all kind of vague," she said, thinking what Rhonda had told her the day before, about Jiggs, and added, seriously, "I'll let you know. Right now, I've got it in Oren's old blacksmith shop. I'll cover it over with some worn-out blankets or something. And we can put a lock on that door, too. I've already told Oren I'm storing it for a friend."

Grover stood up again, stretched and said, "Well, let's get away from all this and go out on the gallery for a while? Maybe admire the stars. It's a beautiful night."

"By all means," Flora said. "All that laughing—and every-

FLORA'S MONEY

thing else; we need a break." Grover went over to the door and stepped out on the gallery. Arie got up too and walked through the door after him. Flora followed, saying, "Gee, what a relief to be with friends like you two."

Grover put two folded blankets on the floor. They all sat down and leaned against the wall, knees up, and just talked—catching up, remembering their growing up days in Hamelet, until Grover said, "Hey, I've got some snacks." He went inside and brought out apples, a bag of hard candies, a former sugar-sack of Maddie's biscuits, and a jar of her homemade apple cider. They snacked, took turns sipping from the jar and kept talking, soothed by the gentle sound of the waves down below.

Their conversation gradually slowed down and the soft breeze let them relax more and more. Grover kept his left arm around Arie's waist as they leaned against the wall. Flora stretched out flat, parallel to the wall, with her arms bent and both hands interlocked to make a finger-pillow under her head. This gave her a good view of the quiet lake and made it easy to look up at all the stars. They stopped talking.

Arie dozed off. Grover continued to hold her safely back from the railing and the edge of the gallery. He felt drowsy, exhilarated and content—yet aroused by the warmth of her head on his shoulder and the soft pressures of her relaxed breathing.

Flora lay there in the moist darkness, thinking, as she tried to sort out everything tumbling through her mind. She finally drifted into a half-sleep, unaware that the gentle breezes off the lake were cooling and beginning to build into occasional gusts. Faint blinks of lightning, unseen by Flora, began to peek through the black merge of water and sky, far off on the western horizon.

"Prohibition has been around for over 13 years. Now it's not a law anymore and Repeal will change millions of lives in America."
The Hamelet Hearsay & Chronicle, Dec. 6, 1933

CHAPTER 31

Only three days after the new Tri-Motor arrived south of Chicago, at their temporary dock on the lake, their new plan of operation abruptly fell apart. Carlos was to go on every flight and be trained on the job to be able to fly the tri-motor. Quent was going to manage all the business and maintenance details for the Goose trips and go along to supervise things. They had completed only two more trial flights, after the day they lost Jiggs, and the Goose proved to be tough and ready to start bringing in loads of bottles. But the newspaper stories about Repeal were heating up, and Quent and his crew had begun to worry about the increase in reports of other bootleggers being nabbed and shut down by the enforcement agencies.

The evening after their last test flight, Quent got a tip

FLORA'S MONEY

from one of his insiders. He called Jed and Carlos to alert them that they might have to cut and run sooner then they thought. And later that same night Gus also called Quent and said, "Listen, I'll be out in front. Pick me up now—as fast as you can get here. We have to get your pilots, fly the bird out, and maybe find a place to disappear. Okay? I'm leaving the house right now. We have to go. Understand?"

"Yeah, Gus. Be right over. What if we fly it south for the winter?"

"Anything. Or maybe—never mind. It's up to you. No time to talk. If I get nailed before you get here, you got yourself a little airline." About twenty minutes later, Quent sped around the corner, a half a block away from where Gus lived, and quickly slowed down when he saw what was happening down the street: Gus, lugging a valise out the front door of his townhouse, was stopped by three men in suits and one of them began handcuffing him. Quent drove on past while purposely looking in the other direction.

The pay phone in the hall, near Carlos's room in the boarding house, rang several times. He roused himself enough to pull on a pair of shorts, open his door, unhook the earpiece and say: "Yeah?"

"Carlos? Quent. Time to bail out."

"Oh?"

"Pick you up in thirty minutes? Bring everything important. We may not get back this way for a while, if ever. Gus has been arrested."

Carlos whistled softly. "Time to scramble?"

"Yup. Already talked to Jed and Hector. Now you got twenty-five minutes!"

FLORA'S MONEY

"Be down on the curb in fifteen. Bye."

~

At the dock, 2:30 a. m. Quent drove his car into the lot next to the warehouse. He and Carlos got out, each carrying duffle bags, and quickly walked out to meet Jed, already out on the dock, putting extra parts and some tools in the skiff.

"Okay, Jed. How we doing?" Quent asked.

"The tanks are full of gas. Oil's okay. Guess I've got all the tools we can handle, right here in the skiff, ready to go out to the plane with us—what you told me on the phone, about Gus, is a shocker."

"Yeah, it sure is. What about Arnie?"

"No, says to tell you sorry, but he can't leave his wife and kid. By now they're probably headed for his folks' farm to stay low. So, what's next?"

"Carlos and I talked this over on the way out here. We've known this might happen some day—and we think its best to get out of this racket too soon, maybe, than too late," Quent said.

"And Gus told him to take the bird and go," Carlos added.

"Right. He did. If we don't go, the cops might grab it and maybe us too. We've tried to keep the operation a secret, but they probably know all about it."

"Leaving the Ford here, Quent?" Jed asked.

"No choice. I was going to sell it—no time now. Gas tank's almost empty anyhow! Let's go!"

Thirty minutes later, with Carlos sitting in as co-pilot, Quent standing between their seats, and Jed at the controls, the Goose taxied out from the shore, picked up speed, and lifted off from the lake. Jed leveled the plane off at five

FLORA'S MONEY

hundred feet and headed east. Visibility was clear with stars poking through all over the night sky.

Quent leaned forward to be heard by the other two and spoke loudly. "Okay, guys, we're on our way—and there are a couple things we should talk about. I want to pick up Hector for several reasons, including there's a good chance he can bring some cash on board that we can use for expenses. Y'know, gas, food, whatever. Also, I'm sure he'll be as anxious as we are to scoot now and start fresh elsewhere. We've talked before about what we would do when the feds finally shut us down. I think he'll join us.

"And the first rule will be stay legit, stay out of trouble—really go into the passenger and freight-flying business—and stay honest. What do you say?"

Carlos turned his head and made a brisk thumbs-up gesture; Jed glanced over at the other two and said, "Great, Quent. We're not fired—let's say we've just been taken over by new management—us!"

"Fine," Quent continued, "We can work out the details, but I think we should keep moving, stay away from congested areas as much as possible, and head south—we need to get to where the blizzards won't shut us down and where cops have no interest in us. After we stop tonight, I hope we'll be able to get in and out fast, maybe set a course to take us toward the Mississippi River, somewhere below St. Louis, to land on the water, wherever we need to while flying basically south. Finding fuel will be the major problem. We may have to set down between towns and look for gas and maybe make some phone calls ahead, to line up refills before we start out from any intermediate stops. Following the river gives us a lot of remote areas to fly over and causes less attention. Next stop could be the Memphis area down-river, than hop over

FLORA'S MONEY

to Mobile Bay—and from there jump over to Key West and so on."

Carlos asked, simply: "Havana?"

"Why not," Quent replied. "All the spots I just mentioned are in our range, roughly five or six hundred miles apart. And the river provides a landing strip all the way down, as long as we avoid floating logs and gators. And Cuba's less than a hundred miles from the Keys. We get that far, then we're out of the country and maybe could look for passengers who want to move around the islands—the Bahamas, the Indies and so on. Business guys, tourists, whatever. And I've got a variety of documents in my bag, made up by the lawyers Gus used, that should give us enough ownership-proof, permits and what-not to satisfy the harbor officials, if any, along the way."

"Hey, boss, you've given this a lot of thought," Carlos said, "Sounds like a fertile area for smart flyboys like us."

"Not boss—partner," Quent said, holding his fist at eye level between the other two. Jed cupped his hand on Quent's. Carlos smiled and laid his on Jed's. Quent quickly pulled his fist away and said, "Okay, gents. Now all we have to do is find that unlit lighthouse in the dark. Enough of my chatter for now."

Shortly after their talk, all three saw the lightening on the horizon and realized that the stars and clear skies were suddenly fading, and a thunder storm had begun moving in from behind them—along with slashes of raindrops driven by a surging tailwind.

Meanwhile, Flora was drowsy but still awake up on the gallery when she realized there were new sounds coming out of the

209

FLORA'S MONEY

black night to the west, and they seemed to be getting louder. Pervasive flashes of lightning, all around her, closely followed by jolts of thunder crashes made her wince. She sat upright. Between the rumbling crescendos came wind and the sounds of churning waves, the staccato beat of driven rain; then the solid hosing of larger raindrops took over, stinging their faces and hammering at the glass windows. Flora jumped to her feet and reached out to help the other two get up. Grover stooped to get the blankets, changed his mind and grabbed Arie's hand as the blasts of wind increased—and a riotous ratcheting began to penetrate the storm noises, dominating everything.

"Is that a motorboat?" Flora shouted, feeling pain from the downpour. Staring out over the black water she shielded her eyes with both hands and saw two white lights, far out and blurred by rain, coming right at them, very low—very fast. Grover and Arie looked around and also stared; all three of them quickly realized that it must be an airplane, and was apparently trying to land on the lake right in front of them. The sounds of the laboring engines continued to grow, with lights glaring, as this scary thing kept coming above the white-topped waves. Insane shadows danced and flickered over the three transfixed figures on the gallery. Grover shouted close to Arie's ear, "IT'S THE TIN GOOSE—TOO CLOSE!" A shrieking increase in the engine sounds overwhelmed anything else Grover was trying to say.

CHAPTER 32

"TOO FAST! Gotta—get 'er back up over the trees—THE TOWER!" Jed shouted, both hands clamped on his control wheel. He, Carlos and Quent each felt a shove as the erratic tailwind suddenly gave the Goose a push ahead. Kicked by an unseen giant, the plane rose wildly out of the lake's black water, tail dipping, and nose rising, as the pilots struggled to regain control.

Out on the lighthouse gallery, the threesome clutched the railing and each other, flinching and ducking as the tri-motor's mass of silvery fuselage lifted from the black water, passed overhead and was gone—leaving behind an abrupt reduction in palpable sounds, total darkness, gusty winds and pounding rain. Flora, Grover and Arie, with shoulders hunched, grabbed at each other and fled inside.

FLORA'S MONEY

Jed managed to regain control, minutes later, as he kept the plane heading east and shouted, "We'll take her over and gain some height, circle back and come in lower next time—if the wind goes down by then—may have to wait it out." Quent continued to hang on wherever he could from his kneeling position between the two pilot seats.

Before the fly-over happened, after Hector had telephoned Quent, he had gone back and sat down on the running board of the Duesenberg and eventually fell asleep in the quiet darkness. Later, he was roused with a start when he felt the first drops of rain—and then heard the increasing winds and identified the sounds of the raucous, straining engines, coming his way. Seconds later he was terrified when he saw the closeness of the sweeping wing lights up in the sky toward the lake, followed by the awesome appearance of the fuselage and the jutting pontoons sweeping overhead, so huge and close. He dropped flat to the ground, his face upturned, staring, eyes blurred by the heavy rain till he squirmed and got his head and shoulders under a running board.

Sprawled in the mud, re-catching reality as best he could, Hec was shocked by the certainty that the plane was doomed to crash—until he heard the engine sounds continue and keep going off into the distance, apparently staying aloft.

Up in the tower, Flora and her friends hurried back in from the gallery, wiping the rain from their eyes, distracted, soaked and shaken. Grover had to pull desperately on the door to get it shut and secured in the squalling wind, while Flora and Arie slammed the windows. Gasping, they all dropped to sit on the floor, breathing hard. The wind continued to howl and scream outside. A few minutes later,

FLORA'S MONEY

Grover was able to light a candle and set it on the floor in front of them.

"Where the hell did that monster plane come from?" Flora asked.

"It's my brother Carlos," Arie said, " and some of the guys he works with—and Grover, do you think they'll come back?"

Grover shrugged and said, "Well, that wind was probably a surprise, just like it was for us, and kind of knocked 'em around. Sometimes we get a mean blow like this, right off the lake with little warning, but it usually doesn't last for long. Maybe they'll fly around for a while and if the weather calms back down, they'll try landing again. We'll have to wait and see."

Several minutes after the Goose had departed, the storm did begin to subside. Within ten more minutes, the rain slowed down to a light drizzle and the wind sounds eased up as well. Up in the lighthouse, Arie got up and began staring out the window and pacing back and forth. Grover and Flora watched her in silence, until Arie stopped and said, "Grover, I just remembered; Hector is probably down there, maybe trying to sleep in that car. He knows how to help them tie up, when they come back—if they do. Maybe we should go down and see if he's there and if he wants any help with the plane."

Grover said, "Good idea, Arie. I'll go down to the car and look for him."

"Who did you say," Flora asked, "Hector?"

"Yes. We talked to him this afternoon," Arie said.

"I know a Hector. Back in Chicago, he's a friend, uh, special."

"I think that's where he's from," Arie replied, noticing

213

FLORA'S MONEY

the eager expression on Flora's face.

"Really. I can't imagine—if it is him—what he'd be doing out here," Flora said quietly, almost to herself.

Grover had just opened the gallery door when they heard someone calling, "Hello up there!"

"Hey, that sounds like Hector calling us," Grover said. He stepped out on the Gallery; Flora jumped to her feet and followed him.

CHAPTER 33

"Hello, lighthouse. Hey!" Hector shouted again.

Grover stepped over to the railing and called down, "Hello, Hector—that you?"

"Yeah! You all okay up there?"

"Yes, wet all over, but we'll dry out. That thing almost shortened the tower."

"It sure scared the hell out of me," Hector replied, "that was a close one. I guess the sudden winds shoved them toward the shore faster than they expected—about like a sailboat coming in with too much wind behind it."

"Looked that way. Are they coming back?"

"Probably, if they can." Hector said, as Flora stepped forward, leaned over the rail so Hector could at least see her silhouette in the dim light, laughed and sang out, "Are you

FLORA'S MONEY

guys gonna gab all night or can I butt in long enough to say hi there, handsome?"

"FLORA? FLORA! What the—how did you get out here in the wilderness? Is that really you? I've been sitting down here, thinking about you, but I had no idea!" Hector shouted, much louder than he had to.

"You have? Since when?"

"Since just before that typhoon blew in, or whatever it was, and we got buzzed by that flyin' whale thing. Hey, how you doing? And what are you doing out here?"

"This is my hometown, honest—and these folks are old friends."

Grover, still standing at the rail, called down, "Do you want to come up and dry out, Hector?" Flora made a face at him and pretended to snarl, loud enough for Hector to hear, "Hey, friend, don't you know this is a private shouting match?" Then she looked down at Hector, and asked with a big smile, "How about I come down there?"

"Sure! C'mon down."

Flora threw him a kiss and ran inside. She flashed a broad smile at Arie as she hurried past, scooped up her shoulder bag without stopping and ran down the dark stairway—one hand on the wall to feel her way and keep going as fast as she dared, until she stepped off on the floor at the bottom. In the nearly total darkness she saw Hector's black shape against the night sky in the open doorway. He lunged forward and blindly bounded over to her, arms outstretched. They collided eagerly, laughing, and managed a quick kiss, slightly off mouth-center in the darkness. Flora pulled her face back and managed to whisper, "Yuck, you're all nice and muddy!"

"And you're all nice and—and—real! But it's nice mud. Try a sip," he suggested. She slipped her tongue out a little

216

FLORA'S MONEY

and gave his cheek a tiny lick. Standing there in the dark, embracing each other, they were individually surprised at the ardor and attraction that pulled them together. Standing so close, Flora realized they were breathing in unison, stomachs moving rapidly at first, then more slowly, gently, and together.

She giggled. So did he, and then asked softly, "What's funny?"

"Us. Finding each other like this—but it's so dark we can barely see. Maybe just as well. We must look like drowned clowns—but it wouldn't matter, would it?"

"Nope, but if someone could turn on a light it might be kind of funny, at that," he said.

"For one thing, we're soaking wet," she said, with a soft laugh.

"You are. I'm also sopped with mud, weeds—and the same clothes I've been wearing for days. And I don't normally go around without shaving for so long."

"Well, I don't think Grover has a light in this whole place, except the candle upstairs. So we're safe."

"That so? Then maybe we could sit down."

"Here?"

"Hey, I know a better place, lovely and dry with soft leather seats and lots of privacy," he whispered in her ear.

"Oh, right. I bet you've got a brand new Ford."

"Want to see it?"

"Sure. I bet if that plane comes back, it'll get kind of crowded in through here."

"C'mon, Flora. Take my hand, I'll lead the way. It's really not a bad jalopy."

~

FLORA'S MONEY

Hector awoke as the first of the daylight began to make a difference in what he could see. He was lying on his back, across the rear seat of the Duesenberg. Flora, lying on her stomach on top of him, woke up at the same time, moved her warm face away from his whiskery chin, placed both hands on his bare shoulders and pushed slowly. She raised her head upright and her breasts about two inches above his chest before she stalled, like a curious rabbit on alert. Her abdomen pressed tightly against his. The four long legs, two of them shapely as those of a posturing ballerina, sans tutu, and two others hairy and chiseled, created a tangled marvel. Hec chose not to move. He rumbled his throat faintly and caressed her lower back with mud-caked knuckles showing, his eyes almost closed. Flo made similar sounds, though more ladylike, and gazed into his face. Her pose, complete with daunting bare breasts, gleamed like a carved and enameled figurehead commanding a taut-sailing square-rigged barky.

She whispered: "Morning, Hec."

"Damn," he mumbled.

"S'matter?" she cooed, exhaling.

"I hear airplane engines, must be the Goose; probably landing way out there."

"Took 'em long enough."

"No it didn't," he said.

Flora moved her head, just a little, to look around inside the Duesenberg for the first time. She saw the underside of the canvas top, and the side window-curtains snapped into place. Strewn across the front seats she saw their clothes in a mixed jumble, some inside out. Her bra had artfully draped itself over the manly steering wheel, like a Picasso work of un-juxtaposed eyeballs. His shirt was lying flat on the driver's seat, with the sleeves carefully folded inside. On the floor in

FLORA'S MONEY

the back, just below her head, she saw her tote bag containing the three Golden's cans of money. She looked to the right side of the floor, surprised to see two more cans lying there, one on its side and partly under the front seat, each with a Golden's Coffee label.

Hec felt that she gently stiffened and was taking deeper breaths. He opened his eyes all the way and saw her looking back toward their legs and down at the floor. She glanced forward at his face for a second and reached over with her right hand to hold up one of the cans so he could see it. She shook it, guessed it was empty, and dropped it back on the floor. He watched, intrigued.

She reached down again, right in front of their heads, and lifted her tote bag a foot or so, for him to see, then dropped it to the floor and pulled one of her cans out of the bag. With the Golden's label in clear view, she placed it on the top of the front seatback.

Hector's eyes questioned; he faked a frown. She felt his ribs vibrate, just a little. Her breasts responded with a few little shakes. Slowly and with a bland look she reached around with her left hand and tweaked his nose. The grating sound of revving engines, loud and close, broke the silence.

"Damn!" Hector said again. Flora sighed.

Getting untangled and upright in the seats was like a taffy pull gone mad—sorting and yanking on the damp clothes was frantic and inefficient. During the struggles, the digni-fied Duesenberg squeaked, just a little, while Hec and Flo became breathless, shy and, in the revealing light of the new day, appreciatively observant of each other.

CHAPTER 34

As the Goose taxied toward the beach, Quent peered through the windshield and saw Arie and a young man on shore, watching. He also spotted Hector and another person as they came running across the sands from the woods behind the lighthouse—then he looked closer, recognized Flora and said to himself, "Well, I'll be damned. How'd he do that?"

Behind them, people from town could be seen, coming across the sand to gawk at the big plane. Jerry and Maddie, determined to have a closer look at the Goose this time, were way ahead of the other locals. Once the plane was tied off in the calm water, with Hector's help, and the pontoons gently touching the sand, Quent walked over to the bystanders and said, "Hi, Arie, Carlos will be out in a few minutes—and hello, Hec, looks like you're right on the job."

FLORA'S MONEY

"Damn right," Hector said, grinning, "And hey, neat landing this time. Quite an improvement!"

Quent playfully pointed a finger at him, then turned, broke into a big smile and cried out, "Flora, my goodness! What a nice surprise. What are you doing here?"

"Just visiting—this is my home town. I grew up here, with Arie and her friend Grover—have you gents met before?" Grover reached over, shook Quent's hand, and said, "Hi—and this is my Aunt Maddie and Uncle Jerry." Quent smiled at Maddie and while shaking Jerry's hand he noticed the badge on his shirt and said, "Well, it looks like Uncle Jerry is also chief of police. How nice."

"Quite a machine you got there. Is Carlos the pilot?" Jerry asked, in a brisk tone.

"Co-pilot. And of course you know him, he's from here, too, isn't he?"

"Yes, Carlos's an old friend. Did that storm last night cause you any problems?"

Quent chuckled and said, "Yeah, some. Those winds were too much—we had to circle awhile and wait until things got calmer before coming in."

"You just passing through or are you going to be here awhile?"

"Not sure, yet. We may be here for a day or two. Depends on what we find when we check the plane over and make sure that nothing was damaged by the storm. A blow like that puts a lot of strain on a plane. Would you two like to come on board and have a look around?"

"Really?" Maddie said, and then she startled Jerry by saying, "That would be wonderful, and after that, how about all of you coming over for some breakfast? Our place is just a little hike down the beach from here." Whoa, Jerry thought.

221

FLORA'S MONEY

This is getting to be too much of a family picnic. These guys are friendly, but what the hell are they doing here?

But Quent spoke to Maddie just then and said, "Thanks for your hospitality—I can take you on board now, but after that we have to get started on checking the plane, and I think the boys and I will need some rest—we've been up all night. If that's okay, just step where I do. Careful or you'll get wet feet!" Excited, Maddie reached and took his hand to make the step over to the float. Jerry followed her without help, thinking well, so far, so good.

Carlos came ashore a few minutes later. He gave his sister a hug and walked along the beach with her, so they could talk in private. "Everything is changed now, Arie," he began, and went on to explain the tentative plans he and the men had for starting a legit business down in the islands. Then he said, "Now tell me what's happening to you—and how's good old Grover?"

Later, Quent brought Jere and Maddie back to shore and said goodbye. Then he found Hector and went for a walk on the beach as he told him about their plans for going to the islands. Hector liked the idea and agreed to go, then he brought Quent up to date and finally said,"—and so, I parked the Duesey right over there in those trees, behind the lighthouse. It's not completely hidden, but I've been watching it pretty close since I got it back yesterday. I even slept in it last night, after you came past—your suit is still in the trunk—now, about the cash."

"Right, did you spend it yet?"

"Hah! It was tempting, but no, I've got it all. The cans each had five thousand, and they were right where we left them under the floor. Now, most of the cash is all right here," Hector said, crossing his wrists and patting his rolled

222

FLORA'S MONEY

up sleeves with his palms, "I counted it last night in the limo, just before I called you. I've got some of it, that wouldn't fit in my sleeves, here in my pockets ."

"Beautiful," Quent said. "Ten total sounds right. It's travel money now, and can do a lot to get us set up down in the islands. I was able to put some dough aside, just in case we had to do exactly what we're doing, and I've got it in my pocket. But it's nowhere near as much, less than a thousand. Jed may have some, too. I haven't asked him yet. But Carlos probably is not very flush."

"So, do you want the shirt off my back now?"

"No, you keep it on. For one thing, our friends are probably not ready for a mixture of your perfume and mine. And besides, you might as well be our treasurer for a while, kind of a human safe. Seriously Hec, I'm grateful, thanks so much. By the way, what's with you and Flora?"

"I need to talk to you about her. She's really amazing—in lots of ways. We just found each other again last night, when she was visiting Arie at the lighthouse. And this morning she showed me three of the Golden's cans she has and—"

"She does! How come? From the bar?"

"I don't have the full story yet—but I'm going to go have a private chat with Flora as soon as you and I are done. I'll bring her over later so you can talk to her too. And don't forget, that beautiful automobile is sitting right over there in that woods. You want to raffle it off, or ship it to the Bahamas on a tramp steamer?"

"We'll talk about that," Quent said, "but right now I wish we could put wings on it."

After Arnie told his boss he had to quit his job as co-pilot for

FLORA'S MONEY

the Goose, he moved his family to his parents' farmhouse outside Muncie, Indiana to avoid the police crack-down on bootleggers back in Chicago. A few mornings later, as they sat in the kitchen having breakfast, his wife handed him a copy of the *Indianapolis News* and said, "Arnie, here's an item in the paper about your old boss, Gus. See there, he made the front page. Did you know he was involved in counterfeit money, too?"

She pointed at a three-column photo of a portly gentleman, wearing a dark suit and tie, staring directly into the camera. He was in handcuffs. A uniformed policeman held him by one arm as they came up some concrete steps. The headline, in boldface type above the photo, said:

NABBED BOOZE KING DENIES
BOGUS BUCK CHARGES.

Part Four ~ Repeal

1934 & Hence

CHAPTER 35

While Hec was talking to Quent right after the plane came in, Flora walked toward the lighthouse and met Grover and Arie headed her way. "There you are! We were coming to find you," Grover said, "we thought we'd start sorting out the money to get it organized and counted, okay?"

"Fine. But first, would you two come with me to talk to the Judge, if he has time?"

When they arrived at the Judge's office in town, he was not busy and welcomed them to come in and sit down with him at the cluttered round table he used as a desk. At first, he looked at each one of them, put his unlit cigar down in an ashtray and, chuckling, said, "My, you sure have serious looks on your faces, and you're all so grown up now. Did you come by to cheer up a lonely old gent? If you did, it worked!

FLORA'S MONEY

But tell me, if this is a business meeting, what can I do for you?"

Flora began talking and briefly explained about coming back to Hamelet, after working in Chicago, bringing back some cash, and wanting to help Oren with his store and start a new business for herself and her two friends. Then she repeated a shortened version of the story she had told her two friends the night before, leaving out most of the details about the cans of money. Then she said, "So, there we are. I have some cash, and I want to use it for the best of everyone involved. And I guess, one of my biggest questions is, can I legally do all this without having to explain how I saved up, and uh, accumulated the money?" Grover and Arie remained silent.

The Judge came right to the point: "Flora, you say you want to help your uncle Oren and also start a little business of your own—and probably hire Grover, Arie and maybe some others from town to work for you. Fine, that's easy to set up. But I gather the source of the funds worries you?"

Flora nodded, and said, "Yes sir."

"And I assume you may want me to handle your legal needs on these projects. Okay, I'd be glad to help. As your lawyer, everything you tell me about your business will be private and safe with me. After we know how much of my time you may need, I'll advise you of my fees. I see you nodding, Flora—so I assume we agree so far. Okay, you've come to my office and briefly told me your plans and that you have funds to invest. Technically, where and how the funds were obtained is not my concern, at this point, but what happens from here on must be accomplished in a completely legal fashion or I cannot be a part of it. Agreed?" Flora nodded.

"Okay Flora, so I can better see the possibilities for you,

FLORA'S MONEY

approximately how much of your funds are you ready to commit to just these projects—wait, don't tell me how much you have in total; I don't need to know that. Are we talking like maybe a thousand dollars?"

"More, much more," Flora said.

"Oh, ten or twenty-five thousand?"

Flora, glanced at Grover and said, "Yes, let's say, twenty-five thousand, that would be good—for starters."

"For starters? Well, can we say roughly fifty thousand dollars for now? And if you have more, you probably should just keep it in reserve until you get more experience."

"Yes sir. That sounds good," Flora replied.

"Well, you know what I'd do if I was as young as you three, and had some funds to invest right now—I'd think about reopening a bank here in Hamelet," the Judge said, leaning back in his creaky desk-chair. "We haven't had a bank here for years. People around here, the storekeepers, everybody, would be delighted to have a safe place to keep their savings, like before the Depression hit us all. Most of them don't have very much, but I know lots of folks worry about trying to hide what they do have under a bedroom floorboard or in a jug hidden in a kitchen cupboard. I think they would really support a bank, especially if it was owned and operated locally by people they know and can trust."

Flora looked at her friends and said, "Golly, a bank. Do you think we could really do that?"

"Well, " the Judge said, "you should hire an experienced manager to set it up, and run things. And, remember this: since 'twenty-nine, hundreds of banks closed in this country largely because they all made the same mistake. Business was booming so the banks loaned out most of their money for mortgages on farms, houses and for businesses, large and

228

FLORA'S MONEY

small, to expand. They did it because charging interest on loans is where banks earn most of their profits—but, as you've heard many times, a series of events depressed business four years ago, the public got panicky and lined up to take back their savings—and lots of banks ran out of cash and had to close, leaving thousands of customers broke and scared of banks.

"But since FDR came in last winter, he's done quite a bit to get Congress to pass new regulations to help banks and depositors—like the Emergency Banking Act and the Federal Deposit Insurance Corporation, among others. Lots of closed banks are re-opening, and new ones are starting, so your timing right now would be good because many people miss the safety and services they used to have from a bank. The public wants to get back to normal, and you would be the first one in this area.

"And kids, this is very important: when you begin dealing with customers, always keep as much of your start-up money as you can in a safe place—and use customer deposits to cover your loan business and operating expenses. Never loan out any of your retained assets; then if another crash comes along you'll be able to ride out the storm. Understand?" All three of them nodded.

"Judge, I have a question," Grover said, "Do you think the old bank building here in Hamelet, that's been boarded up for years, would be a good place for us to buy or rent?"

"Very possibly," the Judge replied, "You might even be able to buy it cheap by just paying the back taxes, or maybe less. I'll find out. I've heard that the old safe is still in there. Maybe it can still be used, at least at first. It's a strong little building, too, all brick and stone. It can probably be repainted, cleaned up and be ready to go fairly soon. You may also want

FLORA'S MONEY

to look into having an actual vault built into the basement of that building as soon as you can, with more up to date electric devices and more fire proofing, but that will take months, maybe longer; be expensive, but a lot safer. I'll let you know when we need to sit and talk again. In the meantime I'll do some checking on a lot of these details so you'll know your costs before we start spending any of your money."

After they left the Judge's office and started to walk back to the beach, Arie laughed and, in a voice filled with awe, remarked, "Flora, I think you summed it up very well."

"I did?"

"Yes, when you said—*golly, a bank!*"

CHAPTER 36

On the way back from talking to the Judge, Flora told Grover and Arie that she wanted to stop off and see her uncle Oren for a little chat, and would meet them at the lighthouse after that. When she walked into the Emporium she found him sitting on a stool behind one of the counters, apparently waiting while a lady customer browsed around at the far end of the store. Flora leaned over the counter and kissed Oren on the top of the head. He grinned and said, "Well, look who's here!"

"Oren, how you doing? Everything okay?" She lowered her voice, so the lady couldn't hear what she said. "Sure," he replied in a soft voice, not sure why, and leaned a little closer to her. "Oren, I may be going away for a while, I'm not sure yet. But it won't be like before, not as long, anyway. And I've

FLORA'S MONEY

had a long talk with your friends, Grover and Arie. They'll be stopping in, once in awhile, to see if you need anything. Or if any problem comes up, send word down to the lighthouse and one of them will come right over."

Oren stared at her with a blank expression. "Going away for a while, all right, but I don't need any nursemaids after all these years."

"I know, but we're all getting older, right?"

He laughed and said, "Maybe you are. I always stay the same."

"You sure do, you toughie. Anyway, there's something else. I think we're going to start a bank, just like Hamelet had before, remember?"

"Of course I do. Kept all our money there. Just down the street. Since they had that robbery years ago, they closed it."

"Well, I just came from the Judge. He tells me it might be possible for me to get it going again. But don't tell anyone yet. We need to keep it secret for now."

"Okay," he said, glancing over his shoulder at the customer still busy at the other end of the store, trying on a pair of work gloves. By now, he and Flora were almost whispering.

"You going to run the bank?"

"Yes, with Grover and the Judge's help."

"Great. Can I put my saved-up money in it and keep it safer?"

"Oh, you have savings? I didn't know. Sure, you'll be able to put it in our bank."

"You want it now? Every morning, first thing, I go check on my money. Got a good hiding place in the moose head upstairs, but I still worry some robber might get it. Or if

FLORA'S MONEY

we have a fire here, it would be too bad," he said, his voice husky and low.

"We're not ready to take in money yet," she whispered, "but as soon as we can, even if I'm still out of town, it'll be okay to have Grover take it over and put it in the fireproof safe. Then you won't have to worry anymore. We'll set up a regular account for you. Is it a lot of money?"

Oren looked at her, nodding emphatically, and said something quietly that Flora couldn't hear, and she asked softly, "How much did you say?"

"Forty two thousand, eight hundred dollars, and then there's the Liberty Bonds I never cashed in," he blurted out—then realizing that maybe he had said it too loudly, he jerked his shoulders up to touch his earlobes and shrugged.

Flora glanced at the browsing customer, now far down the aisle trying on an apron, smiled at Oren, kissed him on the cheek and said, "It's okay, dearie, she couldn't hear you, way down there." After that, Flora could only nod, swallow, gaze at Oren and say, very quietly, "Oooh, Oren."

CHAPTER 37

Gorki sat down on a jutting rock, half-buried in the sand, deep in the wooded area on the north side of Hamelet. It was the morning after he had left the wreckage of his burned truck and hiked around the edge of town, keeping out of sight, and trudging in the direction of the shore. His head still ached and he felt groggy from being hit by Hector.

Before reaching the beach he crossed some abandoned farmland, saw the remains of a dilapidated silo, crawled inside an open hatch at ground level, and fell asleep. When the sudden rainstorm came across the area during the night, the roof leaked badly and left him quite wet. At dawn he got up and tramped on, distracted with hunger, yet determined to find the car and the big guy who slugged him. Maybe I'll sneak up and bash him with

FLORA'S MONEY

a club, he thought, or maybe if I find the car, I'll smash it up — or worse.

He kept walking through more deserted fields and realized he was passing a small orchard of gnarled apple trees with some fallen fruit on the ground. There were also a few shriveled apples still hanging in the trees that he could reach; he quickly snatched several, filled his pockets, and continued his hike, chewing as he went. Once past the orchard he saw a run-down farmhouse facing the dirt road he was avoiding. Behind it was a barn, and from where he was walking he could see a horse standing in a fenced-in area in back of the barn. Prepared to hide or run, if anyone appeared from the house, or a dog raised an alarm, he went over the fence and in the open door at the back of the barn. He found a bridle hanging in a stall and went back out to get acquainted with the tired nag in the barnyard—an easy task for Gorki; even the smell of the barn reminded him of his early days, growing up with horses.

When the phone rang in his Chicago office, Frank picked it up, unhooked the earpiece, jammed it between his raised shoulder and cheek, put his feet up on his desk and said, "Marshall's office."

"Frank, Jack here. Got an update."

"Yeah."

"We've been talking to Morrie and Jake, down on the dock. The so-called fishermen we let go over in Hamelet that night."

"Right. What's up?"

"Jake just volunteered something. When they told us about finding Jiggs's body in the lake, we didn't get the whole

235

FLORA'S MONEY

story—that there was a big seaplane involved. It landed just as they were watching from the shore, and they just remembered today, 'oh yeah, something fell off it, kinda,' that turned out to be Jiggs when they went out in their boat and looked."

"Oh? You say they volunteered this? Uh, never mind."

"Well, it was a little complicated. We were just following up on Jiggs winding up in the lake, to see if we could get any more leads on where he was getting that counterfeit cash—and who might be still passing it around town. Jake goofed and let drop some hints. We made a little deal—after Jake's story about it sort of slipped out."

"THE big plane we've been looking for since we pulled in Gus and his people?"

"Maybe. Not many planes like that around. We don't need to bring Jake in, do we?"

"Naw. But I've got an idea. Talk to you when you come in. Bye."

"Good morning. Hamelet police," Jerry said, as he spooned more sugar into his lukewarm coffee.

"Jerry, Frank here. In Chicago."

"Hi. What can I do for you, Frank?"

"Just checking something out. You know anything about a big tri-motor airplane running around the lake and dropping off booze, or anything else illegal—from Canada or anyplace else?"

There was a pause at Jerry's end. He cleared his throat and said, "Uh, a tri-motor you say? One of those they call the Big Goose?"

"I believe the nickname is the Tin Goose."

"Right. That's it. Well, there was one came in here this

FLORA'S MONEY

morning. I think it was like the one that came in the day after your raid down here. But as far as I know it wasn't involved, I mean—nobody said they had any alcohol on board that one—it never came up. Didn't I tell you about it before, Frank?"

"No. I haven't talked to you since that night when we brought in the power launch."

"Oh yeah—that's right."

"How long was that plane there, Jere?"

"Not long. I think they just landed on the lake to fix something, then they left."

"I see. And you say there's another one there now?"

"Yeah—I inspected this one myself, Frank. Everything seems okay. No sign of any booze. Don't seem to be in any hurry. Said they may hang around and do some repairs."

"Okay, never mind. Talk to you later."

Jerry hung up his phone, got to his feet and began pacing. There was no one else in his office. He let out a big breath, slapped his forehead and thought, what the hell have I done? Why did I screw up the facts so much? But I was all over this plane with Quent, right from when it landed today, and the only booze on that bird would have to be in somebody's pocket flask. Hell, every cop knows that either you catch bootleggers with enough of the stuff in hand to make an arrest, or you can forget it. And, let's see, maybe Maddie was right to invite the crew to breakfast—they are like family, almost: there's Carlos, Arie's brother, who's one of the pilots—and she's my nephew's sweetheart—and there's that big guy I saw driving the Duesenberg yesterday, and coming across the beach this morning with our Flora, who apparently is her boyfriend. And Grover was down there too, acting friendly with them all. What's the harm in them

237

FLORA'S MONEY

having a peaceful look at one of these famous planes?

With that, he walked out of his office, went down to the corner and stared across the beach. In the distance he could see the Goose and the people standing around the shore admiring it, and others hurrying across from town to take a look. Jerry strolled calmly toward the crowd—until he realized that maybe Frank might be rushing out there in the launch or in a truck full of agents. "Damn," Jerry said to himself, "maybe I should go drop a few hints to what's his name—Quent—and then back off."

He began trotting over the hundreds of yards he had to cover, like a veteran fire horse answering an alarm, but he was tiring fast with the drag of the loose sand on his ankle-high shoes. Gasping, he kept one hand on his holstered pistol to keep it from bouncing up and down on his hip.

Quent, standing on a movable ladder on the pontoon, and making some adjustments on the port engine, looked up and saw he had a visitor stepping on to the float. "Why hello, chief," Quent said, "how's the crowd of spectators behaving out there?"

"No problem. Kind of thinning out, actually. Can I interrupt you for a minute? Something I need to tell you."

"Sure." Quent stepped down and turned to face him.

Jerry knew there was no one near enough to hear them talk, but he stepped close to Quent and said quietly, "I'll say this once, and deny it ever after, okay? Just had a call from Chicago—some feds may be coming out here, looking for a Tri-Motor running booze. They'll be in a launch or maybe they're driving. I couldn't deny this big thing was here, too many people have seen it. That's all they know from me. You showed me this morning that you have no booze on board," Jerry continued, "so legally I can't make an arrest or hold you

FLORA'S MONEY

here—even if I wanted to." Quent started to reach out and shake his hand, but Jerry made a negative gesture, palm up, and said, "Take care of your people and uh—that's all I'm going to say." He turned, stepped back on shore, and left.

Nervous about what he had done, Jerry decided it might be wise to find a place to sit down, watch the Goose, and be out of sight if Frank and his agents showed up. He looked across the beach and began to walk toward the tower. From up behind the tower he thought he would have a clear view of the plane, a lot of the beach all the way to town, and off to the south. He also figured that from there it might be interesting to see that big plane take off. Once he got near the lighthouse he turned and walked into the edge of the woods, sat down on a stump, and lit a cigarette.

CHAPTER 38

Later, Hector sat talking to Flora in the last row of seats in the moored Tin Goose. They were alone in the quiet cabin after Carlos gave them a quick walk-through, answered their questions, and then stepped out the door to go ashore. Flora looked intently at Hector and said, "—so you're going to fly south, clear out of the country, with them?"

"Yes, that's our plan now, Flo. We can't go back to Chicago till things settle down, or until Quent contacts one of his friends back there and finds out for sure that it's okay to come back to the States. Quent and I have kept well in the background, and out of the violence since we started in this racket, and it isn't too likely that the police have much reason to want either one of us for anything. But we're not sure. We'll leave here as soon as the plane is ready for a long

FLORA'S MONEY

haul. We have to put a stock of groceries on board and get some blankets, and so on, and refill it with gas—this bird uses about fifty gallons an hour, they say—and they used up much more than they expected to, last night."

"How long will you be down in the islands?" Flora asked,

"For as long as the Goose can support us, I guess. Kind of a wild idea, but it could lead to a good, permanent business for us if we start down there and maybe transfer it up here later—flying folks and freight, no booze, just important stuff and people in a hurry. These guys have a lot of flying experience. And Quent said that maybe they could even train me to become a pilot. Imagine! I like that idea."

"Have you ever gone up before?"

"Only as a passenger, twice, in an old Stearman bi-plane at an air show."

"And I've never tried it. It must be wonderful! It's even exciting to just sit in here. But, hey, you really sound eager about all this traveling," Flora said, "but what about—us?"

"That's easy, Flo, come with me. They say it's a great climate down on those tropical islands. And living without the winter snows sounds good to me. What do you say?"

"You mean, just get up and go with you?" she said, eyes wide.

"Why not? Remember?" He reached up, tweaked his own nose and grinned.

"Oh," she said, "I remember."

"Hah! And what's the story about your coffee cans? I know Manny came looking for you after you left Chicago. Seemed upset, they had him on a leash, sort of—one of their mugs was with him to make sure he didn't skip. Anyway, I was worried about you—even tried to call you, but we had

241

FLORA'S MONEY

to leave and come down here."

Flora frowned, clapped her hand over her mouth for a moment then said, "Gosh! I heard about Manny; Rhonda told me on the phone, yesterday. He came by her shop, too, looking for me. It has to be about the money, doesn't it?"

"She didn't tell him anything, did she?"

"No, she's a dear friend; and I never said a word about those cans to her, ever."

"Well, Flo, maybe you need to get scarce for a while, too. Looks like between us we may have both sides of the law interested in where we are."

"But Hec, I never told anyone in Chicago exactly where I was from, not even you. Do you think any of Manny's bosses would really come after me?"

"Depends, Flo."

"On what?"

"Like how many of the coffee cans you have. The two you saw in the car were full of cash until I took it all out yesterday and hid it for Quent. We brought the cans down in the Duesey for pay-off bribes and so on. Quent got them from Gus before we left. Those guys have been transporting their cash like that for a long time. I guess they thought it was a good way to keep the dough out of sight till it was needed for unofficial business. Now, it turns out we'll be able to grab the money and use it ourselves—like a bonus." Then he shrugged and went on to briefly tell Flora about the first delivery they attempted, using the new Goose, the raid by the feds, the theft of the Duesenberg and how he got it back. He concluded by saying, "That's why Quent flew back to Chicago the next morning without me, and I stayed on here to look for the car and the cash—so the big boss wouldn't hear about it."

FLORA'S MONEY

"And you found it all yesterday."

"Yup, and Quent is delighted we got everything back—especially the money. We had no idea till yesterday that we'd ever wind up with the plane, and need to finance a long trip in such a hurry. I guess we always thought that if and when the cops shut Gus down, we'd all hop a freight and go off into the sunset on the cheap."

"And what about our friend the Duesey, as you call it. That won't fit on this plane, will it?" She said with a wry grin.

Hec sighed and said, "No it won't. That's another thing. We haven't figured out what to do with it, yet. We should sell it, but there's no time."

"How much is it worth?"

"Probably ten, fifteen thousand from a showroom, but now we don't have time to look for a buyer. And if we did, we'd be lucky to get half that or anything much."

"Maybe I could buy it—hide it around here somewhere, and sell it later. That would give you more cash to keep going, wouldn't it?"

"Sure—but really, Flora, do you have that much coffee to spend?"

"Yes, and if you boys need more, I'll loan it to you, since you're such nice fellows to offer me a ride out of here for a while. I'm serious. In fact, Hec, I guess I'm really scared of those city bums now. Actually I managed to leave Golden's with quite a lot of cans. And maybe it's best, for another more important reason, for me to go with you."

"Us?"

"Uh-huh."

"Really?"

"Uh-huh, again!" she said, smiling. "But what about

243

FLORA'S MONEY

Quent, will he let me come?"

"Why not? You'd be our first paying passenger—and maybe our biggest investor! I'll talk to him." Hec leaned forward, keeping his arms folded across his chest and kissed her.

Flo said, in a tiny voice, "Don't I get a hug?"

"Hey, lady, this is a public airplane, or something, people may see us. Oh hell!" He kissed her again, complete with their four arms hugging.

A few minutes later, Quent came in from outside and said, " Hi Flora—Hec can we talk? We got a little problem."

"Go ahead," Flora said, getting up, "I need to go talk to Grover and take care of some things. See you soon." Hec took her hand, got to his feet and gave her a polite tug to help her up.

They smiled privately at each other, and Hector whispered as she slipped past him, "Wait out on the float for a few minutes. I'll talk to him now." The tote bag was still hanging from her shoulder, where it had been all day.

Quent watched her walk out the door, turned to Hector and said quietly, "My, what a big pretty lady."

"Has a big heart, too."

"Everything okay between you two?"

"Great. We just talked about a lot of things."

"And?"

"She wants to fly to the islands with us."

"Why?"

"She's afraid the Chicago guys will come looking for her, for one thing—she apparently acquired so many Golden's cans she hasn't had time to count the money, yet."

"Oh? Whew! Really?" Quent said, "Now that's an inter-

FLORA'S MONEY

esting problem to have."

"And there's some other reasons for her to come, too. She's willing to loan us money to help us start the new business—and she also said she would buy the Duesenberg from us, or have Grover store it here, out of sight, for now."

Quent stared at Hector for a moment, then said, "Those are some pretty sweet reasons for her to come—but it could be dangerous."

"I guess she thinks there might be more danger for her right here. And besides, there is another reason she wants to go."

"Oh?"

"Yeah, she put it in one word, as a matter of fact," Hector said with a little grin.

"And that word is?"

"Us! And Quent, she can cook and is willing to pitch in and help with the business."

"All right. If you're so sure about her, why not? Ask her to have the car hidden for now. And we have to get Jed and Carlos in here to leave this place—fast."

"Great, Quent. I asked her to wait outside—I'll tell her there's no time to pack, and to get back on board."

Hector stuck his head out the cabin door and called, "Hey, baby, c'mon back aboard, and hurry! You're going with us. I only had to tell him a few lies about you. You got those three cans in that shoulder bag?"

"Yes, and Grover can send more money if we need it. The rest is hidden, but he knows where. I have to see Grover and Arie, real quick—say goodbye and, jeepers, what about clothes and all?"

"No time to go pack! We'll buy what we need later. So run!"

"Okay! I'll hurry right back." She squealed happily and

FLORA'S MONEY

started to turn away.

He held up a hand and said, "Oh! Ask Grover to hide the Duesey somewhere out of sight; Quent says you won't have to buy it right now. Here's the key; Grove will need that to move it."

"I'll ask him. He'll do it. Here, keep this for me." She tossed him her shoulder bag, and added, "keep this too," as she threw him a kiss, took a huge step from the pontoon to shore, and began to run as he continued to watch. She still wore the shorts, middy blouse and sandals from the night before as she went charging across the beach toward the tower—like a thoroughbred home-stretching to a big win. Hector, still smiling, turned and ducked as he went back inside the plane.

CHAPTER 39

"GROVER—ARIE, ARE YOU-ooh UP THERE-ere-ere?" Flora's shout echoed up the speaking tube at the light-house.

"FLORA! WE'RE HERE," Grover shouted back, after a short pause while he and Arie came out of the storeroom and up the few stairs to the mouthpiece for the tube. Before he could say more, he heard Flora shouting loud enough to be heard without the tube: "COM-MING UP!" Flora appeared shortly, charging up three to four steps at a time, and joined them at the top.

"Hey, we're on our way! I'm leaving on the Goose with the boys as soon as I get back over there," she blurted, breathing deeply from the climb.

"You're leaving now?" Arie said. Grover stared in

FLORA'S MONEY

silence, mouth wide open.

"Yes! Something came up—they didn't have time to tell me but I'll write you soon as I can, with maybe a phone number where you can call me back from a phone booth. Put a phone in, up here. On me. Golly, I'm so excited—but I trust you to handle things."

"We will, Flora. I got some farm-size milk cans this morning, to put the money in," Grover said, "and we'll get rid of the Golden's cans after dark tonight—I'm going to sink 'em out in the lake—we'll sort the money and tie string around them in packets of the same amounts for each face value—get you a total, and hide it all in the big cans."

"Great, just like a bank," Flora said.

Grover nodded and said, "Sure. The milk cans will be airtight, easy to move around and fire resistant to some extent."

"I hope we never have to find that out," Flora said, "and for now we'll keep the big containers with the money in your storeroom, right?"

"Yes, and I'll get the locks on the doors today, too."

"Oh! Locks—that reminds me," Flora said, pulling the Duesenberg key out of her pocket, "Hector asked if you could find some place to store the car he drove in here—and don't tell anyone who owns it, or anything. But you don't know that, anyway, do you? Can you find a safe place for it? Gosh knows how long it'll be here."

Grover took the key, astonished at this latest request, and said, "Uh, sure. Why not? I'll find a place."

Flora stepped over and swept both of them into her arms, kissed each one on the cheek and said, "Dear ones, this has been the most amazing week in my life! So, you two will be on your own for a while. Pretty soon we'll be able

FLORA'S MONEY

to call each other by long distance—just imagine—to make more plans as we go along."

"Golly Flora," Arie said, "you're about to get into the world's largest airplane and go flying off with your prince!"

Grover laughed and asked, "Shouldn't that be a white stallion, like in the old fairy tales—instead of a silver goose?"

"So there we are, gents," Quent said, standing in the passenger cabin of the plane and talking to Jed, Carlos, and Hector, "We need to leave here now—thanks to the info from our good friend, the local police chief—and hop to someplace else before the feds show up. We'll look for a quiet spot, and set her down to finish the repairs. There are some pulled cables to be adjusted, and some other things that are not too important by themselves, but when taken together they could develop some serious problems. It should be safe to head on down to the islands, as long as we don't pound along too far without doing these things."

"I got a bunch of sandwiches for us from the diner, for now," Jed said. "There wasn't enough time to get anything else."

"Okay, better than nothing; the other supplies we need we'll have to get at the next stop," Quent said, "and Jed, I know you have drinking water, and you figure we have about two or three hours worth of gas?"

"Yes, I hope that's enough to find a small lake, somewhere south of here, to lay over tonight and look for more gas. At least we've still got several hours of daylight left—and we'll need it to spot our next place to land."

"Another thing," Quent said, "Hector's gal Flora will be

FLORA'S MONEY

going with us as a passenger since it may not be safe for her to stay here, either. I'll tell you more later. As soon as she gets on board we go. And she's also going to be bringing along some cash that will come in handy for us down the line—besides that, I hear she's a pretty good cook. And she's willing to pitch in and help any way she can, right Hec?"

"You bet. I'll check outside and see if I can hurry her up," He ran down the cabin aisle, looked out the open door and said, "Here she comes!"

From Jerry's chosen look-out spot the first unusual thing he saw was Flora running from the plane and across the sand, toward the lighthouse, moving with long strides in a smooth and supple display. He heard her call out to Grover and Arie and then saw her dash inside. He glanced back at the Goose and saw Hector moving off and on the pontoon, working with the ropes. A few minutes later, the lighthouse door flew open; Flora ran out and dashed back toward the plane. Jerry looked up and saw Grover and Arie come out on the gallery, lean against the rail, and apparently watch Flora as she ran directly to the pontoon.

She jumped on, then hesitated long enough to turn and wave her long arm once at her friends on the gallery and hurry inside the oval-shaped door; they waved back. Bewildered, Jerry muttered out loud, "Now what the hell is going on?"

When Gorki rode out on the beach, twenty minutes earlier, he had decided to cross to the water's edge to head south toward the old lighthouse before circling back inland from there. He was beginning to feel more and more doubtful of

FLORA'S MONEY

ever spotting the car or the driver, but at least he no longer had to walk. Attracted by the sight of the big plane and the onlookers, he stopped to take a look himself. Then he saw the tall and beautiful woman come running toward the plane, leap on, and run up the steps and through the cabin door. After she was inside, Hector stepped out on the entry ladder and started to pull the door shut—in full view of the astonished Gorki who gasped, leaned forward, and watched in anger as he saw his prey disappear into the plane and the door close. In his excitement in getting Flora back on board and securing the door Hector didn't notice that a spectator, over a hundred feet to the north of the plane, and sitting bareback on an old horse, was his foe from the day before.

At that moment, the pilots began their start-up procedures inside. Already free floating in the calm, shallow water, the plane was ready to move. Gorki slid down off the horse, kneeled down and splashed some of the cool lake water on his face, shook his head and, reaching up to grasp the reins, laid back on the sand, disgusted.

One after the other, each engine emitted a quick puff of smoke, followed by the loud stutter and shriek brought on by the pilot's run-up test. The departure of the Goose roused the few scattered adults and kids still watching from the nearby beaches. Everyone stood up. A few cheered and clapped. Others shouted to each other, unheard because of the engines. The plane edged away from shore and began to taxi straight out, increasing speed; thrashing spray and a spreading wake followed the Goose until it gradually lifted from the lake and kept going.

Back on shore, Jerry also stood up to watch it go, impressed by the performance. He stretched, scratched the back of his head with one hand, shrugged and sat back

FLORA'S MONEY

down—wondering when, and if, the feds might show up.

When the plane began its departure, Gorki heard the rising sounds of the engines. He rose up on one elbow and watched it go. While staring across the water he thought, hey, if that guy is taking off out there—what did he do with the car? Damn, it has to still be around here somewhere, unless he passed it on to someone—but maybe—? He got to his feet, swung himself up onto the horse and let it amble inland, across the sand, while he pondered his choices.

Grover and Arie stayed on the gallery to watch the take off. They saw the plane appear to shrink into a dot, out over the lake, before it disappeared into the haze of the warm afternoon. Then they turned and went inside.

"Thar she blows!" Grover said, then sighed and added, "My, isn't she fun?"

Arie laughed. "What a gal. She's a whirlwind. So which way do we jump first?"

"I should probably put the locks on the doors now. Then go see what it's like to drive something besides Jerry's old police flivver, and move that amazing car for Hector, or Quent, or whoever owns it."

"It sure is beautiful. Bright red, and shiny silver; it made me think, when I first saw it, that it must look like a brand new fire engine," Arie said.

"Yes, all it needs is a rack for the—uh, hoses—hey, fire engines! You know, down at the fire house, they only have one engine, right?"

Arie giggled. "You want to put it in the firehouse?"

"They have an empty space. Jerry parks the police car in there sometimes, mostly in the winter. I could ask him."

FLORA'S MONEY

"You going to let the fire volunteers play with it?"

"Well, they could keep it polished, and maybe they could cover it up with an old piece of canvas. But most of them never go near the place unless there's a fire, and that doesn't happen very often." Grover frowned, puckered his lips, thinking. "Anyway, the firehouse would do for now. Do you want to work on the money cans while I tackle the locks, then the car thing?"

"Yes, maybe I'll bring up one burlap bag at a time, empty the cans on the little table and start sorting, okay?" she asked.

"Sure, and I'll help you finish up when I come back. Last thing, after it gets dark, I'll get rid of the empties."

Late the same afternoon, two hours after take off from Hamelet, the Goose flew low over a meandering river in a rural area of southern Illinois. Quent, Carlos, and Jed peered through the windshield and were satisfied there were no power lines, boats, floating docks, or any other obstacles in their way; after that. Jed circled back, landed on the water, and cut the engines. As they tied off to some trees a farmer drove up in an old truck, got out and walked over to the shore, awed by the big visitor. Within minutes, Quent made friendly contact and arranged for a lift to a general store and gas station, two miles down the road. Jed stayed with the plane while the other four piled on the truck to go buy supplies, including some warmer clothes for Flora and Hec.

CHAPTER 40

Grover left the lighthouse an hour later after installing the new lock on the door at ground level. On the way into the wooded area, to see about moving the Duesenberg, he saw Jerry sitting on the ground, leaning against the stump and gazing out on the lake. Surprised, Grover said, "Hi, Jere. Taking a break?"

Jerry looked around, smiled and said, "Not exactly. I guess I'm on duty—sort of. Where you going?"

"On a little errand—sort of."

"Well, I've been here long enough," Jerry said, getting up. "Hey, that plane going out was something to see, wasn't it? I was right here, then. Saw you and Arie up there—waving."

"Really, you should have come up. Quite a sight—uh, then you also saw Flora run down there."

FLORA'S MONEY

"Yup. That was quite a sight, too—her dashing across the sands. Graceful, fast and uh—?"

"Athletic?" Grover asked with a grin.

"Yeah, that'll do," Jerry laughed, and added, "So where's she off to? I saw her hop right on, and away they went." Grover looked at his uncle, unsure what to say. Jerry waited for a moment, chuckled, and asked, "Complicated?"

"Well, yeah."

"Grover, I need to ask you a question; then I'll tell you a secret. Maybe that will smooth things out some."

"Sure, Jere."

"Do you know why that plane left in such a hurry?"

"No, Flora just said they didn't have time to tell her—and they said they'd go as soon as she got back, and they did."

"Well, Grove, I happen to know that they got a tip some feds might be coming over to talk to them—and apparently Quent thought it best for them to scram." Jerry lit a cigarette, sat down on the stump and asked, "Am I holding you up from something, Grove?"

"No, and I guess you want to know why they wanted to avoid the law guys."

"Oh, I think we both know there is a suspicion here that they are booze runners."

"Not anymore."

"Oh, that's a start. What else can you tell me, Grover— let's say, off the record and before you do, I'll tell you something: I'm the one who warned Quent."

Grover commented silently, with a questioning look.

"And Arie's brother is working for the bootleggers as a pilot, right?" Jerry asked.

"Not exactly. He was hired to do that, but they shut it all down yesterday, and I think they plan to leave the country,

255

FLORA'S MONEY

at least for a while, and go somewhere south and start an honest flying business. I don't know all the details—things are happening so fast. Arie hasn't had time to tell me much about what she's heard from her brother since they landed this morning."

"Wow! Good for them, a flying business. I hope it all works out. And what about Flora?" Jerry asked.

"That's another long story. But for now, I can tell you that she and Hector were friends back in Chicago and he asked her to go with them today."

"Yeah, he's the big fellow I saw driving a Duesenberg yesterday, right through Hamelet. And Arie was behind him, in their truck; meant to ask you about that, too. So what happened to that car? What did he do with it?"

Grover sighed, and said, "Yeah, well, would you like to see it—and go for a little ride while we talk about all this stuff? You know, off the record, like you said."

"A ride? Where the hell is that beautiful machine?"

"Right over there in that clump of pines. In fact, I'll even let you drive it."

While Grover and Jerry talked and spent time gazing at the Duesenberg, back in the trees, Gorki rode the horse to a different wooded area behind the diner and tied the reins to a fence. He went inside and had soup, pie and two cups of coffee, thinking and trying the whole time to put together a scheme that made sense. Frustrated and disgruntled, he left the diner, untied the horse, grabbed its mane and threw himself up on its back. He rode slowly to the main road, slid off the horse and stood on the corner, gazing around, thinking. Head down, the horse snuffled around in the roadside grasses. The reins hung loose and touched the ground as the animal wandered about fifteen feet away.

It was mid-afternoon; there was no one on the sun-baked sidewalk, and the unpaved side street was empty of traffic—until Gorki heard a car coming from down the beach road behind him. He turned and stared; what he saw made him jut his head forward, squint, and mutter to himself—damn, there it is!

The Duesenberg, in all its dignity and dashing aura, was coming right to the intersection where he stood. It slowly passed him, close enough to touch, with two men in the front seats. He restrained himself and stared at the young man on his side of the car—I know him, he thought—yeah, the kid who said he lived in the lighthouse—and I see the driver has a gun holster on his hip, his father, no his uncle—the cop! Grover flipped a quick wave as they went by. Jerry concentrated on swinging into a left turn and never looked at the waiting pedestrian. In seconds, the car was driven away—by the chief of police, no less. Gorki shouted inside his head: enough, enough!

The tired old nag chose that moment to make a large, splashy deposit just a few yards down the street. Gorki ran and hopped on the startled horse, got on the road out of Hamelet, and kept going to where he knew a rail line crossed the road about seven miles to the south. Later, after stopping twice to rest, he reached the place he had in mind, slid off the horse and turned it loose in a nearby field. Then he walked back to the tracks, put his right ear down on a rail and listened. There was a faint sound of a train coming. He stood up and waited—to let the rattling boxcars take him on a new journey.

CHAPTER 41

"So, Grover, you're telling me we have a grand total of—what was it again, four thousand and—no, four hundred and what?" Flora said, breathing heavily into the mouthpiece, excited by what she was hearing.

"Hey, take it easy, Flo, I'll go slower," Grover said, speaking on the new phone recently installed in the top room of the tower. "The total here is four hundred and eighty-seven thousand dollars. The coffee cans are gone. Arie has counted, checked, rechecked and bundled all the cash very carefully, and filled up five milk cans to hold it all. Now it's all in the special room—we decided to call it the dungeon, like Ramsay and I did when we were kids. Be like a code name, just between you and us, okay?"

"Sure, good idea."

FLORA'S MONEY

"The milk cans are against the wall and covered up with a tablecloth, would you believe—that was her idea, too. And she got four extra milk cans to set in front of the full ones for decoys. We also piled my art junk in front of them, to make them less obvious if anyone happens to see in there—but that should never happen. That room and the downstairs door have locks now. No one else knows about the existence or, of course, the total of the cash, except Arie, me, and you. Don't write any of this down."

"Right. Bless you both. What a lot of work. Golly."

"Now, tell me again, where are you calling from?"

"A place called Nassau, one of the bigger cities in the Bahamas—we'll fly on to Grand Turk tomorrow. But tell me more."

"Can you hear me okay?" Grover asked.

"Not bad, some static, but go ahead."

"Okay, tell your friends we have the Duesenberg in the safest place in town—next to the fire engine in the firehouse, which is next door to the police station, as I'm sure you remember. And it's being looked after by the police chief, personally."

"You mean Uncle Jere?"

"Yup."

"I'll tell 'em, but they won't believe me."

"Actually, when I went by there this morning he was washing it," Grover said.

Flora giggled and said, "Amazing. Will he give it back when we come home?"

"Sure, he's storing it, that's all. We had a long talk the day you left about a lot of other things, too. Also, we're making good progress with the bank; the Judge has been a great help. And we haven't touched any of the assets, they're all still in

FLORA'S MONEY

the dungeon. Understand?"

"Yup. Gee, what can I say, Grove—you and Arie are a couple of wizards—give her a big kiss for me. Oh, another thing. Before we left, I saw Uncle Oren and told him I'd be away and about the bank—and he has some savings hidden away that he wants us to put in the bank for safe keeping. So, as soon as the place is ready, talk to him, you know, in private, and take care of his cash. Maybe he'll be our first customer." She giggled and said, "It's a lot of money, so keep it safe."

"Okay, Flora, that's all for now," Grover replied, "maybe next time we'll get you on the phone with the Judge so he can tell you himself about what he's done for the bank project. Bye-bye."

CHAPTER 42

During the weeks that followed, Grover and the Judge moved ahead with setting up the bank across the street from the Emporium. After meeting with Grover and Arie, on Flora's behalf, the Judge purchased the building from the town at a bargain price. The deal he made included exemption from all the over-due back taxes, and no payments to be made until the following year. In addition, he initiated the legal steps needed before the bank could publicly start to accept savings and transact loans. Then the Judge sent a memo to Flora to suggest that Theo, Grover, Arie, and he be asked to serve on the Bank's Board of Directors on an honorary basis, at least at first, to keep the opening expenses down.

Grover and Arie, working together, had the interior and outside of the old bank building repainted, and a locksmith

FLORA'S MONEY

brought in to refurbish the huge floor safe still behind the counter in the main room. At that point, Grover and Arie were the only ones entrusted with the new combination.

At the Judge's suggestion they hired an elderly gentleman to be the new General Manager; he was well-respected in town from the years when he formerly operated the old Hamelet bank before the bank robbers and the Depression forced him to close in 1930. A local lady was also hired, at the manager's suggestion, as a general clerk. Both of these people were put to work right away, working with the Judge on administrative details needed for the bank before it could open. It was agreed that the clerk would become their counter attendant and welcome customers from behind the glass wall, and the little service window, that was installed from the counter top to the ceiling.

At one point, Ramsay came back to Hamelet for a visit, saw what they were doing, and enthusiastically made some suggestions. They should open the bank quietly, he said, as soon as they were ready to just accept deposits and continue to get organized. This would give them several weeks of business, even though all the operating wrinkles hadn't been ironed out yet. Then, with a big smile he added, "So, maybe next spring, you can put on an official grand opening and throw a big public picnic down on the beach—I'll come out and help you set it up, if you want. I love a good party! And maybe Flora and her friends could fly back and join the fun!" Grover told Flora about Ramsay's suggestions, during one of their phone calls, and she heartily approved the ideas.

As soon as the safe was ready to use, and the building was secure, Grover arranged for Oren to bring over his bonds

FLORA'S MONEY

and savings for safe keeping and become their first depositor, even though they weren't yet open to the public. The general manager duly entered the funds in one of their new ledgers and presented his old friend, Oren, with passbook number one as the funds were placed in the bank's sparkling clean safe.

Flora continued to discuss all the bank arrangements by telephone—including naming it the Citizen Bank of Hamelet—from the makeshift office-hut of Floral Aviation on Grand Turk island, the Caicos base of operations for their flight service.

On one of his visits home from his bank job in Chicago, Ramsay showed up the proud owner of a Ford Model-A two-door, with a rumble seat. On Saturday, after lengthy talks with his brother about the plans for Flora's bank, Ramsay suggested that they take a break for a few hours and go for a ride up the lakeshore in his new Ford.

Once out on a dirt road along the lakeshore, headed north, Ramsay drove and gave his brother a flashy demonstration of shifting and accelerating, big city style. Then he got into sliding around curves and showing how to escape the dust raised behind themselves by moving at speeds high enough to stay ahead of the billowing cloud—sometimes going forty-five or faster. A few minutes later he pulled over and said, "Okay, your turn." He left the motor on, hopped out and ran around to the other side of the car and got in as Grover slipped over behind the wheel, shifted gears, and began cruising slowly.

"My, you drive so sedately, like maybe an old farmer going to church," Ramsay said.

"Hey, this is how we avoid getting dust on our cars in Hamelet. Just don't go so fast. Simple. Doesn't raise much

FLORA'S MONEY

dust, see."

"Okay, but going this slow you can get ant bites. Hey, let's pull into that joint ahead—they have a place like this back in Whiting. And look, they have girls to serve you right in the car!"

Grover nodded, slowed down even more and made a wide turn that took the Ford into the dirt parking lot of the drive-in stand. It was a round structure built to look like a giant barrel, almost two stories high and painted bright orange. There were walkways extending out from the building for about forty feet on each side, parallel to the road. Jumbo-sized lettering and hand-painted pictures on the walls featured mugs of frosty root beer, hot dogs and, of course, orange drinks.

A buxom teenager in a short-skirted outfit, the nearest waitress, saw them drive in and scurried over to greet them with a smile and say, "Welcome, gentlemen. Where'd you come from? Not around here, I bet."

Ramsay spoke up first, "We're from Hamelet—way south of here, on the lake."

"Hamelet—is it a big place?" she asked, wanting small talk.

"Depends on the season," Grover announced: "In the summer, the beach gets crowded at times." Grateful to have stumbled on a topic to keep her chatting, he continued, "The downtown is across a street from the beach and runs about six blocks on each side of a grassy park. You get a keen view of open sand and water if you go up or down that street—we call it Blue View Boulevard, now."

"I bet you do!" she gushed. Then she startled Grover with a wink, followed by a nose wrinkle as she struggled with a thought for a moment, and asked, "Uh, what do you mean

FLORA'S MONEY

now? Did they change the name of the road?"

"Yeah, just about every street in town has a new name. Happened last year as part of a big experiment. Maybe you saw it in the newspaper," Grover remarked, trying to sound casual.

Idly, Marge rested one hand on the window sill of Grover's door, leaned forward, and replied, "No. I don't read the papers much, 'cept the comics.'' Then she brightened when another bit of talk occurred to her. She giggled and asked, "How many?"

Grover looked blankly at her for a moment and asked, "How many what?"

"How many street names did they change?"

"Oh, all of them," Grover replied.

"Like how many is that?"

Grover hesitated and looked at the sky, as though pondering, and said, "seventeen streets, five avenues, a couple roads and only one boulevard, of course—and each one was named after a different color and the pavement changed to that same color. Honest!"

"Now, come on, how could they do that? Streets are either black or white. Or maybe brick color. You're makin' this up!"

"No, it's true. Tell her some of the new names, Grove." Ramsay said, hiding a quiet snicker behind his hand.

Grover frowned at him, but began to recite: "Well, the boulevard along the lakeshore is Blue View, like water. Then there's Red Street; runs past the fire house. Get it? Downtown there's Green Street; only a block long, where the new bank has its office—green for dollars, you see. Then there's Buttercup Road, that's yellow since it goes out in the country to the dairy farms where they make butter,

265

FLORA'S MONEY

and—"

"Now wait, a minute. Are you saying the streets are actually those colors, like they're painted, or what?" She interrupted.

"Yes," he replied, "the pavement materials are dyed by a special process we invented. It's much easier to get around in our town now; you can find places easier, even if you can't read the street signs. Just wait, one of these days your street out there will be painted maybe a golden brown and renamed Root Beer Avenue, or something."

She giggled again and stepping back to gaze at the Ford, she asked "how did you get such a bee-utey-full car. Did you steal it, or what?"

Before Grover could answer, Ramsay replied in a remarkably believable manner, "Of course we stole it. Honest!" She stared at him for a moment, her mouth open, then smiled, straightened up and asked: "Yeah, sure—uh, what can I get you gents?"

Ramsay, tossed a quick glance over his shoulder and said, "Let's start with a couple mugs of root beer, hon, large size. And hurry back, please. I think I hear sirens coming this way." She stuck the tip of her tongue out at him, laughed and scurried toward the big barrel.

Later, when they were ready to leave after their snack, Ramsay changed places with Grover and managed a lot of impressive tire squealing as he spun across the lot and headed down the road toward home. Grover looked around and said, "I've heard about these drive-ins. Never saw one before. Looks like a neat way to attract customers. Maybe we could bring Arie for a ride up this way, next time, and you could show

FLORA'S MONEY

off your driving style, again."

"And you and Arie could snuggle up in the rumble seat I suppose."

"Matter of fact—rumble seats are kind of nice."

"Oh. You tried one out already?"

"Yeah

"Who was driving?"

"Nobody. I had to put Flora's Packard behind the Emporium the other night, since they were remodeling things inside, and I parked it facing the lake."

"I get it. Was the moon out?"

"Moon?"

"Well, what happened?"

"I can't tell you that."

"C'mon. You can tell me."

"I fell asleep."

"Oh, fine. What did Arie say about that?"

"Well, after awhile she kinda nudged me awake and suggested we go back to the tower. Said the view was better from up there."

Neither spoke for several minutes. Ramsay guided the car more slowly along the coast road, past the sandy strips of beach bordering the calm waters of the lake. The vermilion sun-ball quickened its dip after touching the horizon.

"You know what, little brother?"

"Hmmm?"

"That Arie. You're a lucky sum-bitch."

CHAPTER 43

With the generous salaries they earned working for Flora, Grover and Arie had several needed improvements begun on the tower, and the shack at the base of it, to make it more livable for their year-around use as their home—adding indoor plumbing, some basic furniture, heating throughout and, the biggest project, bringing electric and telephone lines to the lighthouse.

One evening in November, before a quiet dinner for two atop the lighthouse at the little table, Grover said to Arie, "And now, I have a surprise, actually two. This is the first one." He reached behind a bookshelf and pulled out a chilled bottle of champagne that he had secretly placed in a pail of chipped ice, hours earlier, and said, "This is a gift from Flora's private stock she had left at Oren's. She asked me to

FLORA'S MONEY

go get it for us, when I told her about the second surprise. I also have these." He placed two glasses and a corkscrew on the table.

Arie laughed, and teased, "Are those the second surprise?"

"No, this is." He handed her a small jewelry box. She opened it, gazed at the twinkling diamond ring, took a deep breath, blinked, and gave him a warm smile.

"We can send it back to the catalog people," Grover said, "and swap it for a different design if you want to, or if it doesn't fit your finger—or do you want to keep this one?"

Arie slipped the ring on, kissed it, and whispered, "How about forever?"

Hamelet residents began applying for loan commitments from the new bank by mail, even though it wasn't open yet. Included were a planned tobacco shop, an auto supply store, a second gas station and a Nickelodeon movie house. Oscar, the town druggist, told the bank manager, over lunch at the diner, that he would be in to talk about a loan to enlarge his store, so he could provide more medical items for local customers—and straw hats, postcards and bottled soda pop for the expected increase in tourists.

A retired reporter from Chicago, who heard about the activities afoot in Hamelet from Ramsay, rented a house near the beach, set up an office in a spare room and began publishing a weekly tabloid newspaper he named *The Hamelet Hearsay & Chronicle*. In the first issue he featured a story about six tourist cabins being built next to the diner. He also reported that an abandoned barn was being remodeled into a rustic restaurant, on the main road outside Hamelet, and

FLORA'S MONEY

would be legally selling alcoholic drinks as well as food, as soon as Prohibition ended. Another story hyped the bank installation of a new built-in vault that included lock boxes for customers; the old safe, refurbished, the news item said, would be kept in use for bank papers in the front office.

In December, 1933, the *Chronicle* printed a special feature about the historic Repeal of the 18th Amendment, marking the end of Prohibition. The editor's opening paragraph is reprinted here:

Prohibition has been around for almost fourteen years. Now it's not a law anymore and Repeal will change millions of lives in America. Here are the big headlines from the front page of the famous New York Times, last week, (December 6, 1933) and the three sub-heads of the story:

PROHIBITION REPEAL RATIFIED, NEW YORK CELEBRATES WITH QUIET RESTRAINT;

CITY TOASTS NEW ERA
Crowds Swamp the Legal Resorts,
but the Legal Liquor Is Scarce.

CELEBRATION IN STREETS
Marked by Absence of Undue Hilarity
and Only Normal Number of Arrests.

MANY SPEAKEASIES CLOSE
Machine Guns Guard Some Liquor Trucks,
Supplies to Be Rushed Out Today.

....

FLORA'S MONEY

Early in 1934, Ramsay left his Chicago job and moved back to Hamelet. He rented a small storefront, near the bank, for an office with living quarters in back, and started taking a correspondence course to learn how to sell real estate. A few months later, the *Chronicle* announced that the brothers were going to have ten acres of the woods on their lighthouse property cleared and developed as the site for a guest lodge and an adjoining public park; funding for the project would be handled by the Citizen Bank of Hamelet.

> "Our lake is about 300 miles long, over 900 feet at its deepest, the third largest of the Great Lakes, and it covers over 22,000 square miles. That's about ten percent the area of la belle France."
> *Professor Theo*

CHAPTER 44

May, 1934. Hair tossed askew by the wind, Theo used his forefinger to firmly tamp down the tobacco in the bowl of the pipe he held in the same hand, and said, "All right, Grover, it's a brisk though sunny afternoon in the spring. We're perched here on these layers of stone that support your ageless lighthouse—mesmerized by the waves rolling in. Describe the charm, the attraction of the sounds as you would write them in a story."

"Well first—a man's voice is heard."

"True. I hadn't meant that to be included. What of the waves, the winds, the echoes and the sloshing, the rumbling, the majestic chorus of splash, gurgle, gush and what—hiss and splatter?"

"Professor, that's a bit watered-down, wouldn't you

FLORA'S MONEY

say?'

"Ouch. Of course, and that's a terrible pun. But proceed. Describe this aquatic world hereabouts, for real." Theo faced into the wind, struck a match on the stone he sat on, cupped both hands around the flame and sucked until heady smoke ballooned off in the brisk winds and soared away. A pensive Grover finally asked, "Seriously?"

"Yes."

"Describe the sounds, not the sights, right?"

"Yes."

"Perhaps involving an opposite, the lack of sound?" Grover asked.

"Perhaps."

"How about this: *On these turbulent shores, deathly silences are expunged by lively waters chuckling, sobbing or screaming, always.*"

"Hmm, not bad," Theo offered, "Good. You're so busy waking up our sleepy old town these days, with the new bank and all—but I still like to throw an exercise question about writing at you, now and then, to keep your artistic talents perking."

"And it works, Professor; thank you, as always. I still add pieces to my file of Omnium-Gatherum tablets you've been giving to me for so long—and even these days I work at my writings, when I can, usually early in the morning."

"I thought that. Fine. So what do we hear from Flora's gang down in the storied Caicos Islands, land of pirates and rum, like here, but sprinkled with tropical juices?"

"They're doing very well. Flora calls every week or so, though there's a lot of static and interruptions. Grand Turk Island is still their base. It has no airport, really, so they use an inlet on the north end that lets them land on sheltered water. They island hop and fly folks and freight on special

273

FLORA'S MONEY

charters all around the Caribbean and the south Atlantic in the Goose."

"Any word when they'll come back?" Theo asked.

"Not yet. Flora keeps saying they'll be here for the bank's grand opening, but there aren't many days left."

Two weeks later, at sunset, Arie walked back from a trip to the enlarged Emporium, for groceries, and climbed up to the top room of the lighthouse. She glanced out the window to watch the sun's final display on the lake's horizon, just as the phone rang. She picked it up and heard a loud voice say: "HELLO, WHO'S THIS?"

"FLORA! Is that you?" Arie shot back.

"Hi, Arie! We're on our way. And if the weather holds we'll make it in time for the big day!"

"Wonderful! Everybody keeps asking if and when you're coming. Where are you now?"

"Beside a river in Tennessee somewhere, waiting while the guys refuel the planes. Anyhow, I was delighted to find a phone I could use at a general store just down the road. You all set for Saturday?"

"Yes, I hope so. The whole town will probably be here for the grand opening of the bank and to celebrate that Hamelet is going to have a convenient—and safe—bank, once again to hold their money. Ramsay had a huge open-sided tent brought in and put up right on the beach, near the lighthouse, for the band and where people can enjoy the free hot dogs and beer you're paying for. Some people are even donating homemade cakes and pies, just because they want to. Ramsay said he rented the tent from some traveling miracle-worker outside Elkhart. And he made them loan us

FLORA'S MONEY

a bunch of chairs and—but never mind that—who's coming?"

"All of us. Quent says he got the word that there shouldn't be any problem for us from the feds, or anybody, anymore—we intend to keep our flight service going. But that's not settled yet. Hector and Jed are flying our big ol' Mama Goose today. Quent's with them."

"You said, planes. How many do you have?"

"Two. Mama Goose has a gosling. It's a beauty. Two open-air cockpits, two wings, and it's on pontoons also. It's bright red, and faster than the big mama."

"Who's flying that one?"

"Carlos and me."

"No! Who's the pilot?"

"Both of us, one at a time. Well, Carlos mostly, of course. We take turns. I can't wait to give you a ride. You'll love it!"

"You're kidding, aren't you? You said you were taking lessons, but do you have a license and all that?"

"Yes, no foolin'. Quent bought the little bird for a song, as he says, from some retired guy down here who thought he was too old to fly anymore. Carlos gave Hector and me lessons when he had time. Jed checked us out, too, and we got our licenses in San Juan. Sometimes Carlos uses the baby to fly emergency medicines to another island, or to transport somebody in a rush. But hey, what time does the party start?"

"Roughly noon—but it'll probably go all day."

"Quent says he thinks we can make it by mid-morning, Saturday. We can't fly after dark into strange territory, since we have to find water suitable to land on every time, and that can slow us down—and both planes may not arrive at the same time—it's hard, sometimes, to stay together. Oh,

275

FLORA'S MONEY

Hector's waving at me. Have to go. Bye!"

"Goodbye, Flora. Be careful!"

CHAPTER 45

"CARLOS, THERE'S THE LAKE, I SEE IT! Just a sliver of blue, way ahead, there!" Flora shouted over her shoulder from the front cockpit of the Stearman. She patted her leather helmet, pointed ahead, then turned and peered through her goggles at Carlos, behind her in the rear cockpit and helmeted as she was. He made a quick thumbs-up gesture, smiling at her excitement even though he couldn't really hear what she said.

When they bought the sporty bi-plane from a retired air circus pilot in Bermuda, it came equipped with a skywriting device built to dispense smoke trails to spell out giant letters and symbols in the sky. Carlos and Flora practiced with it on calm days over Grand Turk, at first making meaningless puffs of smoke, but eventually they learned to create mon-

FLORA'S MONEY

ster-sized letters and short words. One day for practice, and to advertise the name of their new airline, Floral Air, they astonished the few local residents as the fluffy letters FLO – AIR were made to float thousands of feet up in the sky, parallel to the ocean.

On this homecoming flight over Hamelet, they planned a demonstration as a skywriting surprise for the homefolks. About a mile ahead, the Goose was beginning to descend to about two hundred feet; the Stearman followed.

As the big plane flew out over the edge of the lake, Hector, sitting in as co-pilot, banked the Tri-Motor and began to follow the shoreline in a northerly direction. A few minutes later, Jed pointed and announced in a loud voice, "There's our friend, the lighthouse!"

It was about eleven-thirty on Saturday morning, the party day. People were scattered around the beach, with most of them crowding close to a big tent near the tower. The Veterans' band stood in a clump near the beer and the food tables outside the tent, and was already playing for the crowd. Large streamers, a yard wide and about ten feet long, each in an alternating color of red, white or blue, flared out from the gallery railing. An American flag swayed and swirled from a brass pole atop the tower. Old timers around the beach gossiped that it was the biggest public party any resident could remember—and it was a free treat from their wonderful new bank.

According to plan, made before take off, the Tri-Motor went straight into an approach glide, touched down on the lake about a quarter mile from the tower and began to taxi the rest of the way to shore.

At the same time, the red Stearman, sparkling in the bright sun, buzzed along the beach at seventy feet as it passed the

FLORA'S MONEY

tower, then climbed to spiral its way to a higher altitude. Arie, Grover, Ramsay, Maddie, Jerry and several friends waved and shouted from the gallery, ecstatic when they realized that Flora was the goggled person waving both arms at them from the front cockpit of the red plane roaring past.

Everyone watched as Carlos put the plane into a circling and climbing pattern to get much higher. The plane went around and around in a loose oval until it exceeded five thousand feet. Carlos glanced down at the lakeshore to make sure they were almost directly over Hamelet, looked at the crude diagram on a pad of paper tied to his thigh, and signaled to Flora by raising one arm.

Watching for this gesture, she pulled the lever connected to the smoke-emitting apparatus. This caused a formula of paraffin oil treated by heat from the engine to discharge white smoke from the tail, under pressure, into the blue sky in a large following trail that strung out behind them, lazily floating along. Some watchers groaned, briefly thinking the smoke meant trouble for the plane.

When Carlos wanted the smoke shut off he used one hand to make a slicing motion under his chin. Flora would then stop the smoke until he maneuvered the plane into the next position and signaled her to release another trail of a white, controlled cloud spreading across the heavens in gigantic letters, readable from the ground and visible for miles.

Down on the beach the crowd cheered and clapped as they stared straight up at the moving plane scribing the white lines on the blue sky. Like a flying red spider reeling out a living web, separate letters formed apace, one after the other. Second guessing what letter would appear next captured the crowd's imagination.

FLORA'S MONEY

Each completion caused a cheer to roll across the beach—with the loudest response released as Carlos made the last turn and the final line squirted out to create a dollar sign from the last floating letter, creating this:

HAM - BANK - SAVE$ -

"Okay. Don't tell me where the money is, or how much." *Quent,* May, 1934

CHAPTER 46

On Monday morning, two days after the big turnout on the beach, potential customers for the bank began lining up in front of the spruced up building an hour before the announced opening at nine o'clock. Others stood on the sidewalk across the street, watching.

At eight forty-five, the Board of Directors made their grand entrance, exploiting another of Ramsay's ideas, put forth by him the day before when he suggested, "Let's chauffeur the Board to the opening. You've got the cars. It's only a couple blocks, but it will be reassuring to your customers to see you all arrive in style."

Jerry, in his full-dress police uniform, drove the glistening red Duesenberg slowly down the street, followed by Ramsay at the wheel of the stately Packard. The little motorcade did

FLORA'S MONEY

a U-turn and eased to a halt in a roped-off place by the front door of the bank. The General Manager rode in the front passenger seat next to Jerry; Flora, Grover and Arie rode in the back; Theo and the Judge rode in the Packard, next to Ramsay. Each car had its top down and displayed a hand-lettered placard between the headlights that read: Citizen Bank of Hamelet.

Flora and Arie, in sedate dresses, hatted and gloved, and all the male members of the Board, including Grover, wearing dark suits, ties and straw skimmers, got out and lined up on the sidewalk to greet everyone with handshakes and smiles. Grover, experiencing his first suit, recently ordered with Arie's help from a Sears Roebuck catalog, tugged often at his starched collar and discovered that his vest pockets made good places to rest his thumbs while standing around. At nine, when the bank door was swung wide, a red ribbon was revealed that stretched across the way in; Ramsay smiled and handed Flora a pair of scissors. Standing there, her beautiful profile and fair skin easily seen over the heads of everyone around her, she snipped the ribbon amid applause and a few whistles from the crowd.

A parade of old friends began to pass in and out of the building. They had come on foot, in farm trucks, flivvers and on horseback, to lay down their private caches in varied amounts and sign up for savings accounts. Others made appointments to come back to discuss personal loans and mortgages. And for the first time in years most of the talk in the bank included relaxed laughter—instead of grim discussion about foreclosures.

The crowd thinned out by noon, the Board members had left their posts out front, and Flora had gone inside the bank to chat and help where she could. An hour or so later

FLORA'S MONEY

she was standing in front of the counter and was stunned to see a pensive Rhonda, her old friend from Chicago, come striding in. When their wide-open eyes found each other, Flora reached out, stepped forward and swept Rhonda off the floor in an enveloping hug. Before Flora could do more than squeal in delight, her friend looked up at her and quietly said, "Hey, baby, we have to talk."

Concerned, Flora sensed that something was not right and, reacting fast in front of the dozen or so people in the lobby, nodded in silence, lifted the hinged counter top and led Rhonda down the short hall to a storeroom in the back. Then she closed the door and said softly, "Great to see you, Rhonda."

"I hope you still feel that way after I tell you why I'm here."

"What's wrong? We just got back Saturday. I tried to call you last week from Miami and invite you here to our beach party for the bank, but anyway I'm glad you made it today. Quent and Hector are here, too—probably down by the planes, on the lake."

"Welcome back, dearie, and I'm looking forward to seeing those two handsome guys again. Anyhow I'm sorry, but I've been busy the last couple days. Fact is, while you were flitting around skywriting the other day, according to what I read in the Chicago paper yesterday, I was talking to—well, don't be scared, because I think in spite of what you might think, he's really one of your many admirers."

Flora asked, concerned, "Who, Rhonda? What are you trying to tell me?"

"Manny, Flora. For the first time in my life I visited somebody in jail. Creepy place and, well—"

"Manny!"

FLORA'S MONEY

"Yeah, he's waiting for trial—for operating a speakeasy. Can you imagine? A few years ago on a pinch like that he would have been set loose by a bent judge and released immediately. But it's all different now. He'll probably get off, but it may take some time."

"Manny? Why would you go there?"

"He wrote me a letter, after he got picked up last fall. Very apologetic about the way he hollered at me when he was looking for you. In the letter he insisted I should come and see him. He didn't mention your name—just wrote, 'It's about your friend. I always liked her. She was so pretty, and friendly.' And Flora, he wrote that he wasn't asking for your address and will never bother you after he gets out—but who knows?"

Flora stared, biting the tip of her thumbnail as she listened.

"Needless to say, I never let on where you were. Remember when you called that one time we agreed it was best I didn't know. Anyway, he also said in the letter that there was something you should know, but he couldn't write about it. I guess he was afraid the cops might read his letter and bother you. And I figured I needed to find out what he had to say about you and pass it on. So, curious, and maybe just being an old softie, I went to see him. He looked awful, pathetic actually, and we didn't talk very long. He thanked me for coming, kind of weepy, and what he said sounded simple, but I still don't understand what it meant. You ready for this?" She took a small piece of folded paper out of the in-between in her bra and said, "In the taxi going back to my place from the jail I wrote it down and hid it here." Unfolding the paper she read it out loud to Flora: "Tell her I knew what she was doing, and be careful because not all

284

FLORA'S MONEY

the coffee is real."

Flora gasped. "That's it? Are you sure that's actually what he said?"

"Here it is, dear," Rhonda said, "It's still warm, keep it."

Two days after the bank opening, Quent, Jed and Carlos had the Tri-Motor ready for the three of them to fly back to the Caicos Islands and return to work. They had also pulled the red Stearman up on the beach on its pontoon wheels, using Carlos's truck, and towed it to the open space directly behind the lighthouse. It was decided that Hector and Grover would have it temporarily tied down and covered with tarps until a shed large enough to house the plane could be found or built nearby, before the snows came. Quent also suggested that they have a mechanic brought in to give it a thorough check up before flying it anywhere. Hector and Flora had also told the others, the night before, that they would stay in Hamelet to work on her local projects, for a while, and return to the islands later on by train to Key West where the pilots could fly over and pick them up.

Early on the day the Goose was to take off from Hamelet, Flora decided to have a frank talk with Quent about the warning Rhonda had brought her from Manny. Till then she hadn't mentioned it to anyone else. She went down to the beach by herself and asked Quent to go for a short walk with her.

"I'm sure you remember Manny," she began, "the manager at Golden's. He's in jail, as you may have heard, and he sent me a note in a kind of code, by way of Rhonda. She has no idea what the note meant, I'm sure of that." She handed

FLORA'S MONEY

him the piece of paper Rhonda had given her and added, "When she arrived the other day she gave me this."

He stopped walking and read it. Flora waited. He gave the note back and said, "Do you have any of the empty cans still around?"

"No. Grover got rid of them all—sunk 'em way out in the lake."

"Then he knows about this?"

She nodded and said, "Yes, he and Arie took all the money out of the cans, and carefully counted and hid it as we were flying out on the Goose in such a rush. Only Arie, Grover and I know what the total is, no one else—but we haven't had to use any of it either, except what I took with us."

"Did Hec ever see more than those three cans you took along?"

"No."

"Okay. Don't tell me where the money is, or how much. And you never checked any of the stash, or the cash you brought with us to the islands, to see if it was fake?"

"Right. Why would we? We had no reason then to be concerned about any of it being counterfeit—and I don't think either of them knows how to detect bad bills from good. I know I don't. In fact, back at Golden's I might have cashed some of the fake stuff, if it came over the bar, without even knowing it."

Quent sighed and said, "Flora, when Hec and I worked for Gus we never got involved in passing phony dough, but we knew there was a lot of it around, all over the country. We stayed out of the rough stuff, too. At least directly. That's how we wanted it, and Gus agreed. He needed us as front men—he had plenty of mugs for hustlin'. But I talked on

FLORA'S MONEY

the phone yesterday with a contact in Chicago and he said there were some stories in the newspapers, that we never saw or heard about down in the Caicos. Seems the Feds grabbed Gus because he was suspected of heading a counterfeiting ring—and not just because he was a bootlegger. I hadn't heard about Manny till now. It sounds like they got him for selling booze, at least, and he must have been one of your many admirers, too."

"But one good thing, the two cans Hector and I had was legit currency. I made sure right after Gus gave them to me for bribes and payoffs. We could have been murdered using phony bills for that. Now, the rest of the money you have stashed should be checked to see how much of it might be counterfeit, and the bad stuff torn up or burned."

"Gee, Quent. What about the money I took to the islands when we left? Do you suppose—"

"Oh, I guess I should tell you now. I went through your cans, looked at every bill and put them all back, honest, when you were snoozing on the plane the second night out. It looked okay to me, so I assumed it was all real receipt money from the bar. And you have my word, I'll never mention any of this to anyone."

Flora took a deep breath and looked down at him, her eyes shiny. She gulped, flashed a little grin and said, "It's scary. All that money—we're helping to start so many projects and giving a boost to so many folks already—maybe we've pulled it off by using very little legal money—and good or bad, none of it was ever really mine. Quent, what about the rest of it we have? You never said anything before about this counterfeit thing."

"There's been a lot going on, as you know, Flora. I did wonder about whether the rest of the money you have was

FLORA'S MONEY

good. But I guess I just jumped to the conclusion you had only dipped from bar sales. But don't forget, a lot of it, or maybe all of it, could be okay. But keep it locked up till you know for sure."

"Golly, is it possible for us to check the money ourselves?"

"I can tell you what to look for, Flora. Then you three can sort out your pile, and whatever you find out will still be your secret. But, hell, you've already got projects going just by creating the right illusions of wealth, and maybe the new money coming in, the deposits, and fees earned on loans and so on will keep you going till you check out your hidden stuff."

Flora nodded and said, "Maybe—we've paid for a lot of things already and loaned out small amounts of cash to good people without having to use our original uh—assets, I guess is the right word."

"Hey kid," Quent said, smiling, "now, you're a regular capitalist—big time!"

As they talked, Quent and Flora strolled aimlessly down the beach then turned back to end up where the Goose was tied off in the shallows at the water's edge.

"Okay, Flora," he said, "let's sit here and I'll tell you what to look for when you check out your cash." They stepped over on to the pontoons and sat down, legs crossed, facing each other. He pulled a small notepad out of his shirt pocket, along with a pencil stub, handed them to Flora and said, "Here, you may want to make a little list."

Flora sighed, nodded and said, "Is it really possible for us to do it? I mean—there are so many bills, fives, tens, twenties and all, to look at and—gosh."

Quent smiled. "Sure, but that's a good problem to have.

FLORA'S MONEY

Right? First, get hold of a genuine bill in each denomination. Look closely and compare them with your bills one at a time. Note the quality of printing. Are the letters and pictures sharp and clear, or ragged and faded. They say you should look for differences, not just the similarities. The good bills are clear and distinct, all the lines unbroken." Flora listened intently, making a few scribbled notes.

"Another thing, every good bill has serial numbers evenly spaced and printed in the same color ink as the big Seal. The paper on your money should look and feel the same as the good ones. That's important. Hold each bill up to the light and compare it with the good bill." Quent went on to explain a few other details, looked at her list, made a few suggestions and concluded, "That should do it. And something I just thought of—maybe you could ask your bank manager, and the clerk lady, in a casual way, to explain what they look for to avoid being stuck with fakes. Sure, even the experts get stung sometimes, but listen to what they have to say."

"Good idea, Quent. I'll have a chat with them." Flora said.

"Fine. I'm sorry I won't be here to help you on this, but you know we really should take off today and head south." They both stood up.

Flora sighed again, gave Quent a weak smile and said, "Here's your pad and pencil." She gently tore off the top sheet of notes she had made, folded it, put it in her blouse pocket, and added, " I've got to have a talk with Grover and Arie—and I better explain all this to Hector, too."

She looked down at Quent. They exchanged warm glances and Quent said, "Sure—Hector came from a banking family, you know. Even worked in his father's bank for a time—and he's part of your team now."

289

FLORA'S MONEY

"He certainly is," she said. "I know you have a lot to do before you leave. We'll all be down here to see you off." She patted Quent on the back, turned quickly, stepped off the float and, heading towards the lighthouse, began walking across the sand.

CHAPTER 47

Grover was taking a break out on the gallery of the lighthouse when he happened to see Flora talking to Quent on one of the floats of the Tin Goose, as it sat in the water in its tie-off place down the beach. She soon stepped back on shore and began walking slowly toward him, head down. When she got closer he saw that she appeared distracted about something. Usually, he thought, she would come along striding fast, head high and full of life. Not so, this time.

Minutes later she looked up, saw Grover, and waved. He raised a palm, with arm extended over his head, pointed at the rock ledges down below where they all liked to sit, then went inside and ran down the steps. She was already perched in the shade of the tower when he came out and joined her.

"Hi Flora," he said, "What's up? I spotted you with Quent

FLORA'S MONEY

over there by the plane."

She nodded and murmured, "Grover, I want to talk for a bit. Is Arie here?"

"No, but she should be back soon. You okay, boss?" he said, thinking to cheer her up.

"They're taking off today—but you already know that." She stared out over the lake at the plane for a moment and idly dragged one finger in the nearby sand, making small circles. He sensed her solemn mood and waited in silence until she continued, "Grove, we have a problem with our inventory up in the dungeon. We still have it all up there, don't we—I mean, we haven't had to use any of that cash yet, have we?"

"No. I would have asked you first—or at least told you by now. That's the way you wanted it, right?" he said.

"Yes. It's just a question, nothing more. I'm not doubting or checking on you or Arie. You've both been wonderful."

"And Flora, the room is always locked—in fact, every time I go up or down those stairs I guess I automatically look at the padlock as I go by. You have a key and I still have the only other one."

"And you and Arie are the only ones who know about our—uh, inventory?"

"Absolutely."

"Grove, tell me about the bank. You've kept me posted on the phone and I assume things are going good. But how do we keep track of the money in the bank vault? I have a vague idea, and I trust you completely, but I'm so new at all this."

"That makes two of us—or three, counting Arie. But she and I have learned a lot since we started. They have several big record books and every day the clerk lists all the incom-

292

FLORA'S MONEY

ing cash from depositors, loan payers and from anything else. They also keep records of all money paid out and they do a count of the cash in the vault on a regular basis. And every few days I sit down with Arie and the manager, in his office, to look those books over as he explains things and tell us what's going on. The judge sits in on some of those meetings too, as a Board member and your legal advisor."

"I thought so, Grove. Then so far, since we opened months back, even before the big beach party and grand opening, you haven't had to go to the dungeon for more, uh, maybe we should call it milk now, instead of coffee." She flashed a little smile and went on, "The bank's doing well, right?"

Grover giggled and said, "Yes, we're off to a great start. We're adding new customers every day. The word is spreading. Business people and working folks are coming in from all over. Also, as the judge told us, we never loan out more than we have in cash in the vault, or readily available, and that's one of the rules they follow. I think the Judge really takes it for granted you have other assets, but it's not included in any of the records. Apparently it doesn't need to be. It's your own private concern, just like he told us at our first meeting. And I get the feeling he's comfortable with the idea that you are well off, financially; to him, your wealth is invisible, but it's there. So, is something wrong? You said we have a problem."

"Yes, we do. You remember that stormy night up there in your tower when I told you and Arie about the money?"

Grover started to reply when he saw Arie walking toward them from the direction of town, and said, "Hey, Flora, here comes my other boss!"

They both watched Arie approach, step up on the ledges,

293

FLORA'S MONEY

bend over to hug Flora, smile at Grover, and then sit down laughing and saying, "If this is a private meeting I'm still barging in, okay Flora? We've hardly had a chance to talk since you got back!"

"Arie, she came over to talk to both of us—right Flora?" Grover said. Flora nodded, so he went on to give Arie a brief recap on what they had been discussing about the bank.

"I'm glad you're here, Arie," Flora added, and said, "Well, to go on. Even now, after months of thinking about it, I'm still not proud of what I did, stealing that money. It was crazy. Why did I ever think I should pull a stunt like that?"

Arie put one hand on Flora's shoulder and said, "Golly— you told us that night that as long as the money was used to help the working folks around here, and perhaps some of the business places in Hamelet, it would all be worthwhile."

"That's true. I did say that." Flora said, almost whispering, "but I still often feel guilty, thinking about it. No matter what, it's wrong to take someone else's money, keep it, control it and spend it yourself."

Moved by seeing Flora so upset, Grover reached out and took her hands in his as he said, "Flora, don't forget, the money had been illegally acquired by gangsters; you knew that. They were the real lawbreakers in this, I think. They took the money, and a whole lot more over the years, for illegally selling booze. And they took it from people who were willing to ignore the law and pay for something they wanted. Besides, we all agree there's no way you could ever return that money to all those speakeasy customers."

"And Flora," Arie said, "just look at all the happy people in this town now. You made it happen."

"Well, I know you both want to help me feel better about all this—but there's still something I need to tell you," Flora

294

FLORA'S MONEY

said, slowly shaking her head from side to side, and then went on to carefully explain that she had just learned, two days before, about the possibility of some or all of the money being counterfeit. Arie and Grover sat there staring, first at each other then at their friend's sad face. Flora continued to talk about her friend Rhonda visiting Flora's old boss in jail and then bringing the note that warned her about the validity of the money, but neither Arie nor Grover really absorbed much of that at first. They were too stunned by Flora's news, and stricken by an anguish she was revealing to them, as never before.

"Flora," Grover asked, "did you say there's a *possibility* that just some of it is counterfeit?"

"Well, yes. Or maybe it's all okay. We just won't know until it's checked out, one bill at a time."

"Did you say Rhonda brought you a note from the guy in jail, but she doesn't actually know about the money?" Grover asked.

"That's right. So far, only you two and I know the total and where it is. Quent and Hector know I had more of the cans, because I mentioned it when I took three of the cans along when we flew to the islands. But I never let on how much money we had after you told me. When I talked to Quent this morning, he repeated that he thought it best if he didn't know how much money there is, or where we hid it. But he did give me some pointers on how to look at each bill and figure out if it's real or phony—I made some notes, but it sounds like an awful job—so complicated. You know, maybe this fake business is some kind of punishment for what I did."

She stopped talking, pulled out a handkerchief, blew her nose and said, "Until this counterfeit concern came up, I

FLORA'S MONEY

was beginning to feel a lot happier the way things were going. Now, I wish those milk cans would just float away, or something. Then maybe I could begin to forget what I did and move on. As I just said, Hector only knows about those three coffee cans I had on the trip, but I haven't told him any of the other details of the rest of the story—not yet anyway. That bothers me, too. It seems wrong for me to keep this kind of a secret from him." All three of them sat quietly, distracted by a gull that fluttered down on a rock outcropping nearby and, twitching its head from side to side, ignored them and began pecking at invisible things in the sand.

Grover finally spoke up, in a soft monotone, almost as if he were thinking out loud. "Flora, maybe—I think I have some thoughts that might help—or maybe not." Arie and Flora sat and listened intently, watching Grover as he talked. "You said you're willing to keep all the money in a special place, for the good of others, untouched, and you're not going to blow it on personal luxuries. Okay, fine, so far; what's so bad about that? In fact, seriously, we could even weld the dungeon door shut so it couldn't be opened—and maybe even brick up the outside window and paint over it—to keep it safer and less of a temptation to anyone. So far you've only spent comparatively little of the cash, and I gather you did that to help pay the emergency expenses for yourself and the others to get safely out of the country last fall. Since then you have just been a kind of custodian, holding the money, or storing it and, most important, keeping it safe—like banks are supposed to do with people's savings. People's savings," he repeated, "that's what the money is now, isn't it? Indirectly, in your mind, it could be like a big anchor of security for the Citizens Bank of Hamelet.

FLORA'S MONEY

"Let's assume it will be there on hold for a rainy day, maybe to donate to help some charity, or to use for whatever else comes along that will benefit the citizens of Hamelet, including expanding the bank services—providing, of course, that it's real money."

Flora listened intently to what Grover was saying then asked, "But should we try to find out now if any of it is fake money? I have some tips from Quent on how to check the money. I tried to write it all down—but there are so many things to look for to be sure it's okay. I don't know—we might miss something, then what?" She took the slip of notepaper from her pocket and held it in her hand.

"Ah, that's the big question," Grover said. "If it's real and you know it, that could understandably be a source of conflict in your mind—why did I take it, you might think—what should I do with it—is it wrong to use it, or not, because—because.

"But if it's worthless, and you know it, your guilt feeling might just fade away—or maybe not. It might just be replaced with other worries—how can I pay my bills, and so on."

With that he shrugged his shoulders, sighed and gave Flora a kindly look.

"Oh, I like what you're saying, Grover," Flora said. She tugged at her left earlobe for a moment and continued, "but what would you do with the money if you were me?"

"Me? Have a good cry if it's fake."

"And if it's good?" she blurted, beginning to smile.

"We'd all have to go hide in our dungeon and check every dollar of it. Then you can spend all the good ones carefully, slowly, make it last!" Grover said, wagging a finger and pointing at her, with a pretend-frown.

Flora sat straighter, chuckled, leaned back, arms reach-

FLORA'S MONEY

ing for the sky. All three of them erupted into giggles and jumped to their feet.

"Grover, Grover, Grover!" Flora shouted. "Forget the bricks and cement—I need to go tell Hector all about this, and to ask him to help us!"

She turned quickly and began running toward town, singing out, "See you soon!"

"Hey, Flora," Grover called after her. "Remember; put those speakeasy days behind you. Before long you'll be saying to yourself, *I just wish everyone in the world was as lucky as I am!*"

EPILOGUE

Within a year, Flora and Hector were married. After three more very busy years for the couple, she was president and he was senior vice president of The Citizen Bank of Hamelet, which by then had seven new branch offices in other small towns around the rural shores of Lake Michigan. The bank also owned the lodge in Hamelet Park, a hundred-seat movie house in Hamelet, a small resort hotel on Grand Turk Island in the Caribbean and the growing Flo-Air airline. Ramsay was vice president in charge of new acquisitions and public relations for the bank and all the other holdings. Flo-Air had three passenger planes and furnished regular service between Florida and several Caribbean islands. Quent was vice president of the airline, Jed was senior pilot and Carlos was operations manager and back-up pilot. At that time,

FLORA'S MONEY

Flora's money was providing employment for 131 people in the Hamelet area, and nine more on Grand Turk island.

Grover and Arie lived in a sprawling log house, designed by him, and built ón the shore in the shadow of the lighthouse. Kept on salary as special consultant to the president of the Bank, Grover was also gaining fame for landscapes he painted in his studio atop the tower and for the historical novel about the Potawatomi Indians he wrote in the paneled den of the log house. Arie had settled down as a housewife and mother of their baby daughter, born in 1937.

Professor Theo, semi-retired, worked with Grover on special planning projects for Flora. In 1938 they completed an extensive survey, primarily for her own information. They found that in the four years after she had started her bank, employment in the Hamelet area had tripled and average incomes had increased substantially. The population of Hamlet was difficult to estimate without a recent census, but it was noted that student enrollment in the Academy had grown from an average total of all grades of thirty to over one hundred.

FLORA'S MONEY

Grover's Omnium-Gatherum. Letter Files.

Dear Grover, old friend –　　　　　*20 April 2006*

Cheers from your newly inspired publisher in Dublin, who still has a mellow hangover from those heady late-night talks in your lofty studio—a retired lighthouse on scenic Lake Michigan, no less. Thank you again, for another stimulating visit and for your warm hospitality.

Today, I had a congenial meeting with our editors and gave them a verbal update about your writings. Our staff send their best and pledge to keep working hard on your prodigious output. When I told them that you are including tales in your next book about Prohibition in your land, one of the junior Veeps did ask a favor: Could you please send a bit of an overview for his own enlightenment about that turbulent era. Yankee bootleggers obviously ruled their fiefs way before his time, and he would like to hear more about those years—especially from someone who lived in a country while they actually had a law against having a taste now and then, itself an inconceivable event for any of my countrymen, young or old.

　　　　　　　　　Cordial regards from Ireland,

　　　　　　　　　　　　Clyde

FLORA'S MONEY

Grover's Private Omnium-Gatherum, 2006 ~ Age 93

Clyde, my wild Irish rogue ~

Thanks for your note—our ubiquitous neighbors, the lake gulls you met during your stay, send their greetings. What busy birdies. This morning, right at the dawning, their shrill garks woke me, as usual. I opened one eye and looked out over the lake—easy to do when your bed sits in a circular room, surrounded by tall low-silled windows, about 65 feet above a sandy shore—and there they were, swooping, flowing and keening all around our shared sky-space. Such emotion, it sounded like one of your old-country wakes, second day.

I sat up, squinted and looked out, mouth agape in the start of a big yawn—that slammed shut and turned into a snicker when one of them winked at me, while gliding past as they are wont to do. Just before he disappeared above my roof, he garked again.

With that, I got out of bed, spiraled down the 87 or so steps for my morning dunk in the lake, thinking about your Veep's request for brief Prohibition facts. I'm attaching some material from my book. Perhaps that will do for now. As you already know, I'm calling the book "Flora's Money" after our dear friend, Flora—at Arie's suggestion—and as I promised to do.

Grover ~

FLORA'S MONEY

Grover's Private Omnium-Gatherum, 2006. History File excerpt.

FACTS ~ Boom, Bust and Bathtub Gin -

In 1919, the U.S. Congress ratified the 18th Amendment to the Constitution and launched new laws, effective in February of 1920, that prohibited the making, transporting or selling of beer, wine and intoxicating liquors in America. Soon after, the Volstead Act was also passed to enforce the Amendment. After years of controversy, sponsors of Prohibition proclaimed that a long list of alcohol-generated health and social ills would finally be corrected, and the making and use of 'demonic' drinks would cease throughout the land—but most of their goals were never achieved, for several reasons.

A major problem was the ambiguity of an important mandate set forth in the Volstead Act: American residents could retain and consume such products, in small amounts for their own use, without breaking the law but no one in the U.S.A. could legally make or import these items in quantities for resale.

And even though illicit suppliers, convicted for possessing or selling alcoholic beverages, faced fines and jail time, their greed and conniving made illegal drinks continue to be available to the public for the more than thirteen

FLORA'S MONEY

years that Prohibition laws existed. Bootleggers thrived on such sales from stocks they smuggled into the country, or procured from the sly operators who cooked, brewed and bottled masses of alcoholic drinks in hide-aways within the United States. Midway through that dry era, then Congressman Fiorello La Guardia said, "It is impossible to tell whether Prohibition is a good thing or a bad thing—it has never been fully enforced—the percentage of whiskey drinkers in the United States now is greater than in any other country."

Millions of Americans regularly bought bottles, jars or jugs of illicit drinks from law-breaking food or drug stores, from neighborhood runners, or patronized illegal bars commonly called speakeasies where they could buy and drink booze—after speaking a password, should the operator insist. Once inside, a 'speak' could be a plank-on-barrel in an old storeroom down an alley, a posh nightclub with a band, dance floor and a chorus of dancing ladies—or any kind of adult whistle-wetting place in between. Widespread making of homebrew beer and bathtub gin, as well as buying of booze of all kinds, became a way of life for many otherwise law-abiding citizens until December 6, 1933, when Congress repealed Prohibition.

This fictional story is set during those real and quirky

FLORA'S MONEY

times towards the end of Prohibition when bootleggers had to either reform, hide, or go to jail; and many honest, jobless folks scrambled to climb out of the economic wreckage of the Depression years. Some of the more creative, or luckier citizens, using cash distilled from murky sources, went on to build legal fortunes—by starting profitable companies having at least the illusion of being lawful—as some capitalists still do.

Grover

About the author ~

Born in Indiana, Ray Rueby served in the Army Air Corps in W. W. II and has a BA from the University of Rochester. During his long career as CEO of the family firm, a successful manufacturer and distributor of promotional products, he wrote management articles for trade journals, including a monthly column for an international magazine.

He resides in western New York State and now devotes full time to writing and illustrating. For this novel he chose the old-style scratchboard method, as well as pen and ink, to show the reader the author's concept of what the locale of the book and the main characters look like.

Flora's Money: Made in America~
Printed by AlphaGraphics, Rochester, NY
Heritage bound by
New Ridge Binding, Rochester, NY

Illustrations: jacket, title & map,
also pages 1, 4, 12, 29, 36, 46, 55, 57, 71,
75, 91, 99, 110, 114, 131, 197, 254, and 268.